LONDON : PRINTED BY W. CLOWES AND SONS, STAMFORD STREET
AND CHARING CROSS.

His Royal Highness Prince Leopold and the Princess Charlotte.

1817

Sampson Low Son & Marston, 188, Fleet Street, London.

MEMOIRS

OF

LEOPOLD I.,

KING OF THE BELGIANS.

FROM UNPUBLISHED DOCUMENTS:

BY ·THÉODORE JUSTE.

Authorized Translation,

BY ROBERT BLACK, M.A.

IN TWO VOLUMES.

VOL. I.

LONDON:
SAMPSON LOW, SON, & MARSTON,
CROWN BUILDINGS, 188, FLEET STREET.
1868.

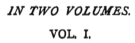

AUTHOR'S NOTE.

LEOPOLD I. wrote more than once : " In political
" affairs, the heart plays a very useful part."
Struck with these words, right worthy as they are
of attention, we made redoubled efforts not only
to bring out the high capacity of the sovereign,
but also to catch, in some sort, the inmost
thoughts of a prince whom posterity, confirming
the judgment of contemporaries, will without any
kind of doubt rank amongst the truly illustrious
personages of the nineteenth century.

Thanks to the numerous communications
which have been made to us, the public is now
initiated into the chiefest solicitudes, and sometimes even into the secret thoughts of the first
King of the Belgians. If these documents, nume-

rous as they are, do not clear up all the questions with which the world is still busy—if they do not throw full light on all aspects of a reign which was one of the longest of modern times—they nevertheless give an insight into the man as well as the monarch. Through them, also, our assertions receive wholesome check and authoritative stamp.

We have to express our profound acknowledgments to the statesmen who, by giving us access to their private collections, have aided us in the accomplishment of a very difficult task. The public will thank them as we do for these valuable communications.

Honoured, as we have been, by the confidence of politicians belonging to different parties, we had a duty to fulfil towards both. Their opinions had to be respected, and the laws of a fair neutrality had to be observed. In other terms, high above party we had to exhibit the constitutional chief, ever faithful to the fundamental pact; intervening, as king and as patriot, in decisive events; constantly preoccupied with the affairs of the whole nation; guiding the country with sure hand through the dangers of rock and tempest; and finally insuring to Belgium, to use his own words, "a political and social existence," which realized the fairest visions of our fathers.

If Leopold I. did not exceed the prerogatives granted to him by the Constitution, he had nevertheless his own views, his own individual ideas. Belgian nationality, to which he gave stability and lustre by his memorable reign, was the object of his incessant solicitude. But because he conceived brilliant and solid hopes for the country of his adoption, because he was justly proud of the high consideration enjoyed by Belgium, he had further so to act that this position should never be compromised or even lessened. He was a pilot of consummate experience; he knew when to reassure and when to admonish.

Profound observer that he was, if he took pleasure in bringing out the valuable qualities of the national character, he found occasion also to point out its imperfections.

Let us not neglect the reflections of a sagacious

and far-seeing mind; let us ever continue to
listen to the wise and patriotic counsels of him
whom Europe and America were wont to call the
Nestor of Kings.

Brussels, August 16, 1868.

TRANSLATOR'S PREFACE.

IF popular enthusiasm be anything more than
windy effervescence, if the clasping of hands be
anything more than the natural consequence of
the drinking of healths, and if frantic cries of
" Vive la Belge!" be anything more than vo-
ciferous ignorance of the French language, then
Englishmen have a kindly feeling towards Belgium. The butts of Wimbledon are silent
witnesses that England takes more than a sisterly
interest in Belgium. Let not Denmark laugh in
her sleeve to think what benefit might under
certain circumstances result to Belgium. England loves Belgium; and if Belgium, then King
Leopold the First, for he, if ever any king, might
say, " The State means me." But Leopold the
First is more to Englishmen than even Belgium

incarnate. He was almost of our bone and our
flesh; he was the husband of her who was once
the flower and hope of our land; he lived
amongst us and became assimilated to us; he
was reproached with being too English; he
caught of us even our native "humour" of
which we boast; and to our Queen he was uncle,
guardian, friend, adviser, co-mourner, and com-
forter. There can be little need, then, to commend to the notice of Englishmen the " Memoirs
" of Leopold I., King of the Belgians." But to
the majority of Englishmen now living Leopold
was known only as the old sage and counsellor of
kings. M. Juste introduces him in the characters
of the dashing dragoon, the winner of decorations
on the field of battle, the observed of all observers
in courtly assemblies, the favoured suitor of a
royal maiden. He was indeed well called Nestor,
whether the name conjure up recollections of him
whose advice was considered like that of "the
" immortals," or of him who fought with the
Lapithæ against the Centaurs. It were unbe-
coming to say here more of the author than that
he has evidently done his best, by the introduction of letters which are all, or nearly all, taken

from autographs, and in other ways, to do justice
to his subject, and of the translator than that he
has endeavoured to do the least possible injustice
to the author.

A few remarks may be allowed by way of
explanation.　The translator has only avoided
being literal when there was a fear of becoming
bald.　From what he has himself experienced,
and from what he has heard others say, there is
scarcely anything more irritating than to find in
what professes to be a translation, words, phrases,
titles of works referred to, etc., untranslated ;
and he has therefore attempted to render into
English *everything*, down to the names of news-
papers, except when a word has become naturalised amongst us, such as "fêtes," "chargé
" d'affaires," and a few others.　He has, consequently, helped to pave a part of the road which
leads to Tartarus ; for certain technical expressions, such as "enclaves," "droits d'aubaine et de
" détraction," and some others, have thwarted all
his good intentions.　He has preferred leaving
such terms alone to giving a long-winded, cir-
cumlocutory, and yet unsatisfactory, rendering ;
for, as they are but few, the careful reader would

probably rather consult a dictionary for himself, and the careless reader would most likely skip the text of a treaty altogether. The translator has Anglicised, or intended to Anglicise, *all* Christian names. He cannot see why some should be Anglicised and some not; the result of that course is a heterogeneous jumble, and he is an advocate for uniformity. If you transform François, Auguste, etc., into Francis, Augustus, etc., why should not Philippe be transformed into Philip? It may shock some persons to see Marie Antoinette turned into Mary Antonietta, and Marie Amélie into Mary Amelia: but there is nothing like carrying out a principle. It is a melancholy fact that a pretty name is thus occasionally made ugly. For instance, Julienne is pretty; Juliana is, to some tastes, hideous: nevertheless it has been introduced into English verse by the poet (Coleridge, it is believed), who sang—

> " Coughing in a shady grove
> Sat my Juliana;
> Lozenges I gave my love—
> Ipecacuanha."

Louis, and Louise, and Josephine, having become naturalised amongst us, have been re-

tained; although Louisa may have sometimes
been written for Louise, either inadvertently or
for euphony's sake. An endeavour has been
made to preserve the general English fashion of
spelling names of places. The titular *De* has
been kept in the case of *purely French* appella-
tions, because it is so often merely an unmeaning
portion of a surname, and there seems to be a
growing opinion in favour of keeping it untranslated. If the translator has erred in these
little matters of detail, he can only regret that
it is too late to correct his error.

R. B.

CONTENTS.

to suspend his march.—Sudden invasion by the Dutch.—The
enemy passes between the two army-corps, of the *Scheldt* and of
the *Meuse*.—The orders of the king for the purpose of effecting
a junction between these two corps are not executed by
General Daine.—Letter to General Belliard once more with
the view of arresting the movement of the French troops.—
Rout of the army of the *Meuse*.—The king falls back on
Louvain with the troops of General Tieken de Terhove.—
He attempts to hold the Dutch in check until the arrival
of the French, to whom a fresh appeal has been made.—
Firmness and courage of the king.—Intervention of the English
ambassador.—The Belgians evacuate Louvain; the French at
Cortenberg and at Tervueren.—Convention of the Prince of
Orange with Marshal Gérard.—Leopold's return to Brussels ;
enthusiastic reception by the people.—The king, however, does
not hide from himself the consequences of this unfortunate
campaign; his grief.—Expressions of Casimir Périer in the
Chamber of Deputies.—Disquietude and susceptibility of the
Cabinet of St. James's.—Part of the French army, at the king's
request, prolongs its stay in Belgium. — Opening of the
Chambers; authority to employ foreign officers.—Missions
of Count Duval de Beaulieu to Berlin, and of Baron J. Vanderlinden d'Hoogvorst to Vienna; both fail.—Fall of Warsaw.—
Suspension of arms with Holland.—Baron Stockmar makes
known the notions prevailing in London.—Confidential mission
of M. Nothomb.—The Twenty-four Articles.—Deliberation
of the Chambers.—Resolution of King Leopold.—Adoption
of the Twenty-four Articles.—The treaty is signed in London,
Nov. 15. — Adjournment of the ratifications. — The Belgian
fortresses of 1815.—General Goblet's mission to London.—
Interviews with the Duke of Wellington.—Discontent of the
French Government. — Painful position of Leopold. — Death
of the Dowager Duchess of Saxe-Coburg.—Convention relative to the Belgian fortresses signed December 14.—Growing
irritation of the Cabinet of Paris. — Letter of King Louis
Philip.—The reproaches addressed to the Cabinet of Brussels
are energetically refuted by King Leopold.—Sequence of the

negotiation intrusted to General Goblet.—Lord Palmerston; violent expressions towards the King of the French.—Mediation of King Leopold; declaration of January 23, 1832.—Tenderness of the three Northern Courts in regard to King William; impatience and protestations of the King of the Belgians.— Reorganization of the national army.—The civil list.—Court of Brussels.—The plenipotentiaries of Austria and Prussia exchange, April 18, ratifications of the Treaty of November 15. —Russia holds back; discontent of King Leopold.—Russia's conditional ratification is given, May 4.—After having accomplished the first half of his task, King Leopold gives his mind to procuring the execution of the treaty sanctioned by Europe.— Judgment of M. Thiers on the first King of the Belgians.

APPENDIX.

INTRODUCTION.

The respect of a free people for its Head must spring from the conviction that he is capable of causing it to attain such a degree of happiness as it aspires to.—*Don Pedro I.*

THE first King of the Belgians is not yet a legendary personage, has not yet entered the regions of the semi-fabulous. It may be said, on the contrary, that he seems still living amongst us, for he asserts his place in our memories.

In attempting to retrace the long and glorious career of him who founded the national dynasty, of the eminent prince who was able, in spite of so many obstacles and so many perils, to consolidate the independence of Belgium, I undertake a laborious, and, perhaps, an ungrateful task. I will do my best, however, to accomplish it.

But let us admit that, as a celebrated

writer has said, for the great dead of yesterday,
the day of completed history has not yet come.
I cannot, then, pretend to pronounce upon Leopold I. the ultimate judgment of posterity.
There is a position, however, to be taken between
Suetonius and Plutarch.   Should I have but the
merit of furnishing future historians with correct
ideas, and with documents of real importance,
the work I undertake will not be without utility.
And for us Belgians is it not also a pious duty
to honour the memory of a king who raised
our country so high in the estimation of the
world?

Let us not forget those noble words of Leopold II.: "Belgium, as I have, has lost a father."

Leopold I. had a penetrating and steady intellect, powerful by its clear-sightedness, but tena-
cious rather than flexible, although he was endowed
with rare address.   He was very well informed,
very enlightened, wise, able, far-seeing, and perse-
vering; and so he indisputably possessed the
principal qualities of a sovereign and a founder.

He had a masterly comprehension of his epoch
and its requirements; but he was not only pro-
gressive and liberal under the influence of certain

political considerations, whatever may have been their weight; he loved progress for its own sake, for the benefits of which it is the source; and he showed on every occasion a loyal, just, and generous spirit.

No doubt Leopold, to the best of his ability, sought and promoted the advancement of the illustrious house whence he sprang; but he was still more ambitious for the State which had placed him at its head. He wished that the Belgian name, so long forgotten, should be henceforth everywhere honoured and respected.

As politician and as king he showed some of the traditional qualities of William III., the liberator of England. He was less lofty in his views; but he recalled the calmness, the patience, and occasionally even the constitutional self-abnegation of the other.

King as he was to the last day of his life, after reigning for more than thirty-four years, he died as it were in harness. If, in his last agonies, one of his officers had asked him for the word, he would have answered with the Roman emperor: *Laboremus* (let us work).

Scarcely has he closed his eyes, when the

praises of his reign fly from mouth to mouth throughout the whole world.

Although the death of the aged king was not unexpected, the news produced an immense and a grievous sensation, because it was understood that the loss of a sovereign who had exercised so great an ascendancy would be felt often and for long.   "Wherever in future times," said the reigning Duke of Saxe-Coburg, "a people shall " struggle obstinately for the acquisition of a con- " stitutional existence, wherever there shall break " out a dangerous conflict between different states, " often and often will resound the cry : Is there no " King Leopold here ?"

The mourning of the Belgians found an echo not only amongst European nations, but even in Asia and in America.   "You will be pleased to hear," wrote the Empress Charlotte, "of the " proofs of affection which were lavished upon me " at the sad loss of my great and much-loved " father, whose name was greeted with acclamation " at Yucatan, in villages where scarcely a word of " Spanish is spoken, by populations that knew not " even the name of the country he reigned " over."

A difficult task, I repeat, is it to retrace the long career of Leopold I. He had witnessed so many great events; he had been brought into contact with so many conditions of men; he had seen so close the most celebrated people of the age.

In his youth the Prince of Saxe-Coburg was present, beside the Emperor Alexander, at the meeting at Erfurt; he conversed with Napoleon I.; he was received on terms of intimacy by the Empress Josephine and Queen Hortensia. He became afterwards one of the chief movers in the delivery of Germany; in 1813 he was with Frederick William III., and backed the efforts of the illustrious Stein and the vigorous Scharnhorst. In 1815 he took part in the Congress of Vienna. Then, what a brilliant prospect opened before him, when, in the following year, he married the heiress to the throne of Great Britain! He was connected with the greater part of the sovereign houses, and, during half a century, was consulted by the most eminent statesmen. He was successively brother-in-law of the Grand Duke Constantine of Russia, and son-in-law of George IV., King of England, and of Louis Philip, King of

the French. He was uncle of Victoria, Queen of
Great Britain, and of Donna Maria II., Queen of
Portugal. George Canning, Lord Grey, Lord
Melbourne, Lord Palmerston, and the principal
leaders of the Whigs courted and liked him.
The Wellesleys, the Duke of Wellington at their
head, showed the highest regard for him. He
had mixed with Prince Talleyrand, Prince
Metternich, Baron Humboldt, and the other
diplomatists of the Congress of 1815. He
knew intimately the principal statesmen of the
monarchy of July, Casimir Périer, Molé, Guizot,
and Thiers. Finally, need I recall the deference
which Napoleon III. openly professed for the
illustrious King of the Belgians? " By his
" wisdom," said he, " and by his lofty intellect,
" he placed himself in the first rank of European
" sovereigns."

Had I but the pen of one of those eloquent
ambassadors of the ancient republic of Venice,
who rivalled Titian's colouring in their celebrated
Reports, then I might endeavour to paint King
Leopold as the last generation knew him. Let
us, nevertheless, collect some traits which will
give an idea of his character.

Leopold I., true king as he was in public, was personally far from exacting. His style of living reminded one of the simple and somewhat rude habits of Germany. Simplicity was conspicuous in his manners and language, as well as in his way of life: he was reserved, no doubt, but he did not affect haughtiness, just as he did not study luxury. A few chairs in covers of a light colour, white curtains, and some small but high tables, at which he wrote standing, formed the furniture of the apartments he inhabited at Brussels, at Laeken, at Ardenne, and at the Giulia Villa on the lake of Como. The same simplicity distinguished his dress: he nearly always, however, wore his uniform of general.

He rose early at all seasons, winter and summer, and worked until two o'clock, only leaving off to take a few turns in the garden before breakfast. State affairs had the precedence. He examined them with great assiduity and regularity; and it was hardly so much as three days before his death that he ceased to attend to them. During the long illness which carried him to the grave, and even amidst the most painful crises, he only once put off—for four-and-twenty hours—the signing of the papers which were in regular course submitted to him. Every day, after having despatched affairs of state, he devoted himself to study. He had always about him an enormous number of works of every kind, and in all languages, for he read fluently French, German, English, Russian, Italian, Spanish, and Flemish.

His librarians had directions to keep him acquainted with the principal novelties. Every Sunday these new books were examined, and the king immediately made his selection. History, fine arts, ethnography, travels, botany, agriculture —all branches of science occupied his attention. All his life he had an inclination for novel-reading; he always had one begun upon his table, and to his last day he never ceased to take a lively pleasure in this kind of reading. In this domain of literature, no striking work ever appeared without being submitted to him; and the fugitive and laconic hits jotted down daily in his diary showed great delicacy of taste and a vivid imagination.

This freshness of his in mind and impressions disclosed itself on every occasion. He enjoyed the beauties of nature in the spirit of a real poet.

The last time he retired to the Giulia Villa, it was with a sort of enthusiasm that he saw once more the neighbourhood of the Alps. He had alighted from his carriage, and as he walked along the road he stopped every moment in an ecstacy which might be termed juvenile. He communicated his impressions to those who surrounded him, delighting as he did to investigate in presence of Nature's grandeur the grand problem of the creation.

He was also endowed with a lively memory. One day, in Switzerland, as he approached a certain bridge, he said, " I passed over this bridge " thirty years ago, and I relieved a blind man. I " am very curious to see if he is there still." The blind man was there.

The king had a will of iron where he himself was concerned. He would not be conquered by grief or by suffering. In the last crisis of his long illness, when he perceived his courage giving way, he surrounded himself with books of light literature, and devoured them night and day to preserve his equanimity.

Indeed, before that time he used to read at night, to beguile his sleeplessness, for he was not a good sleeper. And as he disliked darkness, he was in the habit of always keeping a number of wax candles alight upon a marble table in his bedchamber.

Leopold was naturally kind and beneficent. In 1831, the news of his accession to the throne of Belgium caused consternation amongst the inhabitants of Claremont and the poor of the surrounding districts, who had to regret the loss of an indulgent master and of a benefactor.

In 1865, Duke Ernest II., calling to mind the king's attachment to his native country and his beneficence, wrote: "What Belgium and Europe "have lost in King Leopold, the annals of "history will declare; what he was for Coburg, "will be for ever to be read in thousands and "thousands of hearts."

He never refused to do any good which was proposed to him. He was upright and faithful, and might be trusted in little as well as in great matters.

Next to reading, the king's chief recreation was walking. He held the opinion of Lord

Palmerston, whom he often quoted, and who had said to him, that a man to be well needed four hours open air a day. In his latter days he had given up his horse, although he had been an accomplished rider; but he had not relinquished hunting. He liked to scour the noble plains which lie by the castle of Ardenne, and to track the wolf and the wild boar in the forests of St. Hubert.

He had always shown a special taste for botany, and, in his latter years, he had bestowed much attention upon astronomy.

He generally dined alone, and late. After dinner he liked to make up a family card-party. Being himself a distinguished musician, he had a great fondness for the art adorned by Mozart, Beethoven, Rossini, and Meyerbeer: to the very end of his life he had some of the chief works of the great masters performed nearly every day by his own pianist at the castle of Laeken.

He was attracted to England, not only by his almost paternal affection towards Queen Victoria, but also by a sort of predilection for that country as a place of residence. In London, as well as at the country palaces, he divided his leisure between

conversation and walking. Sometimes he might be
seen, towards two or three P.M., leaving Bucking-
ham Palace by a private gate, alone, and on foot,
and plunging into the heart of the great city, with
an umbrella under his arm, like a simple citizen.
He took its measure in every sense of the
words, and did not return for four or five hours.

His natural tastes prompted him to keep
himself carefully acquainted with the smallest
incidents of general politics.   No one, moreover,
had studied to better purpose Europe and the
men of mark who occupied the stage.   At the
very commencement of his reign he wrote:
" I am better acquainted than the ministers of
" Louis Philip are with Europe and the *masks*
" that govern it."   He was not ignorant that he
was considered the Nestor of kings, the just
arbiter of their differences, and the wisest and
ablest of negotiators.   In his autobiographical
notes, drawn up in 1862, he recalled with a certain degree of pride the fact that he was scarcely
twenty-one when he succeeded in concluding
with Bavaria a treaty advantageous to the duchy
of Saxe-Coburg.   "The future," said one of the
princes who kept up an uninterrupted corre-

spondence with the King of the Belgians, "will
"show us, beyond any conception that we can
"form, to what an extraordinary degree he was
"respected as an adviser amongst the great
"powers of Europe."

His memory, let me repeat, was remarkable.
He was especially retentive of anecdotes, and he
related them with a perfectly English humour,
which added the greatest charm to his conversation.

But diplomacy had not effaced the soldier.
Leopold was proud of having passed a portion of
his youth in camps, and of having taken part in
some of the greatest battles at the commencement of the century. One day, a French lady
asked him if he had been in the army, and he
replied : " I have been a field-marshal forty years
" —that is all, madam."

Such was Leopold I. in the last years of his
life. It is not, however, of this illustrious old
man that I would now call up the image, but of
the prince whom Lawrence painted, the young,
brilliant, gallant soldier, husband of the heiress
presumptive to the throne of Great Britain, and
for a brief moment sovereign of Greece, before he

was called upon by the Belgians to consolidate
their independence. I shall begin, then, with the
youth of Leopold I., and, following him on to
his riper years, recall also the part which he took
in founding the kingdom of Belgium.

LEOPOLD I.,

KING OF THE BELGIANS.

CHAPTER I.

1790—1814.

THE HOUSE OF SAXONY—FIELD-MARSHAL PRINCE OF COBURG
—THE FOUR PRINCESSES OF SAXE-COBURG-SAALFELD—NAPO-
LEON I. WISHES PRINCE LEOPOLD TO ENTER THE SERVICE
OF FRANCE—CAMPAIGN OF 1813—LEOPOLD ACCOMPANIES THE
EMPEROR ALEXANDER TO ENGLAND.

THE House of Saxony, which has recovered so much lustre in our time, is one of the most ancient and illustrious in Europe. It was flourishing and famous at a time when the Hapsburgs alone held the supremacy over the other sovereign families of Germany.

Frederick the Wise, elector of Saxony, and John Frederick the Magnanimous, were the renowned chiefs of the Protestants. They both belonged to the Ernestine or elder branch of the great Saxon family. Their descendants, however, had to suffer the consequences of the defeat sustained, in 1547, by John Frederick at the battle of Mühlberg; they were deprived of the electorate which was their inheritance, and it was transferred to the younger or Albertine branch, the scions of which occupy to this day the throne of Saxony.

It were of no use to set forth here the various arrangements whereby the Ernestine branch, upon losing the electorate (now kingdom) of Saxony, obtained the different duchies which have remained in possession of its descendants.[1] Let me merely call to mind that the formation of the house of Saxe-Saalfeld-Coburg dates back to Duke John Ernest, who died in 1729. He had two sons, Christian Ernest and Francis Josias. The former having died in 1745 without issue, his brother Francis Josias succeeded to the whole inheritance; that is to say, the duchy of Coburg-Saalfeld, which was thenceforth the indivisible appanage of the eldest of the family.

To conform to hereditary tradition, Francis

---

[1] All such details are to be found in a work entitled *History of the House of Saxe-Coburg-Gotha;* free translation, with additions and notes by M. A. Scheler, librarian to H.M. the King of the Belgians (Paris, 1846, 8vo.), *passim.*

Josias at once took service with Austria.   During
the war she waged with Spain he distinguished
himself at the sieges of Messina and Palermo.
The duke was tall and strong, and fond of violent
exercises; and he lost an eye through the pas-
sionate ardour with which he played tennis.
However, he displayed intelligence and capacity
in the administration of his duchy.

The Margravine of Baireuth, sister of Frederick
the Great, described the Duke of Coburg in the
following terms :—" He is tall and well made,
" and his expression moreover is prepossessing.
" He is exceedingly polished, and a prince
" who, besides his great good sense, is also
" very estimable for his kindness of heart."   Let
me add that this Duke of Coburg, so polished
and so sensible, stands out in happy contrast
from the crowd of strange figures, some
comic and some repulsive, which fill up a large
portion of the curious memoirs of Frederick the
Second's sister.[2]

---

[2] Memoirs of Frederica-Sophia-Wilhelmina of Prussia,
Margravine of Baireuth, etc. (Paris, 1811), vol. ii. p. 187.

In another work we read : " I went by Salzburg and
" Passau to Vienna. . . . On this journey I got an idea of

Francis Josias was sixty-three when he died, September 16th, 1764. By his marriage with a princess of Schwarzburg-Rudolstadt he had four sons. Ernest Frederick, the eldest, became Duke of Coburg-Saalfeld. John William, the second, went into the Saxon army, and was killed whilst he was still quite a youth, at the battle of Striegau ; he had taken for his device, " All by " love, naught by force." Christian Francis, the third, served in the Austrian army, in which he reached the higher grades. The fourth, Prince Frederick Josias, likewise entered the Austrian service, and became that Field-Marshal Prince of Coburg who was rendered celebrated by his expeditions against the Turks, and his campaigns against France.

"the mania which possesses all the petty princes and petty "lords of Germany for having Grand Chamberlains, Grand "Stewards, Grand Butlers, Grand Huntsmen, Grand Cooks, "Captains of the Guard, infantry and cavalry, though all the "cavalry and infantry of the petty count or petty baron "would be but some three hussars, four grenadiers, and six "fusiliers. Do not suppose that I invent these stories simply "to amuse you ; I have seen striking examples of what I "have just told you, in Suabia, Franconia, and Westphalia." (*Travels in Various Countries of Europe in* 1774, 1775, *and* 1776, vol. i., *passim.*)

King Leopold had preserved a lively remembrance of his illustrious great-uncle and of
his excellent grandfather.   In his autobiographical notes,[a] he describes Duke Ernest Frederick as debonnair and of an easy disposition, with
sound sense, and an exterior which must have
been remarkable.   Ernest Frederick had married
a princess of Brunswick-Wolfenbuttel (Sophia
Antonietta), sister of the celebrated prince Ferdinand of Brunswick, of Ulrica, Queen of Denmark, and of that poor Queen of Prussia whom
Frederick II. banished far from Potsdam.   The
Duchess of Coburg, according to King Leopold,
was a woman who in a great monarchy would
have been sure to play an important part.
" Coburg," he wrote, "was in all things under
" her orders, and she acted in respect of the little
" duchy as if it had been a great empire. The ex-
" cessive liberality of this princess was productive
" of much harm, for she squandered the revenues

---

[a] These notes, which extend to the year 1830, are to be
found in the form of letters to Queen Victoria, amongst the
pages of a work called *The Early Years of His Royal Highness the Prince Consort, compiled, under the direction of Her
Majesty the Queen, by Lieut.-General the Hon. C. Grey*
(London, 1867). *Appendix.*

" in a fearful manner. The duke stood in great
" awe of his imperious wife. But I dare not say
" much against her, as I was her favourite."

Leopold George Christian Frederick, of Saxe-
Coburg-Saalfeld, born at Coburg, December 16,
1790, was the eighth child of Prince Francis, heir-
presumptive to the duchy, and of Princess
Augusta Caroline Sophia of Reuss-Ebersdorff.
The Emperor Leopold II., who, on the 20th of
the preceding January, had succeeded the great
reformer of Austria, gave his own name to the
child destined to be one day king of the old
Austrian Netherlands. Before long these fine
provinces were invaded by the French armies.
But after his victory in the plains of Neerwinden,
on the 10th of March, 1793, Field-Marshal
Frederick of Coburg re-established the Imperial
authority at Brussels. "This battle," wrote King
Leopold long afterwards, " obliged the French to
" evacuate the Netherlands ; they were so badly
" routed, that after the junction of the English
" and Dutch, the allies might have marched
" on Paris." Field-Marshal Prince of Coburg,
finding himself opposed to the cabinet of the
new emperor (Francis II.), at last took the reso-

lution of freeing himself from a responsibility which weighed too heavily upon him. In September, 1794, he left the Austrian army, and retired to Coburg, where he lived until the 28th of February, 1815.[4]

But it was not the old leader of the Imperialists, the hero of the wars against the Turks, the victor at Neerwinden, that watched over the infancy of Leopold. The aged duchess of Coburg took upon herself this charge, and everything had to bend before her resolute will. Nevertheless, King Leopold had kept his parents in pious remembrance. " My poor father," he said, " whose health had been shattered early, was " a most lovable character; he was affability itself. " He was passionately fond of the arts and sciences. " My beloved mother was an uncommon woman, " and worthy of respect; she had a warm heart " and a fine intellect. Her affection for her " children was profound. Without wishing to

---

[4] *See* the work published, at the expense of King Leopold, by Col. A. de Witzleben, under the title of *Prince Frederick Josias of Coburg-Saalfeld, Duke of Saxony, and Field-Marshal of the Holy Roman Empire.* 3 vols. 8vo., *passim.*

Prince Frederick Josias was born at Coburg, December 26, 1737.

" say anything against the other branches of the
" house of Saxony, ours was certainly the most
" intellectual, in the true acceptation of the term,
" without affectation and without pedantry."

Ernest Frederick filled the ducal throne until
the 7th September, 1800, and the excellent princess, his wife, lived to 1801. Duke Francis, born in
1750, was forty-nine at the time of his accession.
And a mournful accession it was; a grievous
epoch for Germany, distracted by the French
Revolution.

Coburg had become a second Coblentz,
whither flocked pell-mell for refuge the French
emigrants and noble families of the Rhine and
Westphalia, whom the armies of the Republic
sent surging back into Thuringia. All met at
Coburg with a hearty and even a magnificent
welcome. The Grand Marshal of the Court,
Wangenheim, having received orders to fulfil
towards these fugitive nobles the duties of hospi-
tality, displayed an excess of generosity. He
ended by exhausting the resources of the little
duchy. Then Duke Francis, in great perplexity,
had recourse to Baron Kretschmann, finance-
minister of the Margrave of Brandenburg, at

Baireuth.   He was an administrator of capacity
and even of genius, but very rough.   He brought
matters back to some sort of order, but not without exciting against him a lively animosity.   The
reigning duke embroiled himself even with his
only brother, Louis Charles Frederick, who had
been Lieut. Field-Marshal in the Austrian service,[5]
and with his uncle, the hero of Neerwinden.

Prince Leopold grew up in the midst of these
domestic troubles.   From his earliest years, it is
said, he displayed a kindly and docile spirit, and
a serious mind with a leaning towards hard study.
He had been placed early under the guidance of
Ch. Theod. Hoflender, head of the ecclesiastical
department of Coburg, and first professor in the
Casimir College.[6]   By him he was taught Biblical
history, ethics, and the doctrines of Christianity.
The professor also presided at the prince's confir-
mation, which took place on the 12th of September, 1805.   He afterwards taught him Latin, the
rudiments of Russian, logic, and moral sciences.
The prince exerted himself, besides, to master

---

[5] He likewise retired to Coburg, where he died, July 5,
1806.

[6] Founded by Duke John Casimir.   Transl.

French, English, and Italian ; he studied history and the law of nations ; and lastly, by way of recreation, he gave himself up passionately to the cultivation of botany, drawing, and, above all, music. Being destined for the career of arms, he applied himself with the like ardour to his military studies.

Leopold was completing his fourteenth year when Napoleon became Emperor of the French. Whilst he was quietly prosecuting his studies in Coburg, Prince Ernest, his eldest brother, was at Berlin, where he had formed a close friendship with King Frederick William III. and the Queen, Louise of Mecklenburg-Strelitz, no less celebrated for her patriotism than for her beauty. Prince Ferdinand, his other brother, was serving in Austria, in Rosenberg's light horse.

The four princesses, daughters of Duke Francis, were already married.[7]

Princess Antonietta had married, in 1798, Duke Alexander of Wurtemburg, brother of the elector who became king in 1805, and of Maria

---

[7] A fifth princess—Marian Charlotte—born in 1788, died in 1794. Transl.

Feodorowna, second wife of the Emperor Paul of
Russia. Princess Antonietta was, according to
King Leopold, a woman of considerable intellect
and amability, with a great aptitude for command.

Before her establishment in Russia, when Duke
Alexander of Wurtemburg became a general of
cavalry, she lived with her eldest sister, Sophia
Frederica, at *Fantaisie*, near Baireuth, at that time
the residence of a great number of Bavarian families
and of French emigrants. Princess Sophia there
made the acquaintance of a nobleman of Lorraine,
Count Emmanuel of Mensdorf-Pouilly, in the
service of Austria. She married him on the 22nd
of February, 1804, after having refused several
suitors of rank not inferior to her own.

The youngest of the princesses of Saxe-
Coburg-Saalfeld, Maria Louisa Victoria, had
joined her fate, on the 21st of the previous December, to that of Prince Emich Charles of
Linange (Leiningen). The least happy destiny
was that of Juliana Henrietta Ulrica. King
Leopold's account of it is as follows :—" In 1795,
" the Empress Catharine of Russia, being very
" anxious to conclude a match for the Grand
" Duke Constantine, her grandson, applied to

" M. de Budberg, a distinguished minister and
" general.   She received, through his intervention,
" a visit from the eldest three princesses of Saxe-
" Coburg, all three possessing unquestionable
" beauty.   The Grand Duke conceived an affec-
" tion for Juliana, the youngest of the three ; she
" was very pretty, but still a mere child, being
" only fifteen.   Had the choice of Constantine
" fallen on Antonietta, she would have filled
" admirably the position of Grand Duchess. . . . .
" The empress-mother, in her preference for her
" two younger sons (the Grand Dukes Nicholas
" and Michael), did not desire the establishments
" of the two elder to be on a happy footing.
" Constantine himself was terribly cantankerous,
" and to crown the misfortune, the Grand Duke
" Alexander and his wife were Juliana's great
" friends, and supported her in her petty domestic
" differences.   Had it not been for the empress-
" mother's shocking hypocrisy, things might have
" gone on well.   The Grand Duke admired his
" wife very much, and she, with a lovable hus-
" band, would have been an excellent wife.   She
" found herself miserable, and ended by leaving
" Russia in 1802."

In 1805, when Napoleon led his still invincible legions against Austria, Prince Leopold
made his first appearance in the Russian army.
Whilst his brother Ferdinand was fighting amongst
the Austrian hussars, he and his eldest brother
(Ernest) joined the head-quarters of the Emperor
Alexander, in Moravia.   But the battle of
Austerlitz, on the 2nd of December, soon put
an end to the war.

Napoleon, victorious, destroyed the old German Empire, and had himself nominated, in 1806,
Protector of the New Confederation of the Rhine.
Then Prussia, seeing her independence threatened,
united herself with Russia to drive the French
from Germany.   Prince Ernest, heir-presumptive
to the Duchy of Saxe-Coburg, went to join the
army of Frederick William III., whilst the reigning duke, already seriously ill, retired to the fortress of Saalfeld with the duchess, his wife, the
Countess of Mensdorff, and Prince Leopold.

Marshal Lannes, on the 8th of October,
marched across Coburg; the next day but one
he attacked, close to Saalfeld, the advanced guard
commanded by Prince Louis Ferdinand of Prussia.   The Prussians suffered great loss; their

brave leader was killed with a sabre-cut by a
quartermaster of the 10th Hussars; and finally
the fortress of Saalfeld was taken. On the 14th
the French were victorious at Jena.

Duke Francis and his family returned to
Coburg. Everything looked gloomy. The
French were in the heart of Germany; the duke,
getting worse and worse, was at their mercy; and
on the 9th of December he expired.

" The situation," says King Leopold, "was
" very melancholy. Whilst my father lived, the
" French had occupied Coburg, but had not taken
" possession of it. After my father's death this
" question immediately arose : *Where is the new*
" *Duke?* When it was discovered that he was
" with the King of Prussia, Coburg was seized, and
" a military director undertook its administration.
" He was by no means a pleasant person; his
" name was *Villain*, and it suited him. To com-
" plicate matters, a very unseasonable insurrection
" broke out against M. Kretschmann. The French
" thought the movement was directed against them,
" and crushed it. Soon after came a new director,
" M. Dumolart, auditor of the council of state.
" At the same time Colonel Parigot was nominated

" military commandant.   In hopes of getting my
" brother Ernest back, and Coburg entered
" amongst the Confederation of the Rhine, which
" was what the other houses of Saxony had
" obtained for their possessions, my mother
" was for going to Warsaw to see Napoleon.
" But she got no further than Berlin, the
" Emperor of the French disliking visits of
" that kind.   General Clarke, Duke of Feltre,
" Governor of Berlin, was very kind to her.   I
" am sorry to say my cousins behaved very
" badly.   They wished to see Coburg excluded
" from   the Confederation, and consequently
" ruined and lost.   Meanwhile, my poor brother
" was ill of typhus at Koenigsburg.   When he
" had to leave this place for Munich, he fell into
" the river, which he was crossing on the ice.
" Though there may be cases of persons suffering
" from typhus who have been cured by cold
" baths, my brother lingered a while, and only
" recovered his health by slow degrees.   My
" poor mother returned to Coburg, and we
" remained a French possession."

Disastrous as it was for Prussia, the treaty
concluded at Tilsit, July 7, 1807, was less hard

for the Duchy of Coburg. In point of fact it re-established Duke Ernest in full and peaceable possession of his dominions. In the month of November the new duke went with his brother Leopold to Paris, to thank him who at that time held in his victorious hands the destinies of princes. Napoleon gave them a distinguished reception, and they prolonged their stay in the capital of the French empire.

During the spring of 1808, Prince Leopold was very nearly carried off by a typhoid fever, and regained his strength very slowly. In October he again met Napoleon at the Congress of Erfurt, where were gathered together the Emperors of France and Russia, and the four new kings of the Confederation of the Rhine. Leopold backed with all his might the Duke of Coburg's solicitations for an augmentation of territory, but his intelligent moves were not sufficiently supported by the Emperor Alexander.

Leopold was drawn towards the Czar by the ties which bound the house of Coburg to that of the Romanows. He would have liked, therefore, to continue his military career in Russia. Napoleon, however, forbade it, and held Duke

Ernest responsible for the due observance of his
orders.   In vain Prince Leopold endeavoured to
bend the Emperor of the French; in the face of
a threat which meant nothing less than the
dethronement of the Duke of Coburg, there
was nothing left for it but submission. Napoleon
would have liked the prince to take service with
France, but all his offers and all his hints were
always declined or evaded.   Leopold owed his
escape from his embarrassment (as he at a later
period acknowledged) to the friendly intervention
of Queen Hortensia and the Empress Josephine.

Before long Germany was ploughed up afresh
by innumerable armies; they headed towards
Poland; they threatened Russia.   Napoleon
appeared at Dresden.   In his train were the
Emperor and Empress of Austria, the King of
Prussia, the King of Bavaria, the King of Wurtemburg, and all the other princes whom the
powerful master of France considered as his
vassals.   The Duke of Coburg and his brother
Ferdinand also figured in this congress of kings.
But Prince Leopold was "conspicuous by absence."
He judged it advisable not to expose himself to
the fascinations of the great man who wanted

to have him as aide-de-camp. He went to Vienna,
and then to Italy—far away from the scene where
Napoleon was imposing his will.

Leopold felt deeply the humiliation of Germany. "Germany," he said, in after times, "was,
" at the commencement of 1812, in the most
" degrading and humiliating situation. Austria
" and Prussia were reduced to the condition of
" French auxiliaries; all the world trembled,
" except Spain, upheld by England." But the
formidable power of Napoleon was soon to be
hard hit by the frosts of Russia. In November
Germany tingled to hear of the retreat of the
army, and the fearful passage of the Beresina.
On the 18th December, Napoleon re-entered
Paris, where he had been preceded by that
dismal twenty-ninth bulletin which announced
to the world the result of the Russian campaign.

Germany began to rise against French domi-
nation. A ray of hope, as King Leopold said,
came to give the people fresh courage.

The Princes of Coburg took an active part in
the deliverance of the German nation. Already
Duke Ernest had gone off to Berlin, to use his
influence over the mind of Frederick William III.,

who, still irresolute and fearful at this great crisis, had shown extreme displeasure at hearing of General Yorck's defection. The situation of Frederick William was indeed terrible. He was at Potsdam, surrounded by only two or three thousand soldiers of his guard, and at the mercy of Napoleon. The latter, on the smallest suspicion, might have him carried off—him and his —by the division of Marshal Augereau, who occupied Brandenburg. However, the Princes of Coburg were not discouraged. The reigning duke returned to Berlin. Prince Ferdinand went to Vienna, to take soundings of the Austrian intentions. Leopold was off for Munich, to concert measures with another prince, who also showed extreme zealousness for the liberation of Germany. This was the heir-presumptive to the throne of Bavaria (afterwards Louis I.), but lately a general of division under Napoleon, and now one of the promoters of the German uprising. Prince Leopold had contracted a close friendship with him.

Yielding to the energetic pressure of the national party, and to the suggestions of the Duke of Coburg, Frederick William III. left Berlin on the 22nd of January, 1813, and three days

afterwards arrived at the capital of Silesia. But at
Breslau, as at Potsdam, the King of Prussia,
though now surrounded by his own troops, remained undecided, says an historian, between
hatred and dread of Napoleon, between the ambition of re-establishing his crown and the fear of
losing it for ever.[8]   The Duke of Coburg, who
was still at the mercy of France, returned to his
dominions.   But Leopold went secretly from
Munich to Breslau, where he was joined by his
brother Ferdinand, who brought favourable news
from Vienna.   At last Frederick William, catch-
ing some inspiration from the patriotic sentiments
of Baron Stein and General Scharnhorst, gave the
signal for the emancipation of Germany.   On the
28th of February, a treaty of alliance was concluded at Kalisch (in Poland), between Russia
and Prussia.

Prince Leopold repaired to the head-quarters
of the Emperor Alexander at Kalisch.   " I was
" the first German prince," he says, " who joined
" the liberating army."   At the request of his
brother-in-law, the Grand Duke Constantine,

---

[8] *History of the War of* 1813 *in Germany,* by Lieut.-Col.
Charras (Leipzig, 1866, 8vo.), p. 186.

commanding the guards, he was attached to the
staff of that select corps.   As for Prince Ferdinand, he had returned to Vienna and taken his
place again in the Austrian army.

The war of liberation commenced.   The
King of Prussia had at the outset no absolute
confidence in the results.   On arriving at Kalisch
he had expressed to Prince Leopold a fear that
the Russian army would not be strong enough
to sustain the shock of the reorganised French
army.   The prince shared these apprehensions,
which were partially at any rate borne out by
events.   At the latter end of April, the army of
the allies arrived at Dresden on the road to the
Saal.   On the 2nd of May a furious battle took
place in the plains of Lutzen, where Prince
Leopold commanded a body of Russian cavalry.
The allies retired by the line of the Elbe, and on
the 20th of May, at Bautzen, engaged the enemy.
It was a terrible battle, and lasted two days.
" We were not beaten," says King Leopold,
" but, nevertheless, forced to retire into the heart
" of Silesia."   It was he who with his body of
cavalry covered the retreat.[9]

---

[9] Cf. *History of the Consulate and Empire*, by A. Thiers ;
Book 48.

Napoleon, who was still superior to the coalition, committed a great mistake in giving his
consent, on the 4th of June, to the armistice concluded at Pleiswitz, which, being prolonged until
August, allowed the allies to considerably aug-
ment their forces. He committed a still greater
mistake in rejecting the proposals of the Congress
of Prague, in refusing a dominion bounded by
the Rhine, the Alps, and the Meuse. Prince
Leopold, without taking any share in the fruitless
negotiations of Prague, went to reside in the
capital of Bohemia, where he saw the Emperor
Francis of Austria, and lived in the society of
Prince Metternich, Baron Humboldt, and the
other plenipotentiaries.

On the 11th of August, the Congress of
Prague was dissolved ; and next day Austria declared war against Napoleon, and joined Russia
and Prussia. The army of the coalition marched
out of Bohemia, and made for Dresden. On the
26th of August, Prince Leopold distinguished
himself by hurrying with his cuirassiers to the
relief of Prince Eugene of Wurtemburg, who was
attacked by a superior force in his position before
Fort Koenigstein. Three days after, Leopold
had a very sharp affair at Peterswald with a

detachment of French cavalry; being attacked by a superior force he fell back, but not into the hands of the enemy, as was reported at Paris. The same day he had another engagement near Prezen. The allies were threatened with a great danger. General Vandamme, who had 40,000 men under his command, threatened to cut off communications with Bohemia. On the 30th he was himself attacked at Kulm, and in this fight the Russian guard again behaved with the greatest vigour. Vandamme and two other generals, Haxo and Guyot, were taken prisoners. The French lost, besides, from 5000 to 6000 killed and wounded, 7000 prisoners, and forty-eight pieces of artillery.[10] In the evening,[11] Prince Leopold, who had behaved with great bravery, received on the field of battle the decoration of

---

[10] See *History of the Consulate and Empire*, Book 49.

[11] There is evidently a mistake somewhere, for King Leopold himself is represented as saying: " Prince Leopold " received *on the morning of the 30th*, on the field, the Third " Class, etc., and *later* (? later on the same day), etc." [Vide *Early Years of the Prince Consort*, p. 383.] Of course, Mr. Toots would be quite right to say " it is of no conse-" quence." There is a discrepancy also about the duration of the battles (*vide* same place). Transl.

the third class of the military order of St. George
of Russia. It was not long before he added the
Cross of Maria Theresa of Austria, and the Iron
Cross of Prussia.

The armies of the coalition penetrated into
Saxony, and on the plains of Leipzig fought
with the French the most terrible battle of the
early part of this century. It lasted four days
(October 16-19). Prince Leopold, who had taken
part in these fights of giants, took with the
van-guard the Erfurt road. After a short stay
at Coburg with the Grand Duke Constantine,
he repaired to Frankfort, the head-quarters
of the allied sovereigns. The three princes
of Coburg were then all in the army of
the coalition: Leopold took the direction of
Switzerland, with the Grand Duke Constantine;
Duke Ernest was intrusted with the blockade
of Mayence; Prince Ferdinand marched across
Switzerland with the Austrian army to occupy a
position in Franche-Comté. On the 12th January, 1814, the great head-quarters of the Emperor
of Russia and King of Prussia occupied Bâle.
The Grand Duke Constantine, with Prince
Leopold, betook himself to Elfenaau, near Berne,

the place of residence of the Grand Duchess
Anna Feodorowna (Princess Juliana of Coburg).
He desired a reconciliation, but the overtures
made with this view remained without fruit.[12]   It
is stated, also, that Prince Leopold, at the time
of his journey to Berne, became a member of the
freemason's lodge in that town. On the 30th
of January he penetrated with his cavalry into
France. On the 1st of February, he took part
in the battle of Brienne. He afterwards occupied
Troyes. On the 20th of March, at the engagement of Arcis-on-Aube, he had a command on
the right wing. On the 24th, the allies marched
on Paris. Next day Leopold, who was in the
van-guard, distinguished himself afresh in the
bloody battle of Fère-Champenoise. Finally, on
the 31st, at the head of the cuirassiers of the
Russian Guard, he entered the capital of France.

After staying some time in Paris, where he
was rejoined by his two brothers, after having
witnessed the fall of Napoleon and the restoration of the Bourbons, Prince Leopold, as lieut.-
general in the Russian service, accompanied the

---

[12] The divorce, however, was not pronounced by the Emperor Alexander before 1820.

Emperor Alexander to England. He was then
twenty-four. He was tall of stature, and attractive
in features, and he made himself distinguished
also for the maturity of his intellect, rare sagacity,
and extraordinary tact. These qualities were
still further enhanced by the lustre of a reputation
for bravery honourably won in the late battle-
fields.

CHAPTER II.

1814—1829.

GEORGE III., stricken with insanity, had perforce let fall from his thenceforth powerless hands the sceptre of Great Britain. From 1811 his son, the Prince of Wales, had been in possession of the Regency. He, in 1795, had married his cousin, Caroline of Brunswick. On the 7th of January following, the Princess of Wales gave birth to a daughter, Charlotte Augusta.

Joy reigned amongst the English people, and sorrow in Carlton House, the magnificent residence placed at the prince's disposal in 1784, when he attained his majority. Scarcely had the Princess

Caroline recovered from her confinement, when her husband separated from her, declaring that inclination was a sentiment independent of will, and that he found it impossible to force his own. The princess, so cruelly banished from her husband's hearth, retired to a country house at Blackheath. As for the Prince of Wales, who prided himself upon the name of "first gentleman " of the kingdom," English annalists and historians have taken pains to denounce to posterity his barbarous conduct towards his wife.[1]

Charlotte, the only child of the unhappy marriage, was in 1814 in her nineteenth year. She was not only heiress to the crown of Great Britain; she was possessed of unusual beauty, a cultivated mind, and an energetic spirit.

Amongst the aspirants for her hand, the Prince Regent had favoured the pretensions of the Prince of Orange, son of William I., originally sovereign-prince of the United Provinces, and afterwards King of the Netherlands. Such a union might well commend itself to certain statesmen, and even to a portion of the public.

---

[1] *See*, amongst others, Thackeray in " *The Four Georges*."

But the Princess Charlotte declared that she would decide only according to the dictates of her heart. Prince Leopold of Saxe-Coburg was presented at Carlton House, and he became her choice. She distinguished him before all, though he was then neither powerful nor even rich.[a] He lived not in a palace, but on the second floor of a meanish-looking house in High Street, Marylebone. Such were the quarters assigned to him by the Russian ambassador, Count Lieven, who had to find lodgings for the Emperor Alexander's staff.

King Leopold's own description is said to be as follows : " I forgot to mention a subject which has " been talked of as a proof of the great poverty " of Prince Leopold when he was in England in " 1814. He came with the Emperor Alexander, " and as long as the emperor remained himself in " England, the lodgings of the persons who had " come with him were paid by him. The Russian " ambassador, Count Lieven, had the charge of " locating the suite ; and as they lived in Harley

---

[a] We are assured that the personal income of the prince was at this time not more than £400 a year.

" Street, they lodged the people near it, and had
" taken a rather indifferent lodging for Prince
" Leopold, in High Street, Marylebone.   The
" prince had nothing to do with the choice of that
" lodging, and as soon as the emperor had left, he
" lodged himself in Stratford Place, in a house
" where General Count Beroldingen, the Wurtem-
" burg minister, lodged, and where he remained
" till he left London.   He might have explained
" these things before, but he had not thought it
" worth while." (" Early Years of the Prince
Consort," p. 386.)

The Princess Charlotte formally refused the
future heir to the kingdom of the Netherlands,
and took refuge with her mother.[3]   Great was

---

[3] Count Van der Duyn, who, with Baron Fagel, was intrusted with the duty of negotiating in London the marriage
of Princess Charlotte with the Prince of Orange, has explained at length in his *Recollections* the causes of the
rupture. . . . "It was," he adds, "on the occasion of the
" drawing-up of the articles, and when an agreement had
" been made for a residence of the future couple, partly in
" England, partly in Holland, that Princess Charlotte es-
" caped secretly from her father's palace, and fled for refuge
" to her mother, whereupon she herself declared to the
" Prince of Orange that the union could not be thought of.
" A little after, the rupture was officially communicated by

the Regent's irritation against his daughter and
Prince Leopold, but the majority of the public
were in favour of the prince.   He likewise found
support amongst the ministers; the Wellesleys
and Lord Castlereagh were for him ; and in the
royal family the Duke of Kent and the Duke
and Duchess of York showed themselves equally
well disposed towards him.   A contemporary
says that the exterior of Prince Leopold had in it
something which could not fail to prepossess the
English in his favour.   "His manly air," he
adds, " his expressive face, on which were written
" modesty and kindliness, and his simple manners,
" without affectation or pretension, all seemed to
" tell of qualities perfectly in harmony with
" English taste."

After the departure of the Emperor of Russia,
Prince Leopold still prolonged his stay in
England.   He left his humble apartments in
Marylebone, and went to lodge in Stratford

"the English ministers to the ambassadors of the Prince-
"Sovereign of the United Provinces (June, 1814).   The
" Prince of Orange immediately returned to the Hague. . . "
*Biographical Notice and Recollections of Count Van der
Duyn and Baron Capellen, etc.* (St. Germains, 1852), p. 84.

Place, in the house where General Count Beroldingen, Minister of Wurtemburg, lived. The
Regent, who had been convinced that no dishonourable intrigue had been plotted, had soft-
ened towards Leopold, and received him quite
graciously on the eve of his departure from
London. The prince was present at a magnificent ball given at Carlton House to conclude
the season; and he there met nearly all the
members of the royal family, and the reception
they gave him was very friendly.

Family mourning recalled him to Germany.
He crossed Holland to reach Amorbach, the
residence of his younger sister, Victoria of Saxe-
Coburg, who on the 4th of July had lost her
husband, the Prince of Leiningen. Leopold, in
concert with his brothers, arranged for the
guardianship of the two children born of the
marriage death had just dissolved; and then
returned to Coburg, to see his mother once
more.

At the end of August the Duke of Coburg
and Prince Ferdinand took their departure for
Vienna, where the famous congress had commenced its labours. Leopold joined his brothers

towards the close of September. He attracted
the same observation in the midst of those
emperors, kings, and princes, of all the illustrious throng, in fact, which then filled the
capital of Austria. "I for the first time met
"this young man in society," says a contemporary: "he was acquainted with the Prince de
"Ligne, who promptly introduced us. He
"seemed to me then as modest as he was hand-
"some. But never did noble blood and noble
"birth reveal themselves more clearly than in
"the distinguished mien and easy bearing of this
"representative of an illustrious house."[4] He
took a considerable part in the diversions of the
court, and he had his place marked out in the
tableaux vivants and acting charades which were
then in vogue. When the characters of
Olympus were one day to be distributed, Jupiter
fell to the lot of Leopold, whose beauty, says the
same contemporary, was remarkable.

During these fêtes Prince Ferdinand of Saxe
Coburg, at that time a lieutenant-field-marshal,

---

[4] *Fêtes and Recollections of the Congress of Vienna,* by
Count A. de la Garde, vol. i., *passim.*

gained the heart of the rich heiress of the Koharys,[5] to whom he was engaged to be married on the 2nd of January, 1816.

But the amusements at the Court of Austria did not distract Prince Leopold's attention from serious business. Duke Ernest, according to the autobiographical notes of the King of the Belgians, had compromised, by ill-considered proceedings, the hopes he had based upon the protection of the Emperor Alexander. His brother now reopened the negotiations, on condition that the Duke had no hand in the matter. The result was fortunate for the House of Coburg, without, however, realizing the prince's original expectations. He had been obliged, moreover, to struggle against the ill-will of Prussia, by whom Duke Ernest was never forgiven for having opposed her designs touching the King of Saxony. "If Chevalier Gentz had not kindly " informed Prince Leopold that the Prussians had " prevented the arrangement for Coburg from

---

[5] Antonietta Maria Gabriella, daughter and heiress of Francis Joseph, Prince of Kohary, Chancellor and First Grand Master of the Court of Hungary (*History of the House of Saxe-Coburg-Gotha*, p. 253).

" being in the treaty which was to be signed the
" following day, the hopes of Coburg would
" have been wrecked at the last moment; as it
" was, the prince got the Russian and Austrian
" ministers to put into the treaty the paragraph
" concerning Coburg, to the great displeasure
" of Baron Von Humboldt.   From that moment
" the Prussians showed the utmost hostility to
" Coburg, and never executed the part of their
" engagement by which they were bound to ex-
" change the territories which had been assigned
" to Cobourg on the Rhine against some
" detached territories in Saxony, which were
" most desirable for Coburg."   ["Early Years,
etc.," p. 385.]

Napoleon's return from the isle of Elba once
more summoned Europe to arms.   The Duke of
Coburg received command of a corps of observation destined to remain in Alsatia.   Prince
Ferdinand resumed his place in the Austrian
army.   Prince Leopold had to rejoin the Russian
army, to place himself at the head of his division
of cavalry.   But after a troubled reign of one
hundred days, Napoleon was hopelessly beaten on
the plains of Waterloo (June 18, 1815).   The

Russians did not enter France until July; still
the division of Prince Leopold was not to cross
the frontier. He obtained, however, from the
Emperor Alexander, authority to visit Paris.
" He there remained," as he himself says, "occu-
" pied with political affairs, and obtained for his
" brother an augmentation of territory. He was
" treated in the most courteous manner by the
" English. The Duke of Kent, by the medium
" of an officer devoted to his service, facilitated
" the Prince's communications with the Princess
" Charlotte, who showed a disposition to remain
" unshaken in her resolution. The princess and
" her friends desired that the prince should come
" to England. But he, for fear of making affairs
" worse, thought the Regent should not be set at
" defiance. The princess considered that he
" showed an excessive prudence, and was not
" pleased; but the course of events proved that
" the prince had been wise to show patience."
[Cf. " Early Years, etc.," p. 387.]

At the commencement of 1816, Leopold
arrived at Berlin, charged by his brother with
the duty of effecting the territorial exchange
already spoken of; but all his attempts were

useless. It was at the capital of Prussia that he
received, together with an explanatory letter from
Lord Castlereagh, a letter in which the Prince
Regent invited him to return to England. He
was obliged to defer his departure until the arrival
of his brother, Duke Ernest, who was coming
from Vienna, and this delay brought him to the
very middle of winter. At last he left Berlin
during very severe weather; but being attacked
by serious indisposition, he found himself, to
his great despair, obliged to stop at Coburg.
However, as the letters from England became
more and more urgent, he left Coburg in
February, and after being detained some time at
Calais by a storm, he happily arrived in London.
Lord Castlereagh took him to Brighton, where
the Regent received him with gracious courtesy,
and spoke of the Princess Charlotte and his views
respecting her marriage. Soon after there
arrived the Queen (wife of George III.) and the
princesses. With them was Charlotte, whom
Leopold saw again for the first time. The
friends of the heiress to the throne, belonging
chiefly to the Opposition, had inspired her with
a fear that the prince would display too much

humility towards the Regent, and she herself
expressed her apprehensions with some warmth.
Leopold reassured her.   There was no betrothal:
but the marriage was announced as being decided
upon (*Vide* " Early Years, etc.," p. 388).

Early in March the Princess Charlotte left
Brighton, and went to Cranbourn Lodge (Windsor
Park), where she lived with the Dowager Lady
Ilchester and the other persons of her household.

After considerable delay, the marriage, which
was originally to have taken place in April, was
fixed for the 2nd of May.   Prince Leopold, on
whom the Prince Regent had conferred the rank
of general, was already invested with all the rights
of an English citizen, put on an equality, in
respect of titles, with the royal family, and had
settled upon him, by Act of Parliament, a pension
of 50,000*l.* a year (exclusive of 10,000*l.* for the
Princess's private purse. Transl.).

On the 2nd of May, at half-past 7 s. c.,
Princess Charlotte, who had arrived at the palace
of the Queen (her grandmother, Queen Charlotte,
wife of George III.), descended the grand stair-
case, conducted by Princess Augusta on her right,
and Col. Stephenson on her left, and entered the

grand hall, where the Queen joined her . The
Queen got into a carriage with the Princesses
Augusta and Elizabeth ; and the Princesses Mary
and Sophia of Gloucester followed in another
carriage.. The cheers of the people accompanied
them to Carlton House, where the Queen and
Princesses arrived at eight o'clock by the garden
gate. Prince Leopold, on his side, in the full
uniform of a British general, started at half-past
eight from the Duke of Clarence's house, with
two court carriages. In one were Lord James
Murray, lord in waiting, Baron Hardenbroke,
the prince's secretary, and Sir Robert Gardiner,
his equerry. Prince Leopold, accompanied by
Baron Just, Saxon minister at the court of Great
Britain, and Mr. Chester, assistant-master of the
ceremonies, was in the other carriage. When
the prince, on his arrival at Carlton House,
alighted amidst the crowd of spectators, the
women showed great enthusiasm, and did not
confine themselves to waving of handkerchiefs,
the usual mark of congratulation, but coming
close to him, tapped him on the shoulder, as
a sign of their wish for his future happiness,
and showered blessings upon him. The Queen

and the royal family, the Duke and Duchess d'Orléans,[6] and the Prince of Saxe-Coburg, were on their arrival ushered into the Prince Regent's own room. The grand drawing-room, hung with crimson, had been set out for the celebration of the marriage. An altar, covered with velvet of the same colour, had been raised there; in front of it were cushions and prayer-books borrowed from the Chapel Royal, St. James's; the massive candlesticks and plate came from the military chapel at Whitehall. The sergeant of the Chapel Royal exercised his office of verger. At the moment fixed for the cere-mony, the Queen, the Prince Regent, and all the party, assembled in the great hall. Princess Charlotte and Prince Leopold remained in the private room. At last, the assembly being com-plete, and all being ready for the celebration of the ceremony, the Lord Chamberlain returned to the Prince Regent's room, and conducted the Prince of Coburg to the altar. He then went

---

[6] At the time of the events brought about by the return of Napoleon from Elba, the Duke and Duchess d'Orléans had returned to England, and in 1816 were still living at Twickenham.

for the Princess Charlotte. The Duke of Clarence, giving his arm to his niece, conducted her to the altar, where she was received by the Prince Regent. The Archbishop of Canterbury then began the celebration of the rite, and the Prince Regent gave his august daughter away to the Prince of Coburg. The Queen occupied a seat to the right of the altar. On the completion of the ceremony, the royal pair received the congratulations of all persons present, and withdrew, the Prince of Coburg giving his arm to his bride. They started immediately for Oatlands.[7] Salvoes of artillery from St. James's Park and from the Tower announced the happy event to the metropolis.[8]

Prince Leopold, after having looked at several other estates, had chosen Claremont, a beautiful place which belonged to Mr. R. Ellis. It was obtained for the young couple, who came and established themselves there in September, to spend the autumn.

Across the ocean, in the island of St. Helena,

---

[7] The residence of the Duke of York.

[8] This account is taken from the journals of the period.

Napoleon, fallen from the height of his power, was full of the marriage of Prince Leopold and the Princess Charlotte. We read in the 'Mémorial:'

" November, 1816. The public papers which
" had been procured for us spoke of the marriage
" of Prince Leopold of Saxe-Coburg with the
" Princess Charlotte of Wales.

" The emperor said: ' This Prince Leopold
" ' might have been my aide-de-camp: he begged
" ' it of me,[9] and I don't know what prevented
" ' his appointment. It is very lucky for him he
" ' did not succeed: that appointment would
" ' doubtless have lost him the marriage he has
" ' now made: and then that people should come
" ' and tell us about luck and ill-luck (chance)
" ' in men's lives here below ! . . . .'

" The conversation then turned upon the
" Princess Charlotte of England. Some one
" said she was extremely popular in London, and
" gave no equivocal signs of force of character.
" It was a ` saying amongst many Englishmen

---

[9] It has been seen that it was, on the contrary, Napoleon who wanted to get the prince as aide-de-camp.

" that she would be a second Elizabeth. She
" herself, it was maintained, had some notion of
" the kind. The speaker said he was in London,
" in 1814, just when the young princess, after
" the outrages inflicted upon her mother, before
" the eyes of the allied sovereigns, fled from the
" house of the Prince Regent her father, leaped
" into the first hackney-carriage she could find,
" and flew to the house of her mother, whom she
" adored.   English gravity showed itself indulgent
" upon this occasion : people were pleased to find
" an excuse for a somewhat grave indiscretion in
" the moral sentiment which prompted it. The
" young princess would not leave her mother's
" house. The Duke of York, or another of her
" uncles, and perhaps again the Lord High
" Chancellor, had to go and persuade her to
" return to her father, by showing her that her
" obstinacy might expose her mother to the
" extent even of putting her life in danger.

   " Princess Charlotte had already shown force
" of character in refusing to marry the Prince
" of Orange, whom she rejected for the special
" reason that she would have been obliged to
" live sometimes out of England—a national

" sentiment which still further endeared her to
" the English people.

    " She fixed upon Prince Leopold, say the
" English who are here, by her own free choice
" alone ; and she loudly declared that she
" expected to be happy, because she had listened
" to no guide but her own heart. The prince
" pleased her mightily. ' I can easily believe it,'
" observed the emperor; 'for if I remember
" ' rightly, he was the handsomest young man I
" ' saw at the Tuileries.' It was mentioned that
" the English here gave a few days ago what they
" called a proof of the character and dignity
" which distinguished their young sovereign that
" would be. One of the ministers having had
" an interview with her, pending the arrangements
" for the marriage, for the purpose of settling
" some domestic details, made certain proposals
" that she considered were not for her to listen to.

    " ' My lord,' said she proudly, ' I am heiress
" ' of Great Britain ; I shall one day wear a crown :
" ' I know that, and my spirit is equal to my high
" ' destiny ; so do not think you can treat me as
" ' if it were otherwise. Do not suppose that,
" ' to marry Prince Leopold, I could or would

" 'ever consent to be *Mrs. Coburg;* rid yourself
" ' of such a notion,' etc. The young princess
" is the idol of the English, who flatter themselves
" they see in her some promise of a brighter
" future.

  " The emperor, returning to the subject of
" Prince Leopold, who might have been his aide-
" de-camp, said : 'A host of other German princes
" ' solicited the same favour. When I created
" ' the Confederation of the Rhine, the sovereigns
" ' who were parties to it had no doubt but that I
" ' was ready to renew in my own person the
" ' etiquette and forms of the Holy Roman
" ' Empire : and all of them—even the kings—
" ' showed how anxious they were to form my
" ' retinue, and become, one my chief butler,
" ' another my chief baker, etc. About this time
" ' German princes had literally invaded the
" ' Tuileries; they filled its drawing-rooms, and
" ' modestly mingled, and lost themselves, amongst
" ' the rest of you. It is true it was much the
" ' same with Italians, Spaniards, and Portuguese ;
" ' and that the greater part of Europe was
" ' assembled at the Tuileries . . . . The fact is,'
" he concluded, 'that during my reign Paris was

" ' queen of the nations, and the French were the
" ' first people of the universe.' "[10]

Prince Leopold had from the first some apprehensions on the score of his wife's health. She
had suffered a great deal from the sad effect of her
parents' dissensions ; but during her residence at
Claremont a happy improvement had taken place.
Alas! all this happiness was to disappear suddenly.
On the 6th of November, 1817, all England was
thrown into mourning : for the night before the
Princess Charlotte had departed this life, a few
hours after having given birth to a still-born child.
" At one blow," in the words of the ' Autobio-
' graphical Notes,' " all the hopes and all the
" happiness of Prince Leopold were annihilated.
" He never recovered again the feelings he had
" experienced during that short period."

We read in ' Early Years, etc. :' " The
" Princess's health was liable to be a little de-
" ranged. Her nerves had suffered much during
" the last few years. She improved, however,
" visibly at Claremont. From March there began

---

[10] *Memorial of St. Helena* (Brussels, 1823), vol. vii.,
pp. 113-116.

" to be hopes. The Princess's health was in a
" satisfactory state.   She gave, however, up walk-
" ing too much, which proved pernicious.   No-
" vember saw the ruin of this happy home, and
" the destruction at one blow of every hope and
" happiness of Prince Leopold.   He has never
" recovered the feeling of happiness which had
" blessed his short married life."   And in a foot-
note is added : " She died on the 5th, in childbed,
" a few hours after the birth of a still-born son.
" Had she been skilfully treated, her life at least
" would have been saved."

The English people strove to console him by
demonstrations of sympathy. The regent, on
his part, granted him the title of " Prince Royal,"
with authority to bear the arms of Great Britain,
and conferred upon him the rank of Field-
Marshal, as well as the honours of a Privy-
Councillor.

But Prince Leopold would not leave Claremont.   During the lifetime of the Princess
Charlotte the Duke of Kent had offered his hand
to the Dowager Princess of Leiningen (Victoria
of Saxe-Coburg).   This marriage, greatly desired
by the ill-starred Charlotte, was accomplished after

her death. It was celebrated at Coburg, May 29th, 1818, according to the Lutheran rite, and two months later solemnized afresh at Kew, in conformity with the ceremonial of the English Church.[11] The Duke and Duchess of Kent passed the greater part of this year at Claremont, where Prince Leopold continued to live in almost complete retirement.[12]

In September the prince at last resolved to turn his steps towards Switzerland, to visit his other sister (Grand Duchess Anna Feodorowna) : then he went to Coburg, and stayed there until May, 1819. He returned by Paris to England. On the 24th of May, 1819, at Kensington Palace, the Duchess of Kent had given birth to the Princess Alexandrina Victoria, who was destined

---

[11] *History of the House of Saxe-Coburg.*

[12] " The prince being determined," says' one of his biographers, "never to leave Claremont, resolved to finish in " solitude the works commenced by his wife, and to pursue " the course of beneficence he had hitherto shared with " her. A little temple, begun by the princess, in the most " beautiful of gardens, where she had tasted those domestic " joys which are so seldom granted to princes, was finished " by Leopold, and converted into a mausoleum. Under its " vault was placed a bust of the Princess Charlotte."

to reign gloriously over the British empire.
During the summer, Prince Leopold travelled in
Scotland and various parts of England. He
himself says that he was everywhere the object
of the warmest manifestations. But the trip
appeared to displease the Regent, who, besides,
was anything but gracious towards his brother,
the Duke of Kent. The latter, whose health
was impaired, went, by his doctor's recommenda-
tion, to live during the autumn in the milder
air of Devonshire. He took up his abode at Sidmouth, with the Duchess, his wife. In January,
1820, Prince Leopold was at Lord Craven's, when
he received the news that the Duke of Kent had
caught cold during a visit to Salisbury Cathedral,
and that his condition had become alarming.
The prince hastened to Sidmouth, where the
Duke of Kent died, January 23rd, in the arms of
his wife. The despair of the duchess was profound, and with good reason. Not only had she
lost a devoted and affectionate husband, but she
was left without the means of subsistence. Prince
Leopold took the widow and orphan under his
protection. He removed them to Kensington,
established them subsequently at Claremont, and

for several years provided for the maintenance of their household.[13]

Poor George III. died six days after his son, the Duke of Kent. He was succeeded by the Prince of Wales, as King George IV. The new king at first showed himself very well disposed towards his son-in-law. But the latter maintained a prudent reserve; his conduct, according to his own expressions, was regulated with a view to what might happen to Queen Caroline. This unhappy princess was then staying near Lake Como, after her long and adventurous travels through Germany, Italy, Greece, the Archipelago, Syria, and Judea. Scandalous rumours had been set afloat with respect to the relations which it was said had been established during her travels between her and her courier, or equerry, the handsome Bartholomew Bergami. Scarcely was George IV. on the throne, when, through the medium of Lord Hutchinson, he had an offer made to his wife of 50,000*l.* pension, if she would give up her title of queen and any other which

---

[13] In 1825 Parliament voted an annuity of £6000 a year for the education of the Princess Victoria and the maintenance of her household.

would recall the ties which united her to the English royal family, and if she consented never to return within the British Isles. Far from accepting this insulting offer, Caroline embarked for England, and on the 6th of June, 1820, the people conducted her in triumph to London. George IV., in his exasperation, had a charge of adultery brought against the queen by his prime minister, Lord Liverpool, that she might be pronounced unworthy to share the throne. Then there commenced before the House of Lords one of the most celebrated and scandalous trials of the century. On the one side were George IV. and his government, pitiless and unyielding ; on the other the unfortunate queen, defended by the untiring energy and eloquence of Brougham, and encouraged and supported by public opinion. The House of Lords at last pronounced her guilty, by 123 votes to 95. But the ministry recoiled in the very face of their triumph : they considered it dangerous to give effect to the decision of the lords, moved a six months' adjournment, and entirely dropped the prosecution of the bill they had been so anxious for.

During these painful debates the position of

Prince Leopold had been almost insupportable. He had for an instant conceived the idea of going far away from England, to be with his mother, the Dowager Duchess of Coburg, then seriously ill. But how, said he afterwards, could he quite abandon the mother of Princess Charlotte, who had loved her so dearly? He determined, however, not to interfere until the end of the judicial inquiry. This line of conduct seemed to him the fairest. When the moment he had been waiting for arrived, he went openly to Brandenburg House, the residence of Queen Caroline, to pay his mother-in-law a visit. She received him with great affection; but she was restless, agitated, unhappy; her look was peculiar, and she made the most absurd remarks. In the state of indescribable excitement in which the country was, the visit of Prince Leopold made a great noise, and helped to restore public opinion in favour of the queen. It likewise produced a sensible influence on the lords and the ministry, and it was not without effect upon the abandonment of the proceedings. George IV., who, by-the-by, was very vindictive, never forgave Prince Leopold for this step. He had even declared he

would never see his son-in-law again; but by
the intervention of the Duke of York an interview was arranged. George IV., whose curiosity
was irrepressible, begged Prince Leopold to describe the dress Queen Caroline wore on the
occasion of his visit, and to recount other equally
puerile details.[14]

We read in the "Early Years, etc.," p. 391 :
" Prince Leopold's position became unbearably
" distressing between the king and Queen Caro-
" line. A severe illness of his mother, the
" Dowager Countess of Coburg, would have
" given a colour to his leaving England, to keep
" out of the painful struggle which was going on.
" It was much wished by the king, who employed
" Lord Lauderdale in this sad affair; but how
" abandon entirely the mother of Princess Char-
" lotte, who, though she knew her mother well
" loved her very much? The prince determined
" not to interfere till the evidence against the
" queen should be closed, so that whatever he
" might do could not influence the evidence.
" This decision was evidently the most honest and

---

[14] Queen Caroline died, August 7, 1821.

" the most impartial.   He waited till the evidence
" was closed, and then paid a visit to his mother-
" in-law at Brandenburg House.   She received
" him kindly ;   looked very strange, and said
" strange things.   The country was in a state of
" incredible excitement, and this visit was a great
" card for the queen.   It had an effect on the
" lords which it ought not to have had, as it
" could not change the evidence ; but it is certain
" that many lords changed, and ministers came
" to the certainty that the proceedings could
" not be carried further.   They proposed that
" the measure should be given up.   The king,
" who had been, it must be confessed, much
" maltreated during this sad trial, was furious, and
" particularly against Prince Leopold.   He never
" forgave it, being very vindictive, though he
" occasionally showed kinder sentiments, par-
" ticularly during Mr. Canning's being minister.
" He of course at first declared that he would
" never see the prince again.   However, the Duke
" of York arranged an interview.   The king
" could not resist his curiosity, and got Prince
" Leopold to tell him how Queen Caroline was
" dressed, and all sorts of details."

Residence in England became after this far from agreeable for the king's son-in-law. So after the coronation of George IV., which took place in July, 1821, the prince went to Coburg, whence he escorted his mother to Genoa. After remaining some time with her he visited Florence, Rome, and Naples. Early in September of the next year he went to Vienna, to see the Emperor Alexander. Lord Londonderry (Charles), with the design of pleasing George IV., did all in his power to get Prince Leopold a bad reception, and he was backed by Prince Metternich, who had an idea that the son-in-law of the King of England aspired to the throne of Greece. The arrival of the Duke of Wellington put an end to all this chicanery. In October Prince Leopold returned to Coburg, and remained there some time with his family. In December he removed to Paris, on his way to England at the commencement of 1823. He passed a great portion of this year at Claremont and Ramsgate, with the Duchess of Kent and her children.[15] In August, 1824, he

---

[15] " These were the happiest days of the Queen's child-'hood" (*Vide* note by the Queen in "Early Years, etc.," p. 392. Transl.).

returned to Coburg, but arrived too late to pre-vent some painful events.

Duke Ernest I. had married, on the 31st of July, 1817, Louise of Saxe-Gotha-Altenburg, daughter of Duke Augustus, who died in 1822. He had by her two sons, Ernest Augustus, born at Coburg, June 21, 1818, now reigning Duke of Saxe-Coburg-Gotha, one of the most enlightened sovereigns in Germany, the energetic promoter of German unity, and Albert Francis, born at Rosenau, August 26, 1819, an excellent prince, whom England will mourn for a long time yet. In 1826 the Duke of Saxe-Coburg separated from his wife, who went to live at Paris, where she died, August 30, 1831.

Leopold came back from the continent in January, 1825, and returned thither the following year. He went first of all to Carlsbad, and after-wards to Coburg, where he lent his kind offices to secure the arrangements resulting from the death of Frederick II., last Duke of Saxe-Gotha-Altenburg.[16] A convention, signed November 12, 1826, stipulated that the Duke of Coburg

---

[16] He died, February 11, 1825. *Vide* " Early Years, etc.," pp. 41, 393.

should obtain Gotha, in exchange for which he should cede to the Duke of Meiningen the principality of Saalfeld. Prince Leopold and other members of his family felt deeply the loss of Saalfeld and the charming neighbourhood on the borders of the Saal. But Italy also had powerful attractions for Leopold. He returned thither, and spent the winter at Naples, where he had an attack of fever which at one time excited fears for his life. In the spring of 1827 he was back again in England; and he lived the greater part of this year at Claremont, *Cam*bridge,[17] and Ramsgate, with the Duchess of Kent and Princess Victoria.

In 1828, Leopold returned to Paris. Some ardent Royalists, seeing the favour with which he was treated by Charles X., spoke of the advantages which might result from his marriage with the Duchess de Berry.[18] But this project did not at all please the prince, who, moreover, was far from an adherent of the retrograde notions which prevailed amongst the Legitimists. From Paris

---

[17] *Sic* in original : a misprint, no doubt, for *Tun*bridge. *Vide* " Early Years, etc.," p. 393. Transl.

[18] *Vide* " Early Years, etc.," p. 394.

he went to Silesia, to meet the King of Prussia
(Frederick William III.). He was attracted
thither especially by a desire of seeing once more
the best friend he ever had, according to his own
expressions, viz., Prince William of Prussia, the
king's youngest brother.   The Prince Royal
(afterwards Frederick William IV.), on his side,
made Prince Leopold promise to rejoin him at
Naples.   And there, indeed, the latter was in
November, and prolonged his stay on the continent until March, 1829.   On returning by Paris
to England, he became earnestly occupied with a
project which might once more change his destiny.

CHAPTER III.

1829, 1830.

LEOPOLD AND THE GREEKS—OFFER OF THE SOVEREIGNTY OF
GREECE—LEOPOLD'S REFUSAL—DIFFERENT OPINIONS ABOUT
HIS CONDUCT.

As early as 1825 the insurgent Greeks had cast
their eyes on Leopold of Saxe-Coburg. Orlando
of Hydra and Lurioti were deputed to sound
him. They also entered into correspondence with
George Canning, who, since the death of the
Marquis of Londonderry, in 1822, had been
minister of foreign affairs. Canning put before
Prince Leopold the propositions which had been
submitted to him, advising him, however, not to
entertain them. Not only did he consider the
affairs of Greece still too much embroiled, but
he also loudly declared that the prince would

be far more useful in England.[1]   As for Leopold,
he did not recoil before the dangerous, as well as
honourable career open before him ; and perhaps
he would even then have accepted the overtures
of the Greek provisional government, if he had
not seen an almost insurmountable obstacle in
the discord between the powers. Austria in
particular, under the influence of Prince Metternich, did not conceal her aversion for the revolu-
tionists who conjured up the shades of Leonidas
and Demosthenes.

In 1827, France, England, and Russia appeared
to unite for the protection of that heroic people ;
but the treaty signed in London, July 6th,
guaranteed as yet only simple mediation. Greece
was to form a State apart, subject to the suzerainty of the Sultan. The Greeks spurned this
subjection, and the protecting powers were in-
duced to assume a more energetic attitude. The
battle of Navarino (20th October, 1827), and
then the French expedition in the Morea (May,
1828), marked new phases in the tragic annals
of the emancipation of the Hellenes. They rose

---

[1] Vide *The Kingship in Belgium* (by Arendt), p. 60, *seq.*

and rose, until Turkey, after a vain attempt to resist the Russians, submitted, September 14, 1829,
to the conditions of the treaty of Adrianople.

Leopold had not ceased to follow with the
keenest interest the course of events of which
Greece was the scene. He got about him all
books which could give him the most correct
ideas about the country. His sole confidant, it
is said, was Baron Stockmar,[2] who, after having
made the campaigns of 1814 and 1815, as
army surgeon, with the Princes of Saxony, had
accompanied Leopold to England. Such was
the confidence he enjoyed, that after the death of
Princess Charlotte, Leopold had intrusted him
with the duties of comptroller of his household
and with the management of his affairs.

Leopold having before been on terms of pretty
intimate correspondence with Capodistrias, president of the provisional government of Greece,
sent his confidant's brother to the president to
sound his intentions. Capodistrias, in a memo-
randum of May 30, indicated that what he desired
for the future of his country was a monarchical

---

[2] Christian Frederick Stockmar, born at Coburg, August
22, 1787.

government, under a Christian prince, whom the Greeks would require to embrace their form of religion, and to agree with them on the principles on which the country should be governed. He pointed out, moreover, the frontiers which Greece, having become independent, would find indispensable. We are assured that this adroit movement of Prince Leopold, in connection with the president, who had strong Russian sympathies, helped to gain him the support of the court of St. Petersburg.[3]

In November, 1829, the commissioners of the three powers recommenced their conferences in London, having determined to make Greece no longer a tributary but an independent State.

George Canning, who had become Prime Minister, April 12, 1827, had prematurely ended his glorious career, August 8, in the same year. In January, 1828, the Duke of Wellington formed a new cabinet, in which Lord Aberdeen was Foreign Minister. Prince Metternich used the influence which he unhappily possessed over the Duke of Wellington and Lord Aberdeen,

[3] Gervinus's *History of the 19th Century* (French translation), vol. xv., p. 281.

to propose boundaries within which the young state, of which he was the inveterate enemy, would have been, so to speak, stifled. He wished to confine independent Greece to the peninsula of the Morea, and the cabinet of the Duke of Wellington had given in their adherence to that proposal.

Russia, and then France, after the latter had hesitated between other candidates, expressed a formal desire to confer the sovereignty of the new state on Prince Leopold. They consequently begged him to accept a task to which the highest interests of Europe were attached. The Duke of Wellington, however, with his colleagues' consent, rejected the candidature of Prince Leopold, not from personal enmity to himself, but on account of his peculiar position with respect to the King. George IV. happened to be under the influence of his brother, the Duke of Cumberland,[4] the chief of the ultra-Tories, the jealous adversary of the hero of Waterloo. The Duke of Cumberland wished to confer the crown of

---

[4] It is well known that the Duke of Cumberland became, in 1837, King of Hanover, with the names of Ernest Augustus.

Greece upon his brother-in-law, Duke Charles
of Mecklenburg-Strelitz, whilst the Duke of Wellington proposed, as a sort of compromise, Prince
Frederick of the Netherlands, whom the Emperor
Nicholas had originally favoured. As the Duke
of Cumberland had obtained for his candidate
the support of the king, the Duke of Wellington
resolved at last to destroy an influence which incessantly thwarted his policy. He abandoned the
candidature of Prince Frederick, joined the party
of Prince Leopold, and on the 15th January,
1830, assured George IV. that, unless he himself
supported the same candidate, already designated
and accepted by Russia and France, ministers
would resign.

These complications exercised a very sinister
influence upon the ultimate constitution of the
Greek state; for the English cabinet, being
obliged to occupy itself exclusively with the
candidature of Prince Leopold, could not give
sufficient attention to the grave question of
boundaries.

In the "Early Years, etc.," we read: "The
" propositions concerning Greece had now already
" taken a more prominent position. Russia and

" France were particularly favourable, and de-
" sirous to see the prince accept. In England
" matters were also now (1829) progressing.
" Great political events took place in England.
" The Duke of Cumberland had, at that time,
" great influence with the king, and opposed the
" Duke of Wellington's administration most
" bitterly. He took also a violent part in Greek
" affairs, engaging the king to prefer the candi-
" dature of Duke Charles of Mecklenburg-
" Strelitz, the brother of the Duchess of Cumber-
" land.   Ministers pressed the king to accept
" Prince Leopold, and were even forced to
" threaten to resign. This was most unfortunate
" for the Greek affairs, as it rendered it impossible
" for Prince Leopold to press upon a cabinet,
" that staked its existence on the question, those
" measures which many sensible people in Eng-
" land thought necessary for the existence of
" Greece. Prince Metternich had, from the be-
" ginning, wished to ruin the young Greek state.
" Not succeeding in this, he used the influence
" he had with the duke and Lord Aberdeen,
" to propose a frontier which was unaccept-
" able," etc.

On the 3rd February, 1830, the representatives of the three protecting powers[a] having affirmed afresh the independence of the Hellenes, and indicated the frontiers of the new state, resolved to make Prince Leopold an official offer of the hereditary sovereignty of Greece, with the title of *Sovereign Prince*. Before accepting, he desired to confer with the plenipotentiaries and the chief English ministers. On the 9th February, in a conversation with the Duke of Wellington, he declared that he would only consent to become the sovereign of Greece on condition that the Greeks should have the right left them of opposing his nomination ; that he then would demand their free suffrages touching his election ; and that he would besides make his acceptance depend upon a rectification of frontier. And in fact, the note which he wrote from Claremont, February 11th, to the representatives of the three great powers, was at bottom only a conditional acceptance. He therein demanded a more substantial frontier, the intervention of the protecting powers in favour of Candia and Samos, which were going

---

[a] Count Montmorency-Leval, Lord Aberdeen, and Prince Lieven.

to be given up to the Porte, a pecuniary guarantee from the same powers, and an auxiliary force for a period to be determined upon.

But Leopold had higher views. Encouraged by debates in the English parliament, he had expressed a desire that Candia and the Ionian Islands should be made part of the new State. The Duke of Wellington replied that Candia ought to belong to the possessor of the Dardanelles. As for the Ionian Islands, he did not formally oppose their cession; nevertheless, the delays, that were caused with a view of shackling the negotiations, had the same effect as an open opposition.

Finally, the representatives of the three powers, very impatient to be rid of a heavy responsibility, after making Prince Leopold some concessions of secondary importance, and new promises, proclaimed him sovereign of Greece, and officially notified his nomination to the Porte and to the Greek provisional government.

Leopold's acceptance, conditional as it was, had rejoiced the hearts of all who could appreciate his high qualities. One of the first to congratulate him was the celebrated Baron Stein, the

regenerator of Prussia.   He wrote (March 19,
1830): "The election of your R.H. has answered
" the expectations of all friends of Greece, be-
" cause the choice has fallen on a prince of
" illustrious birth, of cool and reflecting mind,
" and with personal experience of eventful affairs:
" a prince who can win hearts and appease pas-
" sions, and who possesses a power of gentle persua-
" sion ; perfectly acquainted, moreover, with the
" political institutions of constitutional countries,
" independent of foreign influence, and for that very
" reason in a position to study only the interests
" of his country."   In his reply, dated April 10,
Leopold showed an honest frankness towards the
illustrious patriot with whom he had many a
time conversed about the eventuality which had
now become realized.   He pointed out, as a
source of great difficulty, the boundaries imposed
upon the new state, notwithstanding his remon-
strances.   He saw another cause for serious embarrassment in the necessity for obtaining from
the powers a full guarantee for the loans that the
melancholy position of Greece rendered indispensable.   "The powers," said he, "will guarantee
" but little more than half what I ask ; on such

" terms I will not accept. It may end in a rup-
" ture; I care not. I am on this subject consistent
" with myself."[6]

This letter was written at Paris, for the prince
left London on the 4th of April for the capital of
France. He was away twenty-five days, and he
did not return to London till April 30. Whilst
he was at Paris he obtained, by great personal
efforts, a guarantee from the three powers for
2,400,000*l*. (60,000,000 frs.) But Lord Aberdeen,
who by-the-by had with difficulty agreed to the
conclusion of the loan, was inflexible as to the
boundaries which the prince made a condition of
his acceptance; he would hear of no modification.

Already undeceived on one point, Leopold
further learned that his election, in its present
stage of accomplishment, met with opposition in
Greece. On the 15th of May he received two
letters from Count Capodistrias, president of the
Provisional Government. They were dated
April 22, and, accompanied by a memorial from

---

[6] *The Life of Minister Baron von Stein*, by S. G. H. Pertz
(Berlin, 1849-55, 6 vols., 8vo.).

the senate, completely destroyed the hypothesis that Greece would give frank and sincere assent to the arrangements of the powers. The senate, on the contrary, made reservations on behalf of the people's rights, and representations against the proposed frontier-line.

The prince no longer hesitated. In a note of the 15th of May, addressed to the plenipotentiaries of the three allied courts, he first summed up the negotiations which had just had so disastrous an issue, and then he put forth the powerful reasons which obliged him to renounce the sovereignty of Greece :—

" When," he wrote, " the undersigned had an " idea of becoming sovereign of Greece, it was " in the hope of being accepted *freely* and " unanimously by the Greek nation, and of being " welcomed as the friend who would repay them " for their long and heroic struggle by assuring " to them their territories, and establishing their " independence upon a permanent and honour- " able basis. It is with the most profound regret " that the undersigned sees his hopes deceived, " and himself forced to declare that the arrange- " ments concluded by the allied powers, together

" with the opposition of the Greeks, depriving
" him of the power of attaining that sacred and
" glorious end, would impose upon him a duty
" of a very different nature; that, in fact, of one
" delegated by the allied powers to hold the
" Greeks in subjection by force of arms.   Such
" a mission would be as contrary to his feelings
" and injurious to his character as it is dia-
" metrically opposed to the object of the treaty
" of July 6, whereby the three powers united for
" the purpose of obtaining the pacification of the
" East.   Consequently the undersigned formally
" resigns into the hands of the plenipoten-
" tiaries a trust which circumstances do not any
" longer permit him to undertake with honour to
" himself, and advantage to Greece and the general
" interests of Europe."

The Duchess of Kent, who had never ceased
to beg her brother not to leave England, welcomed this determination with extreme satisfaction.   Thirty-seven years afterwards Queen
Victoria was writing, further, these touching
words : " The Queen well remembers her joy when
" this took place, as she adored her uncle, and
" was in despair at the thought of his depar-

" ture for Greece."   (" Early Years, etc." p. 396,
note.)

Leopold, however, did not conceal from himself that his conduct might give rise to erroneous
interpretation.   On the 10th of June he sent
Baron Stein another letter, in which he de-
veloped the reasons of his refusal.   " What man
" of honour," said the prince, " would accept the
" sovereignty with the obligation of expelling the
" Greeks from Acarnania and Ætolia, provinces
" of which they are now in complete and tranquil
" possession ?   Sufficiently mature consideration
" has   not   been   given   to   the   consequences.
" Count Capodistrias himself, apart from his
" rightful pretensions in respect of the frontiers,
" has   extemporised   institutions   which   have
" greatly increased the complication of affairs.
" It was with regret that I found myself obliged
" to renounce a position which, in spite of diffi-
" culties, might have been a useful and glorious
" one if the arrangement could have been made
" acceptable to the Greeks.   From the moment
" they considered it hurtful to their chief interests,
" and the powers would make no alteration, it
" became difficult, not to say impossible, to

" expect success. One would have been in the
" painful position of satisfying nobody, whilst the
" sovereign would have been held responsible,
" and have been accused of incapacity. You
" urged me, indeed, when we had our last con-
" versation on this subject, not to accept without
" having the means of success." But Baron
Stein, after having interested himself so keenly
for Greece, and having founded such great
expectations on Prince Leopold's acceptance,
was sure to be disagreeably affected. He expressed his vexation in somewhat absurd terms,
and pushed his harshness to the verge of injustice. He told the prince he should have had
the eye of the believer raised firmly and boldly
heavenward, and reminded him of the struggle
sustained by the Emperor Alexander against
Napoleon. With intimates he was more explicit.
He attributed the prince's determination to selfish
motives, and accused him of pusillanimity. He
wrote: " Instead of facing difficulties, instead of
" finishing what he had begun, he withdraws his
" hand like a coward from the plough, whilst he
" speculates on the changes which may supervene
" on the approaching death of George IV. A

" man with a character of so little resolution is
" not a man to enter on active life with a firm
" step ; he has no tone."[7]

The Philhellenes of France, at that time very
ardent and very influential, showed equal irritation and discontent at the abdication.   One of
the most important organs of the opposition
published a severe estimate " of the conduct of
" Prince Leopold in the affair of Greece."[8]   The
French writer, just as the German statesman, saw
a singular coincidence between Leopold's re-
nouncement and the illness of the king of England.   The letters of Capodistrias, which the
prince had been in such a hurry to send to Lord
Aberdeen, were, according to him, a mere pretence.   " Whoever," says this severe writer,
" knows not what a new perspective the death of
" the king opened to the prince's ambition, would
" find all we could add quite worthless.   Let us
" note, however, that regarded from this new point

---

[7] See *The Life of Minister Baron von Stein,* passim.

[8] *The French Review* (Part for July, 1830), pp. 174-201.
The articles in this collection are not signed ; but it is no
secret that its principal editors were (1828-1830) Messrs.
Guizot and De Barante.

" of view his correspondence no longer shows any
" inconsistency or absurdity.   Ambition being
" admitted as the ruling motive of his conduct,
" it is conceivable that before the end of January,
" the king being well, he should have solicited
" *unconditionally* the sovereignty of Greece;
" that from the end of January to the beginning
" of April, the king being ill, he should have
" sought to gain time, and put off the conclusion
" of the affair; and that, finally, from April 1,
" the king being given over, he should have
" thought only how he might with a plausible pre-
" text back out."   The illness of the King of England, then, was the determining motive of Prince
Leopold's conduct, but not, however, the sole,
exclusive motive.   " If we have not been deceived
" about the prince's character," continued the
French writer, " he is less ambitious than tired of
" idleness; fond of glory, but more fond still of
" the good things of life; and to the German
" fancy which grows so vividly impassioned of
" every new view, unites, as often happens, one of
" those lazy faculties of action which are not the
" less vividly startled at difficulties.   Men of this
" mould are easy to tempt; they are quick to be in-

" fatuated, because they at first see only the beauti-
" ful side of things ; and they are more quick to
" be disgusted, because, having once become
" attached, they can see only the disagreeables."

How ill was the character of Leopold understood by him who wrote these lines ! In the
prince's circumspection he saw nothing but an
inconsistent mind. Leopold was soon to show
that he was capable of founding a State ; that in
intelligent patience, tenacity, and energy, he approached more nearly to William III., called the
Silent, than to those men of vulgar and empty-
pated ambition who build upon sand. The account
given above is believed to be an impartial account
of the negotiations relative to the sovereignty of
Greece. From this account must it not be
concluded, that in his note of May 21, Prince
Leopold unfolded the true reasons, the serious
motives for his determination? " He would not
" be thrust upon a discontented people."[9]

---

[9] The author of the notable *History of the 19th Century*
had inclined to the opinion put forth in 1830 by *The French
Review*. But it appears from a note to the translation
(vol. xv., p. 287), that M. Gervinus has acknowledged some
fresh information, which corrects what he had at first said

Besides, could he guess, could he prophecy the influence the death of George IV. would have on his destinies? This monarch died, June 26, 1830, and was succeeded by his brother, the Duke of Clarence, with the title of William IV. Moreover, William IV. was to reign until June 20, 1837, and at that time the Princess Victoria had attained her majority.

The following letter, given at length, may properly close this chapter :—

----

about Prince Leopold's refusal to accept the crown of Greece. "It will oblige him," says the translator, "to ex- " plain, in a new edition of his work, that the act was the " consequence of external circumstances rather than of per- " sonal motives, in which latter the author had hitherto seen "the only explanation of his conduct." We are, therefore, at one with the eminent professor of the University of Heidelberg.

The hesitation and ultimate refusal of Leopold had, moreover, a happy influence upon the ultimate constitution of independent Greece. This he showed himself, three years after, when he wrote (August, 1833) : "All this diplo- " macy, even when it has no sinister designs, is the very " deuce for pushing you into engagements. I ought to " know something about it, as I have done nothing but " negotiate since November, 1829, nearly four years, and all " that makes a Greek State possible is the result of my weary " work."

" *Renunciation of the Hereditary Sovereignty of*
" *Greece.*

"London, 21st of May, 1830.

" The undersigned, after the most searching
" examination, cannot change the opinion he has
" communicated to the allied courts.   He cannot
" allow that the reply of the President of Greece
" includes a full and entire adhesion to the
" protocols.   The undersigned thinks that it ex-
" presses at the most a forced submission to the
" will of the powers ; and this forced submission
" is even accompanied by reservations of the
" highest importance.

" The character and sentiments of the under-
" signed permit him neither to submit to be thus
" imposed on an unwilling people, nor to be con-
" nected in the mind of that nation with a dimi-
" nution of territory, with the abandonment of
" its military forces, and with the evacuation on
" the part of the Greeks of their lands and houses,
" from which the Turks had up to this moment
" driven them only by a temporary incursion.

" The undersigned always dreaded this result.
" In his communication addressed to the First

" Lord of the Treasury, February 9, he had de-
" clared his inability to govern the Greeks in
" conformity with a treaty which might have for
" its result the spilling of blood and the slaughter
" of their brethren ; he had raised objections to
" the new frontiers, because of their weakness in a
" military point of view, and formally claimed for
" the Greeks the right of opposing his nomina-
" tion.

   " The undersigned must here point out that at
" no time have steps been taken for the drawing
" up of a treaty of which he only regarded the
" protocol (No. 1, February 3rd) as bases, to the
" importance whereof he called the attention of
" the Duke of Wellington in the same note.[10]   If
" this treaty has been retarded it has not been the
" fault of the undersigned ; he never concealed
" from the plenipotentiaries that however disposed
" he may have been to make great personal sacri-
" fices for Greece, no one had a right to demand
" of him that he should enter that country with-
" out obtaining for himself and for the Greeks
" the security which could only be found in the

---

[10] February 9.

" provisions of a solemn treaty. In a *memo-*
" *randum* of May 8, he expressed himself in
" equally positive terms; he declared that it
" would be necessary to conquer the provinces to
" be ceded by the Greeks in order to hand them
" over to the Turks; and that the new sovereign
" could not commence his reign with measures of
" police for the purpose of making the Greeks
" abandon their own hearths and homes.

" If the Greek senate had not manifested any
" opinion, or had manifested such an one as to
" admit of a reasonable hope that it would later
" give in its adhesion to these measures, the
" undersigned might, though unwillingly, have
" submitted to become the instrument of execution
" of these decisions of the allied powers; and he
" would have exerted himself to soften their
" rigour and thwart their tendency, but the lan-
" guage of the senate is as frank as its sentiments
" are natural.

" The undersigned thus finds himself by his
" nomination placed in the painful position of
" being bound by the same deed to coercive
" measures. It will be necessary then that his
" first act as a sovereign should be either to force

" his subjects with the assistance of foreign arms
" to submit to a cession of their goods and pro-
" perties to their enemies, or to unite with them
" in rejecting or eluding the execution of a part
" of the very treaty which places him on the
" throne of Greece.

" It is certain that he will be placed in one
" or the other alternative, because the country
" situated between the two lines, Acarnania and a
" part of Ætolia, which has to be abandoned to
" the Turks, is, as the fortresses also are, in peace-
" able possession of the Greeks. It is the country
" whence Greece can with most advantage provide
" itself with wood for the construction of vessels,
" and it is the country which has furnished the
" best soldiers during the war. The principal
" military chiefs of the Greeks belong to the
" families of Acarnania or Ætolia. After the
" arrival in Greece of the protocol of March 22,
" 1828, and the publication of the adhesion of the
" Turks to the extension of the frontiers fixed by
" the treaty of Adrianople, all the families which
" had survived the war reappeared, and began to
" rebuild their houses and towns, and to cultivate
" their fields. These people will never submit

" afresh to the Turkish yoke without resistance,
" and the other Greeks will not and cannot
" abandon them to their fate.

" Under these circumstances, the duty of the
" undersigned towards Greece is quite plain. In
" all transactions he has only had an eye to the
" interests of the country ; he has constantly pro-
" tested, in his written communications and per-
" sonal interviews with the English ministers and
" with the plenipotentiaries of the Allied Courts,
" against the project of forcing the Greeks into
" any arrangement whatsoever which they would
" consider contrary to their wishes, and destruc-
" tive of the rights on which, as the president[11]
" justly observes, their great sacrifices permit
" them to insist.

" When the undersigned entertained the idea
" of becoming the sovereign of Greece, it was in
" the hope of being recognized *freely* and unani-
" mously by the Greek nation, and of being
" welcomed by it as the friend who would com-
" pensate it for its long and heroic struggle, by
" the security of its territory and the establish-

---

[11] Capodistrias.

" ment of its independence on a permanent and
" honourable basis.

    " It is with the most profound regret that the
" undersigned sees these hopes deceived, and that
" he is forced to declare that the arrangements
" fixed by the Allied Powers, together with the
" opposition of the Greeks, taking from him the
" power of attaining this sacred and glorious end,
" would impose upon him a duty of a very
" different nature; that, in fact, of one delegated
" by the Allied Courts for the purpose of holding
" the Greeks in subjection by force of arms.
" Such a mission would be as contrary to his
" sentiments and injurious to his character as it is
" opposed to the aim of the treaty of July 6,
" whereby the three powers united to obtain the
" pacification of the East. Consequently, the
" undersigned resigns formally into the hands of
" the plenipotentiaries a trust which circumstances
" do not permit him to take upon himself with
" honour to himself and advantage to the Greeks,
" or to the general interests of Europe.

                        " LEOPOLD."

CHAPTER IV.

1830, 1831.

BELGIAN REVOLUTION — CROWN OFFERED TO DUKE DE NE-
MOURS—IS REFUSED—PRINCE LEOPOLD ELECTED KING OF
THE BELGIANS—TRIUMPHAL PROGRESS FROM OSTEND TO
LAEKEN — INAUGURATION OF LEOPOLD I.—DUKE OF WEL-
LINGTON'S SPEECH.

IT is very probable that Prince Leopold, having
refused the throne of Greece, followed with lively
interest the circumstances of the Belgian revolu-
tions.

On the 4th October, 1830, the Provisional
Government determined that the Belgian provinces, forcibly detached from Holland, should
constitute an *independent state,* and convoked a
national congress at Brussels. At the beginning
of the following month a Conference, composed
of the representatives of France, England, Prussia,
Austria, and Russia, met in London at the

request of the King of the Netherlands. It proposed, on the 4th November, to Belgium and
Holland a cessation of hostilities under the intervention of the Powers, assigning to Holland, as
the line of the armistice, the boundaries she had
before the meeting, that is before the treaty of
Paris on the 30th of May, 1814. On the 10th
the Provisional Government gave in its adhesion
to this armistice. The same day the constituent
assembly of the Belgian people met at Brussels.
It proclaimed on the 18th, unanimously, the
independence of Belgium, save the relations of
Luxemburg with the Germanic confederation;
decreed on the 22nd that the form of government
should be an hereditary monarchy; and pronounced, on the 24th, the exclusion for ever of
all members of the House of Orange-Nassau
from all power in Belgium.

From that time, the name of Prince Leopold
of Saxe-Coburg had been mentioned. At the
meeting of the Congress charged with establishing
the independence of the old southern provinces
of the kingdom of the Netherlands, the Prussian
ambassador gave the prince to understand that
King Frederick William III., if he were not

restrained by his family connections with the House
of Orange, would gladly see him at the head of
the new state.   At Brussels, M. Van de Weyer,
member of the Provisional Government, and
other influential men, had likewise called attention
to him.[1]   But the Cabinet of St. James's kept up
an extreme reserve, or, rather, it had not yet
despaired of seeing Belgium established under
the viceroyalty of the Prince of Orange.   Lord
Aberdeen, Secretary of State for Foreign Affairs
in the Duke of Wellington's ministry, formally
declared that he had never admitted more than
an *administrative separation* of the two countries.[2]
On the 16th of November Lord Grey formed
the Whig Cabinet, in which Lord Palmerston
took the place of Lord Aberdeen; but it was
only by degrees that the new ministry gave in its

---

[1] *The Belgic Revolution of* 1830, by Charles White,
vol. iii., chap. 2.

[2] " We reject in the most positive manner the assertion
" which renders us responsible for having sanctioned the
" independence of Belgium.   The only separation we ad-
" mitted was an administrative separation of the two
" countries. But the principle of government was to remain
" the same. . . ."   Lord Aberdeen in the House of Lords
(27 [26 ?] January, 1832).

adhesion to the absolute independence of Belgium.
Nor was it in any hurry to rally to the aid of
Prince Leopold's candidature, regarded with dis-
favour from the first by the court, and the object
even of certain jests on the part of its avowed
organ.

As for the French Government, it had yet to
keep in order the party of movement who coveted
the Belgian and Rhenish provinces.

The Conference of London continued its work
of pacification.   On the 17th November, it made
the armistice of unlimited duration.   On the
20th of December, it proclaimed the dissolution
of the kingdom of the Netherlands, at the same
time that it claimed for itself the right of inter-
fering, even against the will of both countries,
to regulate the conditions of partition.   King
William protested against this protocol; the
insurrectionary government subscribed to it
conditionally.   The Conference, going a step
further, decreed, by new protocols on the 20th
and 27th January, 1831, bases of separation
between Belgium and Holland.   The Congress,
in its turn, protested energetically against those
acts which dispossessed Belgium of Luxemburg

and the left bank of the Scheldt. King William, on the contrary, agreed to the conditions of partition.

Such was the state of things when the congress approached the important question of electing a Head of the State. Louis Philip had at first declined all proposals which aimed at placing the Duke de Nemours on the new throne. But when Duke Augustus of Leuchtenberg, son of Eugène de Beauharnais, had met with a large number of supporters in the heart of the national assembly, the French Cabinet, for fear of Bonapartism, did all in its power to insure the election of the Duke de Nemours. This young prince was proclaimed on the 3rd of February.[3] Louis Philip,

---

[3] The principal promoters of this election were, in Brussels, MM. Bressen and De Lawoestine; at Paris, Count de Celles, member of Congress and of the diplomatic committee. M. de Celles had married Mdlle. de Valence, granddaughter of Mdme. de Genlis, whose aunt, Mdme. de Montessu, had been married morganatically to Louis Philip's grandfather. At Paris the commissioner-general was named who was to have governed Belgium during the minority of the Duke de Nemours : it was M. Teste. With respect to Duke Augustus of Leuchtenberg, it is known that he afterwards married Donna Maria, Queen of Portugal, and died in 1835.

having then to choose between a general war and an attempt to erect a throne for one of his sons, declared, not without having hesitated for some time, that he would imitate neither Louis XIV. nor Napoleon.   On the 17th he solemnly refused the offer of the Belgian Congress.

The following extracts from letters find appropriate place here :—

*" M. Behr to the President of the Committee on
" Foreign Relations.'*

"London, February 8, 1831.

"Everybody was expecting the nomination of " the Duke de Nemours, and nevertheless it has " produced a great sensation. The *Courier* ap- " peared on Sunday evening, to announce the " news, a thing which never yet happened. Im- " mediately after the arrival of the despatches, " the Conference assembled. Talleyrand de- " clared that the King of France would never " consent to give his son, and he has repeated

---

' M. Behr had been appointed First Secretary of the Legation in London, December 26, 1830; but this mission had not been officially recognized by the English Government.

" this declaration in writing. On the other hand,
" M. de Flahaut said quite the contrary to the
" Marquis de Wielopolski. . . . ."

" *M. Behr to the President of the Committee on*
" *Foreign Relations.*

" London, February 15, 1831.

" The expectation of a decision on the
" Belgian affair keeps everybody in suspense.
" The formal assurances given by M. de Talley-
" rand had reassured the ministry and the Con-
" ference, but the extraordinary turn affairs took
" a few days ago, and above all the conduct of
" M. Bresson, break up all the combinations. . ."

During the hot discussions which arose in
Congress as to the choice of a Head of the State,
M. Paul Devaux, who had already acquired considerable influence over his colleagues, expressed
himself as follows (January 12, 1831) :—

" It seems to me that the question has been
" rather contracted : we have had presented to
" us no alternative but a French prince, Duke
" Augustus of Leuchtenberg, or Prince Otho of
" Bavaria. I believe, however, there are other

" princes who would suit us equally well, and
" over whom we have passed too lightly,
" perhaps; and amongst them I would mention
" the Prince of Saxe-Coburg.   I know the
" prejudice which exists in this assembly against
" an English prince; I know that all trade
" interests revolt against such a choice.   But we
" forget that the Prince of Saxe-Coburg is
" English only by marriage connection : if he were
" to connect himself with France, on accepting
" the crown of Belgium, he would become more
" French than English.   History teaches us,
" moreover, that no prince sacrifices the interests
" of the country he is called to govern to those
" of the country to which he becomes a
" foreigner.   General opinion, further, is un-
" favourable to this prince, because it pronounces
" for a Catholic prince.   The manner in which I
" have voted on questions, partly political, partly
" religious, which have been submitted to the
" assembly, give me a right to express my
" opinion freely on this subject.   I then thought
" that the law should be neither Catholic nor
" anti-Catholic, but simply just and liberal; and,
" in the same way, I cannot understand the

" exclusion of a non-Catholic prince. If he is
" a Catholic, good; if he is not, good again;
" and I will say further, that if in the election
" there could be preference, it should be for a
" non-Catholic prince; for, according to the
" basis of our future constitution, there is but
" one kind of oppression to dread—that of the
" majority. All our political organisation, in
" fact, rests upon the elective system, and the
" elective system is government by the majority.
" The majority amongst us being Catholic, it
" were desirable, perhaps, that the head of the
" executive should not be."[5]

But at this period France rejected almost
churlishly the candidature of the Prince of Saxe-
Coburg, and, as M. Devaux said a little later,
European diplomacy dared not offer him. In
its perplexity the Provisional Government had
sent to Paris one of its members, M. Alexander
Gendebien, to learn the definitive determination
of the French Government. At the commencement of January, Louis Philip, having received
the Belgian envoy, declared that he could not

---

[5] *Discussions in the National Congress*, vol. ii., p. 129.

accept the vote of the congress if it should confer the crown on the Duke de Nemours. Then
M. Gendebien sounded him as to the eventual
election of the Prince of Saxe-Coburg, and a
marriage with one of the princesses of the House
of Orleans.   Louis Philip was loud in the prince's
praise, but held out no hope of bringing about
the proposed combination, or of concurring in its
being brought about.[8]   In a final and very warm
conversation which he had, on the 8th of January,
with Count Sébastiani, minister of foreign
affairs, M. Gendebien said to him: "Whom
" do you recommend ?   Prince Otho of Bavaria
" or a Neapolitan prince—both mere children.

---

[8] ". . . . I told the king that the second object of my
" mission was to ask his consent to the election of Prince
" Leopold of Saxe-Coburg, and a marriage with a princess
" of Orleans. The king answered: 'I have known Prince
"' Leopold a long while; he is a handsome fellow, a perfect
"' gentleman, very well informed, very well educated ; the
"' queen also knows him, and appreciates his personal ad-
"' vantages. But . . . . there is a *but* which means nothing
"' derogatory to the prince's person and qualities : there
"' are family objections, prejudices perhaps, which are in
"' the way of the projected union.' " *Historical Revelations
touching the Revolution of* 1830, by Alex. Gendebien, in the
Liberté, third year, No. 11.

" Two children ! Two children to realise for us,
" to guarantee for us, at home and abroad, the
" results of our revolution, the promises of
" 1830. . . . . The candidatures of the Duke
" de Nemours and of the Prince of Saxe-
" Coburg are alone worth thinking about; yet
" you reject both absolutely. There is but one
" way for us out of the perilous position in which
" your double refusal places us—to go to
" London and propose the candidature of Prince
" Leopold and a French marriage; and if the
" King of the French persists in his refusal, we
" will go a step further—we will take Prince
" Leopold without the French princess." The
minister, rising, answered angrily : " If Saxe-
" Coburg sets foot in Belgium, we will fire on
" him."—" Very well, we will beg England to
" return your fire."—" There will be a general
" war."—" So be it; we prefer war, even a
" general war, to a restoration, to a humiliation
" without interval or end."[7]

In spite of Louis Philip's formal declaration,
his government, as has been said, found itself

---

[7] *Historical Revelations, etc.*, third year, No. 12.   Cf.
Discussions in the National Congress, vol. ii., pp. 83, 106.

brought over to support—by all and every means —the candidature of the Duke de Nemours, when an important part of the Congress showed a strong disposition to confer the crown upon Augustus de Beauharnais, Duke of Leuchtenberg.[8] The Duke de Nemours triumphed, but his election ended in nothing, as Louis Philip would not face a general outbreak for the sake of dynastic interests.

Leopold, then, was quite right to maintain later that the tardiness of his election was a great misfortune for Belgium. Had he been proclaimed in November, 1830, or even in January, 1831, he might, he considered, have saved our country from a painful crisis and great sacrifices. He attributed the postponement of his candidature far less to the objections of the autocratic courts, and their family relations towards the House of Orange, than to the ill-will and the by-ends of Louis Philip's government.[9]

---

[8] *See*, amongst the rest, *Memoranda to serve towards a History of my Times*, by M. Guizot (Leipzig edition), vol. viii., p. 218.

[9] "The affairs of Belgium would have been put on a very " different footing then, and she pays dearly for her leanings

After the institution of the regency, the Prince of Saxe-Coburg was mentioned more frequently.[10] In the instructions given to the Belgian envoys at Paris and London (M. Le Hon and Count d'Arschot) respecting the definitive Head of the State, M. Van de Weyer, then minister of foreign affairs, drew their attention particularly to Prince Leopold of Saxe-Coburg. The Conference of London had not confined itself to pronouncing the exclusion of the Duke of Leuchtenberg and the Duke de Nemours: it had declared, in its protocol of February 19, 1831, that the sovereign of Belgium must, by his personal position, correspond with the principle of existence of Belgium itself, and give satisfaction for the security of the other states. Such was, in reality, the vocation of Prince Leopold. M. Lebeau, M. Van de Weyer's successor in the ministry of foreign

---

" at that time, towards France. Prince Talleyrand, France, " and the Belgians, have to reproach one another; but it is " painful to think what Belgium might have been without " the miserable intrigues of that period. . . ." (Leopold to M. Le Hon, June 19, 1832.)

[10] Suchet de Chokier, president of the National Congress, was appointed Regent, February 24.

affairs, resumed the negotiations sketched out by
the former president of the diplomatic committee,
and determined to bring them to an issue. He
had been the most ardent promoter of the Duke
of Leuchtenberg's candidature; he had supported
it energetically against the Duke de Nemours,
after having, however, at first recommended
another combination, according to which Prince
John of Saxony would have received the crown
of Belgium.[11] But the time for illusions was past.
M. Lebeau, in concert with M. Paul Devaux, a
member also of the council of ministers, undertook resolutely to end the revolution by the
choice of Prince Leopold as definitive Head of
the State.

He lost no time in seeing Lord Ponsonby,

---

[11] M. Lebeau expressed himself in the following terms
(National Congress, Session of January 11, 1831): ". . . .
" There is yet another question to be handled: I have not
" forgotten that there was a question of giving us for king a
" prince of Saxony, and so reuniting the Rhenish provinces
" to Belgium. This combination was discussed by the French
" cabinet, who discarded it only a few days ago. I should
" like France to be again consulted by our commissioners
" about this reconnection." *Discussions in the National
Congress*, vol. iii., p. 101.

commissioner to the conference at Brussels, and
General Belliard, Minister Plenipotentiary of the
King of the French accredited to the regent, to
be assured of their dispositions. The former
declared frankly that he would not mention the
Prince of Orange to him again. " He risked his
" party," said he, in allusion to late events, "and
" he has lost it irretrievably." M. Lebeau having
begged the commissioner to tell him straight-
forwardly whether he might count on sincere
co-operation in the negotiations he was about
to enter into with the Prince of Saxe-Coburg,
Lord Ponsonby formally promised his support.[12]
With respect to General Belliard, he then gave
his assurance that his government would see

---

[12] Mr. Charles White, who was Lord Ponsonby's secretary,
says : ". . . . It was not, however, until after the accession
" of Lebeau's ministry that the question was reproduced in a
" tangible form. On the 12th April, after a consultation with
" MM. G. de Jonghe, H. Vilain XIV., and other members of
" the congress, a renewed communication on the subject was
" privately made by Mr. White to Sir Edward Cust, one of
" Prince Leopold's equerries ; for Lord Ponsonby declined
" being the vehicle of any direct communication until he had
" submitted the matter to his own government, and received
" their instructions." *Belgic Revolution of* 1830, vol. iii.,
chap. 2.

without displeasure the election of the prince. There could be no better proof of the revulsion of feeling which had taken place in the French ministry from the time that Casimir Périer became its head.

Indeed, from the commencement of April, the new president of the council, in concert with his colleagues, had given adhesion to the combination which was soon to acquire European importance.[13] On the 12th of April the Belgian envoy wrote from Paris to M. Lebeau :—" There " is no longer any doubt but that the Prince of " Saxe-Coburg will be recognized here as else- " where.   I have it to-day from a high authority " that the desired marriage [14] might be agreed to " within a reasonable time, say a year or two, " after the accession of the new sovereign; but " that it must not be calculated upon as a con- " dition or certain consequence of the election; " and that, though policy might see no obstacle,

---

[13] M. Le Hon to the Minister of Foreign Affairs (at Brussels), from Paris, May 3, 1831.

[14] The Cabinet of Brussels had pointed to the prospect of an alliance between the Prince of Saxe-Coburg, in case of his election, and a princess of Orleans.

" everything would still be made subordinate
" here to the inclination of the princess.   I have
" to repeat that the sentiments of the king and
" queen towards the Prince of Coburg personally
" are excellent."

For a long time friendly relations had existed
between Louis Philip and Prince Leopold.   It
will not be forgotten that, in 1816, the Duke
and Duchess d'Orléans had been present at the
prince's marriage with the heiress of Great
Britain.   On his side, Leopold paid the Duke
d'Orléans and his family visits, which were no
longer simply matters of duty and courtesy; for
the relations commenced in 1816 had become
more intimate during the prince's stay at Paris
in 1828 and 1829.   In May, 1829, Leopold,
moreover, had as his guest at Claremont the
Duke d'Orléans, accompanied by his eldest son,
the Duke de Chartres.

In a letter of April 16, the Belgian envoy at
Paris specified clearly the dispositions of England
and France.   Lord Granville, ambassador from
the court of St. James's, assured him that England would recognize for Belgium any independent sovereign, that is, whose elevation to power

would not be equivalent to a union with France, and that there was no preference for any particular candidate.   Count Sébastiani had just expressed the same sentiments in favour of the election of anybody who would not be hostile to France, were he the Prince of Coburg or any other.

The Belgian Congress had adjourned on the 14th of April, to leave the ministry at liberty to proceed more actively with the new negotiations, the object of which was no longer a secret.   It had been thought at first that it was expedient to make one more attempt with the cabinet of St. James's, which would not follow the example of France in recognizing the Regent of Belgium. But Lord Palmerston over and over again declared to Count d'Arschot that all official relations with England were impossible so long as the Congress of Brussels rejected the protocol of January 20, which contained the basis of separation between Belgium and Holland.   "In this "posture of affairs," he added, "England will "recognize the choice of no prince, were he the "Duke of Cambridge."   M. d'Arschot having spoken of Prince Leopold, the chief of the Foreign Office was loud in his praises, but soon broke off;

reiterating once more his declaration that it was useless for the time being to think of him or of any one else.

At that time M. Lebeau proposed to the Regent to immediately recall M. d'Arschot from London, and to nominate certain members of Congress who should be expressly intrusted, in the name of the Minister of Foreign Affairs, with an official mission to Prince Leopold. The minister chose for this purely official mission MM. Count Felix de Mérode, the Abbé de Foere, Henry de Brouckere, and Hippolyte Vilain XIV. The departure of these commissioners was heard of with satisfaction amongst the public. From that time the candidature of the Prince of Saxe-Coburg gained friends every day, even in the province of Liège, where union with France had been desired but lately by many of the industrial classes, and at Antwerp, where the House of Orange had possessed numerous and influential adherents.

The French Cabinet, on its side, at the same time that it humoured the Prince of Capua, the avowed candidate of Queen Mary Amélia, his aunt, continued to show itself well disposed towards the Prince of Saxe-Coburg.   Count Sébastiani wrote to General Belliard that entire freedom must be left to Congress; neutrality must be observed between the Prince of Capua and the Prince of Coburg; but that energetic opposition must be made to the candidature of the Duke of Reichstadt, if he should be put for-ward.[15]   M. Le Hon wrote to M. Lebeau: "The "French ministers are convinced that amongst "all the candidates, the Prince of Coburg is pro-"bably, in the eyes of Belgium and the other "powers, in a position to make the best offer of "guarantees for being a genuine *Belgian* prince." He added: "The general opinion here is that " circumstances were never so favourable for our " establishing a Belgian State.   The victories of " the Poles have paralysed, so far as we are con-" cerned, Russian policy and influence, and to-" gether with them the repressive schemes of " Austria and Prussia.[16]

On the 20th of April the Belgium deputies

---

[15] Count Sébastiani to General Belliard, April 25 and May 2, 1831.

[16] M. Le Hon to the Minister of Foreign Affairs, Paris, May 9, 1831.

arrived in London. After a preliminary conference with Baron Stockmar, Leopold's confidant, they were received on the 22nd at Marlborough House. The prince listened to them
attentively, and replied that the message with
which they were intrusted was infinitely flattering
to him, and the more so as they belonged to a
nation known for its sentiments of fairness and
frankness, to a nation surpassing most peoples in
civilization.   Turning   towards   the   Abbé   de
Foere : " I am glad to see above all," he added,
" that   Belgium   is   deeply   religious :   a   nation
" which   is   attached   to   its   religion   is   generally
" moral, and it is far more easy to govern it."

The prince had already read, studied, and gone
to the very bottom of the constitution voted by
the Belgian Congress in the preceding February ;
and, admirer   though   he   was   of   the   great
and free institutions of England, he considered
that the constituents of Brussels had far outdone
the famous Bill of Rights.[17]   He had communi-

---

[17] *See*, with respect to the prerogatives of Belgian royalty,
a speech of M. Faider, former Minister of Justice, in the
Bulletin of the Royal Academy of Belgium, 2nd series,
vol. xxi.

cated his fears and scruples to his confidant. He,
some years before the revolution of February,
1848, recalled the incident, and was good enough
to relate it. " After a careful examination of the
" constitution of the new kingdom of Belgium,
" his Majesty," said he, " asked me whether, in
" a state governed by such laws, liberty and order
" —two conditions necessary to every public com-
" munity, but inseparable—could exist. ' My
" ' dear Stockmar,' said Leopold, ' do read the
" ' constitution and give me your opinion.' I
" went through this constitution with the utmost
" care ; I compared its several articles, and I found
" that the power of the government was really
" very limited : however, my firm confidence in
" the people reassured me. Then I spoke to that
" intelligent and enlightened prince in pretty much
" the following terms. ' Yes, without a doubt, the
" ' power of the king and of his ministers is kept
" ' within very narrow limits by the constitution.
" ' See, however, whether all this liberty is not con-
" ' sistent with order : try if you cannot govern
" ' according to the spirit of the constitution, com-
" ' bined with great tenderness of conscience.
" ' Make trial of these new institutions, let a certain

" 'time elapse, and if you then find good govern-
" ' ment incompatible with such laws, send the
" ' chambers a message frankly acquainting them
" ' with the results of your essay, and the flaws you
" ' have noticed in the fundamental compact.   If
" ' you have acted conscientiously, and with good
" ' intentions, the people will support you, and
" ' willingly accept all changes the necessity for
" ' which shall be demonstrated.' "[18]

Leopold remembered this advice in his first
interview with the Belgian deputies.   He asked
them whether, in case it should be considered expedient to make some change in the Constitution,
such a proposal would meet with obstacles.   He
added that he should not desire this change in
the interest of power; but as power should have
for its sole aim the interest of the country, it was
for this very end that a change might be desirable.
The deputies answered that it would possibly be
imprudent to propose such a thing just then;
but that the Constitution had foreseen such a case
as the prince spoke of, and pointed out the course
of proceeding.   Leopold did not dispute the

---

[18] *German Annuals of Politics and Literature* (Berlin,
1863), vol. 8, pp. 315, *seq.*

justice of this observation; he agreed that experience alone could show what changes, if any,
would be necessary. He said, on this subject,
that his wish was to show perfect candour in his
dealings with the deputies, and he begged that
the candour might be mutual. He then pointed
out the obstacles opposed to an immediate acceptance. "To make my election possible for myself
" and useful for you"—these were his own words—
" it must carry with it the solution of your terri-
" torial and financial difficulties; Belgium and
" her king must be in a position to be recognized
" by Europe. I could not accept the sovereignty
" of a state whose territory is disputed by all the
" powers; this would be, without any service to
" you, to place myself, the moment I put my foot
" on Belgian soil, in a state of hostility with all
" the world." The deputies having reiterated
their entreaties, he added: "It would be impos-
" sible for me to give you an answer to-day; but
" all my ambition is to promote the happiness of
" my fellows. Young as I still am, I have been
" in so many extraordinary and difficult positions,
" that I have learned to regard power only from
" a philosophical point of view. I never desired

" it but for the sake of doing good, and the good
" that lasts.   If certain political difficulties, which
" seemed to me opposed to the independence of
" Greece, had not arisen, I should be now in
" that country; and yet I never attempted to
" conceal from myself how embarrassing would
" have been my position.   I feel how desirable
" it is for Belgium to have a Head as soon as
" possible : the very peace of Europe is concerned
" in it."[19]

M. Lebeau, having had cognizance of the
details of this interview, ordered the commissioners
to press again for an immediate and uncondi-
tional acceptance.   " Your boundaries," the prince
had said to them on the 24th of April, " are the
" great difficulty.   The protocol of the 20th of
" January is a thing quite irrevocable; the five
" great powers are determined to support it, and
" even France, who at first hesitated, now admits
" it without restriction.   It were desirable, then,
" that you should put yourselves thus far in
" harmony with the powers, at least relatively to
" the principle ; as for putting it into execution,

---

[19] These conversations are related from accounts written
in London itself by the deputies.

" we might enter upon a negotiation. Then I
" might accept the flattering offer you are good
" enough to make me; but on condition that a
" large majority take part in my election, for I
" would not be, from the very first, a cause of
" disunion."   The deputies answered that the
moment they were assured of his acceptance, they
would not hesitate to give him a guarantee that a
large number of voices would unite in calling him
to the throne.   Long explanations were given
touching the two provinces disputed to Belgium.
" You perceive," objected Leopold, " how painful
" my position would be if I were now at the head
" of your affairs.   Let us admit that there would
" be a necessity for giving up a portion of terri-
" tory; the proposal would have to come from
" the government, and from that moment
" suspicions would be raised against me; it might
" be supposed, although very wrongly, that I
" listened to interests other than yours.   But if
" it pleased Congress to conclude an arrangement,
" the nation itself would be considered to have
" made it, and no suspicion would be possible.
" My present position is just that in which I
" found myself when the throne of Greece was

" offered me; then also the powers wished to
" separate Acarnania and Ætolia from Greece:
" the Greek senate would not consent. Seeing
" on the one hand the impossibility of carrying
" the views of the senate to a triumphant issue,
" and on the other not wishing to appear the
" tool of the powers, I preferred to decline the
" throne."

In a fresh interview which took place on the
30th, the prince kept the same reserve. Being
pressed, on the 2nd of May, by the deputies to
give them a definitive reply, he declared he would
accept with great pleasure after a preliminary
arrangement with the powers ; but that his position would be too grievous, insupportable indeed,
if he were obliged to take the responsibility of a
curtailment of Belgian territory. On the 10th of
May, M. Devaux, member of the cabinet, went
to London to hasten on the solution so im-
patiently desired. The prince told him, as he
had told his colleagues, that he had every disposition to accept their offers ; and then he repeated that he could not give his acceptance so
long as the State of Belgium was a vague and
uncertain geographical term ; and, above all, so

long as the Belgians were not on terms of good
fellowship with the principal powers of Europe.[20]

In a general committee which was held on the
21st of May, M. Lebeau brought to the cognizance of the members of congress the intelligence received from London touching the favourable dispositions of the Prince of Saxe-Coburg.

To paralyze the last resolutions of the Conference, it was necessary to profit by these dispositions. A protocol of the 17th of April had
declared *fundamental* and *irrevocable* the arrangements concluded in those of the 20th and 27th of
January; and it had placed the Belgians in the
presence of the forces of the Germanic Confederation, if they did not withdraw the troops which
were in the Grand Duchy of Luxemburg. On
the 10th of May the Conference decided that the
official communication of this protocol should
be made by their commissioner to the Belgian
Government before the 1st of June. Instead of

---

[20] Prince Talleyrand to Count Sébastiani, 12th of May,
1831. The extreme circumspection of Leopold was blamed
by some, praised by others. Baron Stein wrote to M. de
Gagern, May 27 : " Prince Leopold's hesitation is a con-
" sequence of his situation, but still more of his character."

strictly obeying this injunction, Lord Ponsonby started for London, to set before the Conference the real state of things, and to try to obtain less harsh conditions. Being now better informed, the Conference declared, May 21, that the five powers promised to open with the King of the Netherlands negotiations, the aim of which should be to assure to Belgium, if it were possible, and for proper compensation, the possession of the Grand Duchy of Luxemburg, which however should keep its present connection with the Germanic Confederation.

At this conjuncture the immediate election of the Prince of Saxe-Coburg was, at M. Lebeau's suggestion, proposed to Congress, May 25, by ninety-five deputies. " This candidature," said M. Van de Weyer, "is not hostile to the institu-
" tions of Belgium. The Prince of Saxe-Coburg
" has lived in a country which has long enjoyed
" a constitutional government; he can appreciate
" its advantages, and he has before his eyes the
" example of the King of England, who has just
" put himself at the head of the liberal movement
" for the purpose of bestowing upon the nation a
" long-desired reform. . . . . By deferring the

" election to June 1, even supposing it were not
" followed by acceptance, we should in no way
" have compromised ourselves : on the contrary,
" we should have given the Powers a further
" proof, a new guarantee of our firm intention of
" remaining Belgians, of not losing our inde-
" pendence by annexation to a foreign power."[22]
Counter-propositions had been laid before the
House at the same time, one for postponing the
election, the other for taking possession by force
of the territory still occupied by the Dutch.   The
sections deliberated, and it was resolved, May 27,
to propose to Congress that the question of
choosing a Head of the State should be put in the
order of the day for June 1.

May 26, in the evening, Lord Ponsonby
returned to Brussels.   He determined, of his own
motion, in spite of the formal injunctions of the
Powers, not to notify the Belgian Government of
the protocol of May 21, but to replace it by a
private letter, in which he would give positive information of the Conference's favourable intentions in the matter of Luxemburg, but at the

---

[22] *Discussions in the National Congress*, vol. iii., p. 139.

same time represent the dangers to which Belgium
would expose herself if she persisted in her resistance and isolation.[23]   M. Lebeau exerted himself
in vain to get Lord Ponsonby to suppress this
letter, the tone of which was harsh, and occasionally threatening.   The Commissioner of the Conference replied that it did not rest with him to
withdraw the communication.   On the 28th,
M. Lebeau, having failed in his efforts, mounted
the tribune, and in a faltering voice read the
letter.   It concluded as follows, making the members of the national representative body jump :—
" . . . . . The hesitation displayed by H. R. H.
" Prince Leopold, in the replies he made to the
" deputies who sounded him touching the sove-
" reignty of Belgium, is sufficient proof of the
" disinterested character of H. R. H.'s principles,
" and proves that he would not accept a crown
" which might be offered him, if he could not wear
" it with honour to Belgium and honour to him-
" self.   However, he is now convinced, to his
" entire satisfaction, that he is abundantly justified

---

[23] Mr. White's account of the matter differs considerably
from this. Vide *Belgic Revolution*, vol. ii., p. 263 (London,
1835).

" in awaiting with confidence the equitable and
" prompt execution whereby the Conference will
" assist in a satisfactory arrangement of the affairs
" of Luxemburg; and the prince is disposed to
" take upon himself, as sovereign, the completion
" of this matter. Could there be better proof of
" the change which has lately operated in the
" opinion and resolutions of the Conference? It
" is but a week since the Conference considered the
" preserving of this duchy to the House of Nassau,
" if not necessary, at any rate extremely desirable ;
" and now it is disposed for mediation with the
" avowed intention of getting this duchy for the
" sovereign of Belgium. The honour of Belgium
" consists in getting Luxemburg, and not in
" fighting for it, and ruining the Belgians by the
" struggle. The Conference does not pretend to
" interfere in what concerns the rights, inde-
" pendence, and interior organization of Belgium :
" but the Conference will maintain the rights of
" the other states against all aggression, under
" whatever pretext. . . . . I have confidence in the
" good sense of the Belgian Government and in
" the country; I flatter myself they will calmly
" consider and wisely decide the great question

" which is before them, and that they will refuse
" to rashly throw themselves into difficulties which
" would be unnecessarily created, and which
" might bring about even the extinction of the
" Belgian name." A proposal, laid before the
House by M. Nothomb, conjointly with MM.
H. de Brouckere and Ch. Vilain XIV., happily
came to avert the storm. It had for its special
object to declare the election of a Head of the
State null and void, if acceptance were made
dependent upon the cession of Luxemburg and
a part of Limburg; and it further authorized
the government to propose to the Conference and
to King William to terminate, on consideration
of pecuniary sacrifices to be borne by Belgium,
all territorial disputes. On the 2nd of June this
proposal was adopted.

Next day Congress commenced the debate
on the choice of a Head of the State. The
discussions between the adherents of the Prince
of Saxe-Coburg and the war party, the latter
strengthened by the Republican minority, waxed
occasionally very hot, without, however, exciting
a real storm. A young abbé (M. de Haerne),
who but lately had voted for the Republic,

pretended that Catholic opinion pronounced
against the candidature of the prince. This
assertion, which Count Felix de Mérode had
already warmly disputed, was now taken up by
two other ecclesiastics, the Abbé Boucqueau de
Villeraie, of the diocese of Malines, and the Abbé
Andries, of the diocese of Bruges. " In politics,"
said the latter, "my creed is the constitution;
" and as it makes no stipulation about the
" religion which the Head of the State should
" profess, I am not more exacting than it; and
" indeed I think it is a mark of great wisdom to
" make no demands on that head. Religious
" freedom is sacred for all Belgians; why should
" it not be for the king ? . . . ." These protests
caused the greater sensation in Germany because
a positive belief prevailed there that the Catholic
party was opposed to the election of a Lutheran
prince. The principal organ of this party,[24] however, had already expressed itself with great
frankness and a blunt common sense. It had
said to its coreligionists: " . . . . Do not delude
" yourselves: with our charter, it will not be the

---

[24] *The Courier of the Meuse* (1831).

" king that will have the power and sovereignty;
" the sovereignty will be entirely with the cham-
" bers, or, more correctly speaking, with the elect-
" oral colleges. If you would have your sovereign
" Catholic, try to gain the victory in the electoral
" battles; there is no other way of procuring this
" advantage. A Catholic king would be for you
" merely a Catholic functionary, a functionary
" who could do nothing for you if parliament,
" the real sovereign, were bigoted philosophers.
" Your sovereign will be Catholic if you are in a
" majority at the Palace of the Nation at Brussels;
" Liberal, if you are in a minority. Count up
" yonder, if you would have your counting worth
" anything. . . . ." The debate, opened on
June 3rd, was concluded the same day. One
hundred and ninety-six members, out of the two
hundred who composed the Congress, were
present on the 4th at the Palace of the Nation,
to proceed to the election of the king. As his
name was called, each deputy mounted the
tribune, and delivered his ballot, signed, to the
president. On counting the votes it appeared
that Prince Leopold of Saxe-Coburg had obtained one hundred and fifty-two. The President

of the Congress, therefore, in the name of the people, proclaimed him King of the Belgians, on condition of his accepting the Constitution.

Mr. White, secretary to Lord Ponsonby, immediately started for London, to announce to the prince the decision of the National Assembly. Leopold was awaiting this news without the slightest impatience, for his part had been a strictly passive one: he had taken no step to gain partisans in Congress, had not spent a shilling to bestir the people in his favour.[26] He was, as was said, ready, rather than anxious, to become king, and showed in his very ambition a

---

[26] ". . . . Although the British Government and the "monarch-elect had been in some measure prepared for the "issue, Lord Ponsonby deemed it expedient to despatch a "confidential person to communicate this important intelli- "gence to both. The prince, who had left town for Clare- "mont, was, therefore, apprised of the honour conferred on "him at an early hour on the 6th. The impression that "such an event would otherwise have been calculated to "make was somewhat neutralized by previous anticipation; "but H.R.H. nevertheless manifested deep emotion on being "informed of the various circumstances attending the elec- "tion, and on being assured that the dissentient votes were "political—not personal." *Belgic Revolution of* 1830, by Charles White, vol. iii., chap. 2.

patient moderation which seemed to reach the verge of indifference. Congress nominated a deputation to deliver to the Prince of Coburg the decree of election.[26] The Regent, on his part, appointed M M. Deavaux and Nothomb to open with the Conference the negotiations authorized by the Assembly.

Whilst the deputies of Congress and the Commissioners of the Regent were crossing the Straits, sinister news spread about. It was said (and the rumour was not destitute of foundation) that Holland, on the eve of losing the old southern provinces of the kingdom of the Netherlands, had put forward a project of partition with France and Prussia; and it was added that Prince Talleyrand himself favoured the notion.[27]

---

[26] Besides the President, this deputation was composed of MM. Felix de Mérode, Van de Weyer, the Abbé de Foere, D'Arschot, H. Vilain XIV., Osy, Destouvelles, Duval de Beaulieu, and Thorn.

[27] In a confidential letter written a little subsequently, M. Le Hon informed the regent that he had some warm discussions with Casimir Périer and Count Sébastiani on the subject of the conduct attributed to Prince Talleyrand. "It is avowed," said he, "that after the Prince Leopold

On the 8th of June the Regent's two Commissioners had their first interview with Leopold, at which they put themselves in concert for undertaking the negotiations which were to save Belgian nationality, and seal the triumph of the Revolution of September, 1830. They have elsewhere been set forth in detail.[28] It will be enough here to say that they culminated in the drawing up of those preliminaries of peace so celebrated in modern history under the name of *The Eighteen Articles.*

The deputies of Congress awaited, for the fulfilment of their official mission, the result of the deliberations of the Conference. Prince Leopold, however, saw them frequently, but in private, and conversed freely with them. " If I " had to choose amongst a thousand," the President wrote to the Regent, " I do not believe I

" combination, the only way to make an end of it is reunion " or partition ; and, as Périer does not want the first, if it " must infallibly cause war, it is not astonishing that Prince " Talleyrand spoke, in the first moments of irritation, as if " partition were, in default of reunion, one of the conse- " quences to be looked for from the occupation." M. Le Hon to the Regent, Paris, June 19, 1831.

[28] *History of the National Congress*, vol. ii., p. 234, *seq.*

" could do better." " If he accepts," wrote
another deputy, " Belgium will have a dis-
" tinguished sovereign, who appears deeply
" conscious of this great truth, which he has
" several times repeated, that the first duty of a
" king is to labour to obtain for the people he
" governs the greatest possible amount of happi-
" ness." But the deputies saw that the prince
still had misgivings about the constitution.
One day he said to them with a smile : " Gentle-
" men, you have dealt a little hardly with the
" royalty which was not present to defend itself,
" —your charter is very democratic ; however, I
" believe that, with good intentions on both sides,
" we may get along."[29] The elect of Congress
knew probably the sentiment expressed in 1551 by
a Venetian ambassador about the English parliament : " These parliaments are useful and safe, as
" things which are the work of the counsel and
" consent of all; and because they turn kingly and
" absolute power into a lawful and regular power,
" in presence whereof every man is free."

---

[29] *The Brussels Journal,* July, 1856. The article from
which these words are borrowed gave the recollections of
one of the members of the deputation of 1831.

On the 24th of June, in the evening, the definitive drawing up of the preliminaries of peace, contained in eighteen articles, was concluded, at Marlborough House, between Prince Leopold, Lord Palmerston, and the two Commissioners of the Regent of Belgium. Leopold having failed in his efforts to get the territorial integrity of the country he was to reign over admitted, *i.e.*, to get Belgium recognized with the boundaries fixed by Congress, did not lose heart. The crown which a people had offered him he decided to accept under the conditions presented to him as definitive, and as bound to insure his recognition by the great powers and by all Europe. On the evening of the 26th, the two Commissioners, who had put up at the *Brunswick Hotel*, received from the Foreign Office a packet containing the official text of the eighteen articles, signed by the representatives of the five powers.

At nine the deputation from Congress went officially to Marlborough House, to deliver to the Prince the decree which called him to the throne of Belgium. M. De Gerlache, the president, expressed himself in these terms: " . . . . It is a

" rare and noble spectacle in the annals of nations
" when four millions of free men, with one accord
" and of their own will, offer a crown to a prince
" born far away from them, and whom they know
" solely by the fame of his excellent qualities.
" Your R. H. is worthy of this summons, worthy
" of replying to this mark of confidence. The
" happiness of Belgium, and perhaps the peace of
" all Europe, are now in your hands! As the
" meed of a noble resolution, sir, we are not
" afraid to promise you glory, the blessings of a
" good and true people, ever attached to their
" Heads so long as rights have been respected,
" and finally, a memory dear to the most remote
" posterity." The prince replied: " I am deeply
" sensible of the meaning of the vote of which
" the Belgian Congress has made you interpreters.
" This mark of confidence is the more flattering
" as it was not sought by me. There is in human
" destiny no task more noble or useful than to be
" called upon to maintain the independence and
" consolidate the liberties of a nation. A mission
" of such high importance might of itself decide
" me to give up a position of independence, and
" separate myself even from a country to which

" I have been attached by the most sacred ties
" and recollections, and which has given me so
" many proofs of sympathy.   I accept, then,
" gentlemen, the offer you make me, with the
" understanding that it shall devolve upon the
" congress of the representatives of the nation to
" accept those measures which alone can establish
" the new state, and thereby insure recognition
" from the states of Europe.   It is only so that
" Congress will give me the means of devoting
" myself entirely to Belgium, and of dedicating
" to its well-being and prosperity the connections
" I have formed in the countries whose friendship
" is essential for her, and of insuring for her,
" so far as it will depend on my co-operation, an
" independent and happy existence."

The same day, further, the prince wrote to the
Regent, that after the adoption by Congress of
the preliminaries proposed by the Conference of
London, he should consider the difficulties
removed from his path, and could start immediately for Belgium.   The deputies from
Congress and the Regent's Commissioners left
London at midnight, disembarked on the 27th
at Ostend, and went on to Brussels.

Next day M. Lebeau read the eighteen articles to Congress. It was now for the National Assembly to throw down the last obstacle which was still in the way of enthroning the king-elect, —to decide the destinies of Belgium. It was not unequal to its high and patriotic mission.

July 9, after discussions, and a scene which recalled sometimes the most stormy days of the National Convention, Congress adopted the proposal, the object of which was to accept the eighteen articles, *i.e.*, the preliminaries to the treaty of peace between Belgium and Holland. Whilst the minister of foreign affairs set about transmitting the decree to the Conference, the Assembly nominated deputies, who, after announcing to Prince Leopold the acceptance of the eighteen articles, were to accompany him to Belgium.[30] They left Brussels, July 10, at 11 A.M., and arrived in London the next day at midnight.

On the 12th, in the morning, Prince Leopold went to Claremont, to put his seal to his papers there. On his return in the afternoon to Marl-

---

[30] The deputation was composed of MM. Lebeau, who had just resigned the portfolio of Foreign Affairs, Felix de Mérode, Fleussu, De Muélenaere, and Joseph d'Hoogvorst.

borough House, he received first the representatives of the five Great Powers. " Is it the
" intention of the Great Powers to recognize me
" at once ?" he asked.   " Is it their intention to
" recognize me if I go to Belgium without waiting
" for the adhesion of the King of Holland ?"
" In any case," replied Count Matuszewic, representative of Russia; " and if he refuses, we
" will find means to make him consent."   The
resolution of the prince to yield to the wishes of
the Belgian people was then irrevocable.   At
9 P.M. he received the deputies from Congress,
who delivered to him a letter, in which the
Regent expressed himself thus : " After an
" eleven days' debate Congress has just consented
" to the proposals submitted to it by the Con-
" ference of London.   Your R. H. having stated
" your acceptance of the crown of Belgium to
" depend on this consent alone, there is no longer
" any obstacle to your arrival in this country,
" as you assured me in the letter you did me the
" honour to write to me on the 26th of June
" last.   By appearing as soon as ever you can in
" the midst of the Belgian people, you will best
" crown its hopes, best calm its anxieties . . . . "

The prince answered that he was already making his preparations, and that in a few days he would be ready to leave England. He added, with a smile, that as he was on the point of moving, he could not do the deputies the honours of London, but that his sister, the Duchess of Kent, would fill his place.

On the 15th, the king-elect addressed to Lord Grey his renunciation of the pension of 50,000*l.* a year granted him by the English parliament. "As sovereign of Belgium," said the prince, " my intention is not to take out of England " any portion of the revenue which was granted " me by Act of Parliament at the time of my " marriage." He made up his mind also to pension off all the people of his household, and to take with him only one officer, to whom he would give neither rank nor title.

On Saturday, the 16th, the prince bade adieu to Marlborough House, and left London at 6 A.M., accompanied by Sir Henry Seton, his aide-de-camp, the deputies from Congress, and M. Jules Van Praet, who was already fulfilling the delicate duties of secretary. M. Van Praet had come to London with Count d'Arschot, remained with the Commissioners of the Minister of Foreign Affairs, been admitted to the late negotiations, and from that time gained the confidence of Prince Leopold, and was to preserve it during the entire duration of the long reign which was about to commence. At half-past two Leopold arrived at Dover, under a salute from the guns of the fort. A few minutes after he embarked for Calais on board the steamboat *Crusader*, which had hoisted the royal standard. When the *Crusader* hove in sight of Fort Rouge, a salvo of artillery announced that the King of the French accorded to the King of the Belgians the honour due to crowned heads. Leopold was received on the quay by the mayor and authorities of the town, and afterwards complimented in the harbour itself by Lieutenant-General Count Belliard in the name of the King of the French. He passed the night at *Dessin's* hotel.

Next day, in the morning, the weather being magnificent, Leopold started for Dunkirk. On arriving at the boundary which separates France from Belgium, he found there the deputation which had been sent to meet him by the Regent.

General Wautier saluted the king-elect in the name of the army. "I rely entirely," answered the prince, "on its courage and fidelity."[31] An eye-witness relates that this first meeting of the national authorities and their new king, on the shores of the ocean, beneath a radiant July sun, in the presence of the representatives of a friendly people, excited emotion in every bosom.

So soon as the king-elect had crossed the frontier of Belgium, his passage became a veritable ovation. At Ostend, where he arrived towards 6 P.M., he found in front of the parish church of St. Peter, the Bishop of Ghent, clad in his pontifical robes. The prelate offered to the future sovereign the homage and good wishes of the Catholic clergy. Bruges gave him a splendid reception. There was an inclination to persuade

---

[31] It is said that in London, Prince Talleyrand, at one of his last conversations with the king-elect, advised him to give up all military display, and content himself with 4000 or 5000 men for the maintenance of a police in the interior. The king looked at M. De Talleyrand with his quick, profound eye, and penetrated the real meaning of an idea, the bearing of which there was an attempt to conceal from him under the most honied words. *Opuscules of S. Van de Weyer*.

him not to include in his tour the other capital
of Flanders, where it was said he might be
exposed to demonstrations of ill-will. "The more
"reason," rejoined Leopold, "for going by
"Ghent." This noble confidence was not misplaced: Ghent joined in the general joy.

An account is given elsewhere,[32] from the
recollections of one of the members of the
deputation from Congress, of the principal
incidents and the significance of the triumphal
progress. "Certainly one could not but admire,"
it is there said, "the splendour and unanimity
"of the manifestations in the towns which the
"retinue passed through; but what raised most
"emotion was the reception which the sovereign
"met with in the country. When one saw a
"village pastor, with white hair and venerable
"face, come to salute, in the person of a Lutheran
"prince, the protector of Belgian independence,
"the restorer of that Belgian nationality which
"had been so long oppressed, this mixture of
"a patriotism which was connected with the
"traditions of the past, and of a tolerance which

---

[32] *History of the National Congress of Belgium, etc.,*
vol. ii., p. 341.

" belonged to the liberal principles of the re-
" volution of 1830, made a deep impression upon
" the witnesses of so admirable a sight. When,
" further, one saw the branches of trees and the
" garlands which adorned the cabins scattered
" over the high roads, when one remarked the
" simple and spontaneous joy of the poor
" inhabitants flocking to the thresholds of their
" cottages, one might say that the ; people
" instinctively understood the nature of the
" occasion. They felt that this prince, elected
" by the suffrages of the National Assembly, was
" bringing back confidence, peace, security,
" commerce, and public and private prosperity.
" One could also recognize, in these populations
" of Flanders and Brabant flocking out to meet
" the king, that old respect for monarchical
" power which the Belgian people have always
" known how to unite with an invincible love of
" freedom."

On the 19th, towards evening, the party
approached Brussels, and the crowd increased
incessantly. More than once Leopold replied, to
the felicitations of which he was the object, that
in sight of an enthusiasm so general, he felt

himself fortunate to have been the freely elected
king of the Belgian people. More than once he
was seen to rise up in his carriage, saluting and
thanking the countless population which had
thronged to meet him. At half-past ten the
party arrived at last at the Castle of Laeken.
The prince there received the felicitations of the
Regent of Belgium, of the ministers, of the
members composing the Board of Congress, and
of the high functionaries of the State.

The inauguration of the first King of the
Belgians was fixed for the 21st. Leopold passed
the eve of this great day in conversing with some
of the personages who were soon to be his chief
assistants in the government of the country. He
showed especially the most kind confidence in
M. Lebeau, who had contributed so much to his
election and accession. During a conversation
with this former minister of the Regent, the
prince drew from his pocket a paper, and begged
him to look over it. It was the speech which
he proposed to make after taking the oath.
M. Lebeau read it, and confined himself to
suggesting certain purely grammatical altera-
tions. The memorable speech at the inaugura-

tion was and remained the work of the king exclusively.[34]

On the 21st of July, Brussels in holiday guise was illuminated by the rays of a joyous sun. All the population were in the streets or at the windows, to lend their presence to the solemn entry of the first king of the Belgians. Leopold, who wore the uniform of a general in the national army, entered on horseback, by the old William Gate, the capital of the new kingdom, and at the head of a brilliant staff made his way towards the Place Royale.

A stage, raised against the Church of St. Jacques-sur-Cardenberg, was occupied by the Regent of Belgium and the members of Congress. At one o'clock Leopold, having arrived in front of the church, dismounted from his horse, ascended the steps, and took his place between the Regent and the President in front of the throne. After the venerable Regent had laid down the powers with which he had been invested on the 24th February preceding, one of the Secretaries of Congress (M. Ch. Vilain XIV.), standing in front of the king, read the Constitution of the king-

---

[34] This incident was related to the author by M. Lebeau.

dom of Belgium.   When this was over, another
secretary, M. Nothomb, presented the form of
oath imposed on the king by the fundamental
compact.   Leopold I. said, in a steady voice: *I
swear to observe the constitution and laws of the
Belgian people; to maintain national independence
and territorial integrity.*   Whilst the king was
signing the official report of the swearing in, the
seats which occupied the front of the platform
were removed.   The throne was left in sight.
The President of Congress, turning towards the
king, said: "Sir, ascend the throne!"   The king
standing on the higher platform, surrounded
by generals and ministers, made the following
speech :—

"The alacrity with which I set foot upon
" Belgian soil must have convinced you that,
" faithful to my word, I deferred coming to you
" only until I had seen you yourselves remove
" the obstacles which hindered my accession to
" the throne. The different considerations un-
" folded in the important debate which brought
" about that result will be the object of my
" liveliest solicitude. I have met, since my
" entrance upon Belgian soil, proofs of touching

" kindliness; I am still equally moved by them
" and grateful for them.   At the sight of those
" populations ratifying by their cheers the act of
" the national representatives, I felt that I was
" called by the wish of the country, and I under-
" stood all the obligations that such a reception
" imposes on me. Belgian as I am by your
" adoption, I shall make it a law to myself to be
" so also in my policy.   I was likewise received
" with extreme kindliness in the part of French
" territory I traversed, and I fancied I saw in
" those demonstrations, which I highly value, a
" happy presage of such confident and friendly
" relations as should exist between the two
" countries. The effect of all political commotion
" is to damage for the time being material
" interests.   I understand their importance too
" well not to give my immediate attention to
" helping by the most active solicitude to re-
" habilitate commerce and industry, those vivify-
" ing principles of national prosperity; but I like
" to think that the Belgian people, so remarkable
" at the same time for right feeling and for resig-
" nation, will make allowances for the government
" on the difficulties of a position which is due to

" the state of uneasiness with which almost all
" Europe is afflicted. I intend to surround
" myself with all possible lights, to draw forth all
" views tending to amelioration; and it is on the
. " very spot, just as I have begun to do, that I
" mean to gather the best notions to shed light
" in this respect upon the course of the govern-
" ment. Gentlemen, I only accepted the crown
" you offered me with a view of fulfilling a task
" as honourable as it is useful, that of being
" called to consolidate the institutions and main-
" tain the independence of a noble people. My
" heart knows no other ambition than that of
" rendering you happy. I must, on so solemnly
" touching an occasion, express to you one of my
" most ardent wishes. The nation is coming out
" from a violent crisis. Oh! may this day efface
" all hatred, extinguish all resentment! May
" one single feeling animate all Belgians, a feeling
" of frank and sincere unity! I shall esteem
" myself happy in contributing to this happy
" result, so well prepared for by the venerable
" man who has devoted himself with such noble
" patriotism to the salvation of his country.
" Gentlemen, I hope to be to Belgium a pledge

" of peace and tranquillity; but the previsions of
" man are not infallible. If, in spite of so many
" sacrifices for the preservation of peace, we were
" threatened with war, I should not hesitate to
" appeal to the courage of the Belgian people;
" and I hope it would rally, one and all, round
" its Head, for the defence of the country and for
" national independence."

All present promised, by reiterated cheers, to
aid the definitive Head of the State in main-
taining the independence of Belgium.

Leopold descended from the platform, and
passing the serried ranks of the people, went on
foot towards the royal palace. At six he presided
at the banquet to which he had invited the
members of Congress. He was seated between
the late regent and the president of the assembly. The latter gave the toast, "Leopold I.,
" King of the Belgians!" The king replied:
" Gentlemen, I thank you, and I drink to the
" future of Belgium; may it be one of happiness
" and independence."

At this very moment Lord Grey was officially
announcing to the House of Peers the determination of the King of the Belgians to give up the

pension he received as a member of the English
Royal Family. After the venerable lord had
read the letter the prince had addressed to him
on the 15th of July, loud cheers resounded in
the house. The Duke of Wellington, as the
mouthpiece of his colleagues, said that the
Belgian people, over whom Leopold had gone
to reign, would see in this determination proof
that their sovereign was above any suspicion of
dependence upon foreigners.

Some days later similar homage was paid to
the new king by the French Government.
" Where," said the minister of foreign affairs,
speaking from the tribune of the chamber of
deputies—" where are the English armies which
" now occupy Belgium ? Is not the prince who
" has gained the throne of that nation tied down,
" as all the constitutional princes of Europe are,
" by the bonds of a constitution ?"

ʳ

CHAPTER V.

1831, 1832.

LEOPOLD I. REVIEWS HIS ARMY—SUDDEN INVASION BY THE
DUTCH—DISASTERS OF THE BELGIANS—FIRMNESS AND COU-
RAGE OF KING LEOPOLD—THE TWENTY-FOUR ARTICLES—
BELGIAN FORTRESSES — STRONG LANGUAGE OF LORD PAL-
MERSTON—M. THIERS' OPINION OF LEOPOLD I.

LEOPOLD signalized his accession by liberal
donations from his private purse, which were
distributed between Brussels, Ghent, Antwerp,
and Liège, for the assistance of the families
which had suffered by the late events. He lost
no time, moreover, in visiting the Place of
Martyrs, wishing to do honour to the memory
of the citizens who had fallen gloriously for the
independence of Belgium.

July 28th he went to Antwerp, where he was
received with enthusiasm; next day he reviewed

at St. Antoine the army-corps of General Tieken de Terhove.   On the 31st, in the neighbourhood of Hasselt, he inspected the other army—of the Meuse, as it was called—which had been placed under the command of General Daine.   Being saluted with cheers by the troops, he let no symptom of his anxiety peep out.   Nevertheless, vague rumours of the threatening movements of the Dutch army had reached him, and though he did not entirely believe them, he would have to be in readiness.   And what a prospect was his!   Instead of the sixty-eight thousand men the "shells" made out, he found—at St. Antoine and at Hasselt—only twenty-five thousand at the outside.

He made his entry into Liège on the 1st of August.   His design was to continue his progress to Verviers, and thence to Namur.   But the news from Holland becoming more alarming, Leopold communicated from Liège with his war minister,[1] who had remained at Brussels with all his colleagues.   Next day, August 2nd, in the afternoon, he received, through the minister of

---

[1] General De Failly.

foreign affairs,[2] a copy of a letter in which General Chassé, commandant of the citadel of Anvers, had given notice the preceding evening to the military commandant of the city that hostilities would be recommenced on the 4th, at half-past nine, P.M.

Leopold did not lose his coolness. As he was at Liège without any minister, he sent for M. Lebeau, who had resumed in that city the functions of attorney-general in the Court of Appeal. Handing him the declaration of General Chassé, he said: "See what I get by way of "welcome. Still, if I could have given a few "months to the organization of the army, I "should not fear the struggle. Perhaps it would "be rather a matter of congratulation; for a "success would increase the attachment of the "army and the country to their nascent na- "tionality, and to the leader who had fought at "their head. But to have been caught so un- "prepared is very unfortunate. What do you "think of the condition of the army? Could it "sustain, do you think, the shock of the enemy,

---

[2] M. De Muelenaere.

" and fight a pitched battle?" The former
minister of the Regent replied frankly, that in his
opinion the new army left much to be desired in
the way of organization.[3] Consequently his
advice was to at once claim from the English
and French Governments execution of the
engagements entered into by the two powers,
viz., the guarantee of Belgian independence,
stipulated in the eighteen articles.

"It costs me a struggle," replied the king,
" to have recourse to this plan; I should have
" liked to lead an army against the Dutch. A
" success would produce upon our soldiers and
" the whole country an impression most favour-
" able to the nationality and the dynasty; but I
" believe with you that it would be risking too
" much." M. Lebeau, assuming all responsibility for his advice, wrote forthwith to MM. le
Hon and Van de Weyer, the representatives of
Belgium in Paris and in London, to claim in the

---

[3] M. Lebeau agreed with the generals who, on the previous
22nd of June, had deliberated in presence of the Regent
and ministers on the possibility of renewing hostilities. *See*
the revelations made to the Chamber of Representatives by
Barthélemy, former Minister of Justice. (Session of November 10, 1831.)

king's name the armed intervention of France
and England. Leopold, on his side, addressed
private and pressing letters to Louis Philip, and
Lords Grey, Palmerston, and Durham. The
king was back in Brussels on August the 3rd, at
4 A.M. Next day, in an energetic proclamation,
he said to the people: " I, Belgian as you are,
" will defend Belgium. I count on the civic
" guard, on the army, on the courage and devotion
" of all. I repair to my post." In the evening
he went to sleep at Antwerp, which was threatened
with a second bombardment, and did not leave
until he was quite reassured as to the fate of this
great metropolis of commerce. Head-quarters
were moved to Malines.

Upon hearing of the abrupt aggression of the
Dutch, the cabinet, at the head of which was Casimir Périer, which had been declared dissolved a few
hours before, came to the resolution of remaining
in power to prevent a restoration in Belgium.
On the 4th, at 8 A.M., M. Le Hon, whose energy
and zeal at this conjuncture was beyond all praise,
received the letter written in the king's name
from Liège. He repaired forthwith to Count
Sébastiani, and demanded the armed intervention

of France, according to the terms of the guarantee promised in the preliminaries accepted on both sides. At two he was received officially by the King of the French, as minister plenipotentiary and envoy extraordinary from the King of the Belgians. An hour afterwards the *Monitor*, pasted on the walls of Paris, announced the armed intervention of France in favour of the Belgians.

Two corps, the total force of which must have been 50,000 men, were concentrated at Lille and at Givet, under the command of Marshal Gérard. But, according to a formal declaration made by Count Sébastiani to the Belgian minister, the commander-in-chief of the French army had positive instructions to waive his own claims entirely in Belgium, and place himself under the orders of the king.

As early as August 3, the English cabinet, warned by its minister at the Hague of the movements of the Dutch army, had sent orders to Admiral Codrington to repair with his fleet from Plymouth to Dover. Next day, *i.e.*, on the very day of M. Le Hon's official reception at Paris by Louis Philip, M. Van de Weyer was likewise received, in the capacity of envoy extraordinary and minister plenipotentiary from the King of the Belgians, by William IV., King of Great Britain. The courier from Liège having subsequently handed him the letters sent by King Leopold, he forwarded them immediately to Lords Grey, Palmerston, and Durham, as appears from his own words.

" *M. Van de Weyer to the King of the Belgians.*

" London, August 4, 1831.

" . . . . . The news of this abrupt resolution of
" the King of Holland reached the English
" Cabinet on the evening of the 3rd, in a despatch
" from Sir Charles Bagot, who announced from
" the Hague that he had it on good authority
" that the Dutch troops were being put in
" motion. The English Cabinet at first attached
" the less faith to it, that it was in contradiction
" with two facts of recent and almost the same
" date, *i.e.,* the arrival in London of M. Van
" Zuylen Van Nyevelt, and his delivery to
" the Conference of full powers to the utmost
" extent, authorizing him to discuss, sign, and
" conclude with the five powers a definitive treaty
" of separation between Belgium and Holland.

" It needed the arrival of official papers proving
" General Chassé's renunciation of the suspension
" of arms, papers which I at once put before
" Lord Palmerston, to convince him of the truth
" of the news, which might well appear incredible.
" The cabinet met immediately; and Lord Dur-
" ham, whom I saw this morning, communicated
" to me confidentially that the council's first
" resolution was to send, by telegraphic despatch,
" orders to Admiral Codrington to move with
" his fleet from Plymouth to Dover. This was
" confirmed by Lord Palmerston, who calculated
" that Admiral Codrington would have effected
" his movement by Sunday, or Monday early, at
" the latest. The Conference was summoned the
" same day, and the session was prolonged up to
" 9 P.M., without any definitive resolution being
" taken, as I am informed by Lord Palmerston,
" whom I saw an hour afterwards. Its first care
" was to summon to its presence the two Dutch
" commissioners, MM. Falk and Van Zuylen,
" and demand of them an explanation of their
" sovereign's strange conduct.—The Dutch pleni-
" potentiaries replied merely that they did not
" know the motives which had decided the king

" their master to take this step; and that they
" had no authority to give any explanation on
" that subject.

"It is certain that the English Government
" is but little satisfied with the conduct of the
" French Cabinet since your majesty's accession
" to the throne of Belgium   After having warmly
" and with apparent sincerity co-operated in that
" accession, it is on its part that all difficulties
" now arise, whether about the German Con-
" federation, or the fortresses; and France's last
" determination not to recognize our envoy until
" after our adhesion to the dismantlement of the
" fortified places, has particularly encouraged the
" King of Holland in the step he has just taken.

" Two A.M.—I am at this moment in receipt
" of the letter and papers which M. Lebeau ad-
" dressed to me from Liège (where your majesty
" then was), as well as the three letters addressed
" to Lords Grey, Palmerston, and Durham.   I
" shall not wait for daylight to send them; they
" shall have them at once."

The most singular, the most fatal illusions
prevailed amongst the Belgians. By those about

the king's own person opinions were pronounced with great warmth against the intervention of the French. The minister of foreign affairs set the example of this rash susceptibility. Sceptical, but, above all, terrified at his responsibility,[4] M. de Muelenaere begged Mr. White, who had repaired to head-quarters at Malines, to tell the king that " he implored him on his knees " to prevent the execution of a measure which " was calculated to compromise the military " honour of the country." With an imprudent condescension, Leopold consented to have instructions sent on the 6th to Marshal Gérard to suspend his march.[5]

The army which suddenly invaded Belgium comprised 45,000 infantry, 6000 cavalry, and seventy-two pieces of artillery. To this imposing force Leopold could oppose only the 25,000 men composing the two corps of Daine and Tieken, between which there was a distance of several

---

[4] Article 121 of the Constitution is couched in these terms : " No foreign soldiery may be admitted into the " service of the state, to occupy or traverse the territory, " but by virtue of a law."

[5] *Belgic Revolution of* 1830, by Charles White, vol. iii., chap. 3.

leagues totally devoid of troops. It was by this
gap that the enemy was about to advance into
the heart of the country. On the 2nd of August
all the Dutch army had crossed the frontier; on
the 3rd, the Prince of Orange arrived at Turn-
hout; on the 5th, the Dutch occupied Diest.
Penetrating the designs of the Prince of Orange,
Leopold had, from Malines, sent a pressing order
to General Daine to move from his camp at Hasselt
in the direction of Diest, to form a junction with
the division of Tieken, who would move by Lierre
on this same line. On the 8th, Tieken arrived
in the environs of Diest, and finding this town
in the hands of the enemy, fell back on Arschot.
Leopold, at the head of a corps of the Civic
Guard, joined him at the village of Westmeerbeek,
close to Waterloo. Pleased at the enthusiasm
which burst out amongst the troops, and counting
on the approaching co-operation of General
Daine, he renewed his resolution to abandon at
any rate for the present the idea of French intervention. He wrote to General Belliard, at that
time at Louvain, that he hoped to carry Montaigu
early next day, and march on to meet Daine;
that, circumstances being so favourable, he

thought it was urgent to arrest the advance of
Marshal Gérard; and that to maintain good
feeling amongst the powers, it was quite desirable
that the marshal should not be set in motion
until the pressure of affairs should require it.
He shared in fact the opinion of the army, which
wished to fight without foreign aid. His spirit
shows itself in his letter.

" *King Leopold to General Belliard.*[8]

" Arschot, August 9, 1831.

" MY DEAR GENERAL,

" I arrived here pretty early. I took 1500
" Civic Guards of different cantons, and twenty
" gendarmes, and repaired with all military pre-
" cautions to Westmeerbeek, close to Waterloo.
" There I had the good fortune to join General
" Tieken: he, whom I have brought on here,
" has very nearly 13,000 men under arms. I
" was received by the troops, who were tired to
" death, with cheers and extreme joy. I think
" of mustering here early to-morrow—with a
" view of carrying Montaigu and marching to

---

[8] See the *Essay, Political and Historical, on the Belgian
Revolution,* 3rd edition, p. 187.

" meet Daine, who appears to have had suc-
" cesses—about 17,000 men and twenty pieces of
" artillery.

" I breathe again, now that I have this good
" large force, which is animated by the best
" possible spirit.

" Circumstances being so favourable, I think
" it urgent to stop the movement of Marshal
" Gérard; the feeling is very strong in the army
" —and I consider it natural—to fight without
" foreign assistance.

" I think that, for the sake of good under-
" standing amongst the powers, it is above all
" things desirable not to put the marshal in
" motion until the urgency of the case shall
" demand it.

" Believe me ever,

" My very dear Count,

" Your sincerely devoted friend,

" LEOPOLD."

But when, next day, Leopold made for
Montaigu, to dislodge the enemy and unite with
Daine, he learned that that general had not fol-
lowed the formal instructions transmitted to him,

and that the army of the Meuse, as it was called, existed no longer. The troops, marched back by their commander upon Hasselt, lost all confidence, and threw themselves upon the Tongres road; there, being attacked by superior forces, they made for Liège in the most shocking disorder.[7] The Dutch being enabled to march without difficulty on Brussels, Leopold resolved to make a last attempt to bar their way to the capital.

He fell back on Louvain, and, with Ticken's corps, took up a position in front of that town. The Belgians bivouacked on the 10th, in the evening, before Louvain. Next day the heads of the Prince of Orange's columns appeared at Bautersem. If they had not been so extremely slow, the Dutch might easily have anticipated

---

[7] " . . . . The army of General Daine is completely " routed without having fought. . . . Belgium, it must be " owned, has no regular army; it is an armed mob and " nothing more. We have no real military capacity; we " have no want of muscle and individual courage, but very " great of an organizing head. What is happening justifies " those who, in the face of a furious minority who vociferated " for war, accepted the suspension of arms, the armistice, " the preliminaries of peace." The Minister of Foreign Affairs to M. Van de Weyer, August 11, 1831.

King Leopold, and on the evening before have
crowned the heights which command Louvain.
The situation of the King of the Belgians was,
nevertheless, terrible; for he had to cover Brussels, whilst keeping in check the whole Dutch
army, until the arrival of the French, to whom a
fresh appeal had been addressed on the 9th, after
the dispersion of the army of the Meuse. On
the afternoon of the 11th, the van-guard of the
little Belgian army, led by the king in person, dis-
lodged the troops which occupied Bautersem, and
caused them to recoil as far as Roosbeek. Accompanied by some officers, the king had passed his
advanced posts in a reconnaissance, pushed for-
ward by way of Beauvechain, and when he was
pressed not to expose his person, he replied, " I
" *must* show an example to these young soldiers."
But a new and terrible disaster was, nevertheless,
to be feared, seeing the enormous numerical dis-
proportion between the two armies. On the
12th of August, at 4 A.M., the Dutch advanced,
surrounded in some sort the little Belgian army,
got possession of the Brussels road, and pushed
their vedettes as far as Cortenberg and Tervueren.
Forced to give way to numbers, the Belgians

retired towards Louvain leisurely, for they took seven hours to march two leagues. At this almost supreme moment, the king continued to distinguish himself by his firmness and bravery. Many a time, to use General Belliard's terms, he did subaltern's duty, and several times he was in danger of being killed. He gave orders to the columns, he posted the artillery, he directed all the movements. " Without him the Belgian army " had been annihilated."[*] Read the—

" *Opinion of General Frederick de Gagern on* " *the Courageous Behaviour of King Leopold* " *before Louvain.*

" . . . . . The King of the Belgians, though " scarcely yet at home with his new army, on " this day gave repeated proofs of intrepidity and " presence of mind. In a reconnaissance pushed " forward to our lines he exposed himself to the " utmost danger, and had not our cavalry been so " fatigued, would have fallen into their hands." (Life of General Frederick von Gagern, vol. i., Amsterdam, 1858, p. 394.)

---

[*] General Belliard to the Minister of Foreign Affairs (Count Sébastiani), August 14, 1831.

The Prince of Orange was making his arrangements for turning his forces against the last refuge
of the national army, when he received a visit
from Lord William Russell, sent by the representative of England, Sir Robert Adair, who on
the 9th had joined the head-quarters of the King
of the Belgians. Sir Robert demanded a suspension of hostilities, and informed the prince
that the van-guard of the French army was already
at Wavre, and would soon be at Brussels. The
prince ordered one of his aides-de-camp to accompany Lord William, and to make sure of the
approach of the French troops. But as the
Dutch troops continued, nevertheless, to advance,
Sir Robert himself mounted his horse, and at the
peril of his life traversed the fire of both armies
to get to the Prince of Orange. He obtained a
suspension of hostilities for twenty-four hours, on
condition that the Belgians evacuated Louvain
and abandoned the town to the Dutch. Leopold
bade General Goblet draw up an agreement to
this effect. As for himself, who had not on this
fatal day lost for an instant his presence of mind,
he put himself at the head of the cavalry and
gained the Malines road, making his way through

the division of Saxe-Weimar, which by its hostile demonstrations hoped to increase the humiliation of the Belgians.   General Tieken put himself at the head of the infantry, and rejoined the king at the bridge of Campenhout.

On the morning of the 13th, the French vedettes showed themselves at Cortenberg and Tervueren, in front of the Dutch.[9]   It was soon agreed between General Lawoestine, acting for Marshal Gérard, and the Prince of Orange, that the Dutch army should immediately commence its retrograde movement, and be followed by the French as far as the frontier. This agreement was literally carried out. By the 20th, the Dutch had re-entered the boundaries of northern Brabant.

As for the English fleet, it had not made its appearance in the Scheldt.[10]

---

[9] The Minister of Foreign Affairs wrote, on the 11th, to M. Van de Weyer: ". . . . Happily France has answered " our appeal with that perfectly French precipitation which " at first disconcerted us, but on which we should now feli- " citate ourselves.   The French troops have arrived at " Namur and at Mons. . . ."

[10] M. Van de Weyer sent word, on the 13th, to the Minister of Foreign Affairs, that he had lost no time in reiterating to

It was not in the character of the vanquished that Leopold reappeared in Brussels. On seeing him again, on the 16th, the cheers of the people were in honour of the courageous leader who had not despaired of the republic, of the sovereign who by his presence at the head of the army had probably prevented the annihilation of Belgian independence.[11]

But Leopold could not hide from himself the

Lord Palmerston a demand for the prompt appearance of the English fleet in the Scheldt, and that Lord Palmerston had replied that the news arrived from the Hague, and written assurances, submitted to the Conference by the plenipotentiaries of King William, rendered this measure useless. "The sending of an English fleet, consequently, " appears to Lord Palmerston a perfectly useless step, and " he earnestly begged me to tell you that he is in possession " of all guarantees possible on the part of the Dutch " Government, to the extent even of a declaration from " King William, that he never had any intention of attack- " ing Antwerp. . . ."

[11] A military writer, severe in his judgments, thus expresses himself: "If we suffer our imagination to wander " over the state of confusion to which Belgium was a prey " from the 1st to the 30th of August, we cannot but attribute " to the king alone the honour of having saved the country." *Political and Military History of Belgium* (1830, 1831), by P. A. Huybrecht, retired field-officer (Brussels, 1856, 8vo.), p. 131.

deplorable consequences of this fatal campaign.
Long afterwards he still said: "That unfortunate
"campaign of 1831 causes me daily fearful
"trouble." [12]

On the 9th of August, Casimir Périer, on
announcing the French intervention to the
Chamber of Deputies, had expressed himself in
these terms: "How many times, as you must
"remember, has the kingship of Belgium been
"predicted as the cause of rupture with all
"Europe! Certainly, when we entered upon the
"ministry, the refusal of the crown for the Duke
"de Nemours, and the exclusion of the Duke of
"Leuchtenberg, left a very limited choice of a
"sovereign whose destiny it would be to at last
"give reality and unity to this nascent kingdom.
"The choice made by Belgium was politic; the

---

[12] He wrote, August 30, 1833: "We suffer in every-
"thing from that unfortunate campaign of 1831. . . . It is
"a misfortune over which I groan daily; but without the
"surprise of the attack we should have come out better—
"the will was good, it deserved more success. . . ." Then,
September 10, ". . . . That unfortunate campaign of 1831
"causes me daily fearful trouble, and I would give a great
"deal to commence afresh the 2nd of August, 1831. We
"are now bearing the shame and sorrow of it. . . . "

" personal character of the prince who was the
" object of it rendered the choice desirable.
" France could not but accept it with satisfaction,
" for she does not share in shadowy suspicions
" for which there is nothing but an apparent
" cause. . . . . The independence of Belgium
" was guaranteed, none the less is its neutrality.
" Both will be, at need, defended. The last
" decisions of the French Cabinet have just proved
" it.   A French army has received orders to enter
" Belgium, to repel the unexpected aggression of
" the King of Holland. This expedition, which
" we resolved upon at the first despatch from the
" King of the Belgians, is the result of the con-
" cert existing between all the great powers of
" Europe." But the cabinet of St. James's, so
soon as it was sure that the Prince of Orange
would evacuate Belgian territory, lost no time
in desiring and demanding also the prompt
evacuation of Belgium by the French army.
Lord Palmerston reckoned, for the solution of
this delicate and important question, on the good
faith of Louis Philip's government and on the
active co-operation of the King of the Belgians.
In the eyes of the English ministry, a prolonged

stay on the part of the French must be attended
by the gravest inconveniences.[13]   But the too
passive attitude of the Cabinet of St. James's
had hurt and disconcerted the government of
Leopold.[14]   In reality, he had at that time only
the effectual support of France to insure the
security of the country.   Accordingly, when, on
the 21st August, Marshal Gérard announced to
the King of the Belgians that he had received
orders from his own government to commence
his retirement with the army under his command,
the ministers in council, taking into consideration
that the national army was not yet reorganised,
demanded that some French corps should prolong
their stay.   These regiments protected the Belgian
territories until September 17.

---

[13] M. Van de Weyer to the Minister of Foreign Affairs,
London, August 13, 1831.

[14] M. De Muelenaere wrote to M. Van de Weyer, August
16 : " . . . . The English Ministry by their delays, hesita-
" tions, and misplaced fears, have lost for the present all
" moral influence in Belgium.   Whilst in London they were
" deliberating, they were acting at Paris. . . . England
" might have counterbalanced French influence by holding
" Antwerp after causing the evacuation of the citadel.   She
" did nothing of the kind, and contented herself with the
" King of Holland's words. . . ."

On the 8th of this month Leopold repaired in state to the Palace of the Nation, to open the first session of the Chambers. He was, on this occasion, the object of a fresh ovation: the representatives of the country mingled their applause with the sympathetic demonstrations of the people. In his speech the king thanked the nation for the proofs of affection and devotion it had not ceased to give him since the day he first set foot on the soil of his adopted country. The legislature, on their side, did not refuse the Head of the State means for promptly re-establishing the army.

A law of September 22nd authorized the king to take into the Belgian service, till the conclusion of peace, such number of foreign officers as he judged to be useful or necessary for the good of the country; and he had further the power of employing foreign officers, who, without giving up their rank and privileges in their own country, might offer to serve for the duration of the war.

Being already formally recognized by France and England, could the King of the Belgians have believed that the other powers would not follow their example? He was however bitterly deceived in his expectation.

Count Duval de Beaulieu had been instructed, August 21st, to notify the accession of Leopold to the King of Prussia, the King of Saxony, and the reigning Duke of Saxe-Coburg-Gotha. A like mission was intrusted, on the 25th, to Baron Joseph Vanderlinden d'Hoogvorst at the courts of Austria, Bavaria, Wurtemberg, Hesse-Darmstadt, and Baden. On arrival at Berlin, September the 1st, after being cordially received by the reigning Duke of Saxe-Coburg-Gotha, Count Duval had, on the 3rd, a conversation with M. Ancillon, Minister of Foreign Affairs, and a devoted instrument of the absolutist party. Whilst allowing that there had been implied and even explicit recognition of the King of the Belgians by the powers met together at the Conference in London, M. Ancillon did not think that the reception of his envoy—what he called the *patent act*—could take place before all the arrangements with Holland were concluded. The Prussian minister at the same time disclosed a conformity of views on the part of Austria and Russia. " There is reason to

" believe," he added, " that this is also the
" opinion of Austria, and that Russia will not be
" more hasty. It is not Prussia's place to take
" the initiative; she must have regard to her
" allies."[15] M. Ancillon had perfectly correctly
indicated the course of Prince Metternich. The
Chancellor of the Austrian Empire having, on
the 4th of September, begged the Belgian envoy
to call upon him, asked M. d'Hoogvorst if he
were intended to reside in Vienna. The latter
answered that his mission was confined to
notifying the accession of the king, and that he
had orders to afterwards repair for the same
purpose to the other courts which he mentioned.
" The Emperor," rejoined Prince Metternich,
" has ordered me to communicate with you on all
" business just as if you had been received; but
" this formality cannot take place till after pacifi-
" cation with Holland ; and according to the news
" received to-day from London, that cannot be
" long.". M. d'Hoogvorst tried in vain to shake
this resolution : it was a view taken not only at
Vienna, but also at Berlin and St. Petersburg, to

---

[15] Count Duval to the Minister of Foreign Affairs, Wittem-
berg, 9th September, 1831.

say nothing of the other courts of Germany. M. d'Hoogvorst, with Prince Metternich's approbation, determined to go and wait for instructions from his government at the baths of Ischl.[16] The two envoys, of course, had to be recalled.

The prevalent feelings are to be gathered from the expressions in the following extracts:—

" In London there were doubts about the " early retirement of the French, who had " hastened to the assistance of Belgium ; and in " Belgium again there were doubts about the " diplomatic consequences of the fatal campaign " of August. The king had furnished M. No- " thomb with letters intended to reassure the " English ministers desirous of seeing the French " depart.   M. Nothomb carried away from " London the conviction that the *eighteen* " *articles had perished at Louvain*, and that the " fault lay in Belgium's military condition. The " king, who had believed he would find an army " in Belgium, had just been cruelly undeceived."

---

[16] Baron Joseph Vanderlinden d'Hoogvorst to the Minister of Foreign Affairs, Vienna, September 4, 1831.

" *Note addressed by Count Duval to M. Ancillon.*

" The undersigned envoy extraordinary and
" minister plenipotentiary of H. M. the King of
" the Belgians, has the honour of informing
" H. E. the Minister Secretary of State for
" Foreign Affairs, that he is charged by the
" king his master with the duty of notifying
" H. M.'s accession to the throne to H. M. the
" King of Prussia.

" He begs his Excellency to have the
" kindness to take his Majesty's commands, that
" he may be informed of the day on which the
" king will be pleased to receive him.

" The undersigned has the honour of adding
" to the present note copy of the credentials and
" notification of which he is the bearer, and he
" begs his Excellency to have the kindness to
" accept, etc.

" Berlin, September the 2nd, 1831."

" *Answer of M. Ancillon.*

" Berlin, September the 4th, 1831.

" SIR,

" At the visit you were good enough to pay
" me, I had the honour of developing to you the

" reasons which do not permit the king as yet to
" receive your credentials.   We join you in
" wishing that the day when every obstacle will
" be removed may not have to be very long
" waited for, and that your reception may take
" place under the happiest auspices.

   " I can but refer to that conversation; and as
" it is not customary for the minister of the king
" to take cognizance of the credentials of foreign
" ministers before they have been called upon to
" deliver the originals to his Majesty, I must
" return you the copies you addressed to me.

" Accept, etc.

" ANCILLON."

   " M. Behr, intrusted by M. Lebeau, Minister
" of Foreign Affairs, with a mission to Berlin—
" wrote to him April the 30th, 1831 : ' Since my
" ' stay in Berlin I have seen many persons more
" ' or less intimately acquainted with the policy
" ' of their country.   What they say, added to
" ' the results of my preliminary proceedings with
" ' the Minister of Foreign Affairs, gives me the
" ' conviction that for the present all diplomatic
" ' relations between the two governments is

" ' absolutely *impossible*. . . .' On the 12th of
" June he expressed himself in these terms: ' I
" ' have just learned from the papers the choice
" ' of Congress. At the date of my residence in
" ' London I was of opinion that Prince Leopold
" ' offered the elements of a political combination
" ' likely to bring Belgium peace and happiness.
" ' The proceedings of Lord Ponsonby in favour
" ' of the Prince of Orange, supported by an
" ' article inserted in the *Court Journal*, and not
" ' contradicted, forced me at the time to re-
" ' nounce all hope on this score. May it now
" ' be realized. . . .' "

Peace was the desire of the Belgians, but it
could not have worn a smiling face for King
William after a campaign which he looked upon
as a triumph. Having refused adhesion to the
eighteen articles before the enthronement of
Leopold, he was not disposed to accept them
after having nearly succeeded in upsetting the
new throne. He had nevertheless acquiesced in
a suspension of hostilities for six weeks, the
conditions of which had been settled by the Conference in their protocol of August 23. The
day before, whilst sending M. Van de Weyer

full powers to convert the preliminaries of peace
into a definitive treaty, the Minister of Foreign
Affairs said to him : "Your powers do not per-
" mit you to negotiate outside of the eighteen
" articles understood in the sense which was put
" upon them by the Belgian congress."[17] But a
reaction had taken place in the feelings of the
Conference. The fall of Warsaw (September 6)
had raised again the pride of the powers of the
north; the unfortunate ten days' campaign in
Belgium had excited the suspicions and awakened
the scepticism of England.

King Leopold wrote to his minister in France :
" Circumstances are serious, but I think that
" with courage and moderation we shall pull
" through. I am making all my preparations as if
" there must be war on the 10th of October : the

---

[17] He had already written to him on the 16th of August :
" The English Ministry ought to bind themselves to obtain
" from the King of Holland, both the evacuation of the
" citadel of Antwerp, and the adoption, pure and simple, of
" the eighteen articles. They know that it was on these con-
" ditions that the Prince of Saxe-Coburg accepted the
" throne of Belgium. England chiefly guaranteed him those
" conditions ; she ought not to have forgotten it so
" soon. . . ."

" former surprise did us so much harm we cannot
" permit a second."

The suspension of hostilities was, however,
prolonged from the 10th to the 23rd October,
for the Conference to bring its labours to a close.

Dreading the issue of them, Leopold had
sent to London Baron Stockmar, as *confidential
agent*. But this faithful servant was soon obliged
to acknowledge that all his efforts would come to
naught before the ill-will of the absolutist courts
and the apprehensions of England. " That un-
" fortunate campaign," said he, " has revived the
" old English principle that Holland must never
" be weakened. It has awakened all the English
" distrust and jealousy of the ulterior designs of
" France. It has furnished the absolutist party
" in the Conference with pretexts sufficiently
" powerful to colour the general views Dutch.
" It has, moreover, created in the mind of one of
" the English ministers—of great influence—very
" strong prejudices, which did not exist before,
" against the national character of the Belgians."

M. Nothomb was likewise intrusted with a
confidential mission to London. He returned
with the conviction that the eighteen articles had

perished at Louvain, and that Belgium would pay for its defeat. Notwithstanding that the disposition of the northern courts was so favourable towards Holland, the new act of the Conference was nevertheless completed without the cognizance of the plenipotentiaries of King William. The Belgian government, on the contrary, had been warned that it would be deprived of the right bank of the Meuse in Limburg, as well as of the German part of Luxemburg; that it would keep indeed, in the latter province, only the districts of Marche and Neufchâteau. It then made an attempt to keep Ruremonde, and failed; but, on the other hand, it got a concession that the town of Arlon and the Longwy road should be detached from the German part of the grand-duchy, which had already been assigned to the King of the Netherlands.

On the 15th of October the Conference fixed, in twenty-four articles, the new conditions of separation between Belgium and Holland. These decisions were declared to be *final* and *irrevocable*. Belgium was subjected to the law of the vanquished. True, France had protected her, but was not inclined, after setting the territory free, to aggrandize her, or even preserve her integrity, at the risk of having to confront a European war. As for the cabinet of St. James's, Lord Grey declared, October 18th, in the House of Lords, that it was England's interest to provide first for the defensive position of Holland; and then, in the second place, to assure to Belgium the advantages of an independent nation.

On the 26th October, by order of the King of the Belgians, the Minister of Foreign Affairs proposed to the legislature the adoption, as a measure of public safety, of the treaty imposed by the Conference of London. He did not attempt to conceal the gravity of the situation, and the fearful perils that a rejection would entail. " Having to choose," he said, " between giving " up some members and the annihilation of the " whole family, our choice was not free." The first consequence of rejection must have been the military intervention of Germany, and from that intervention it was not a long step to a restoration, and even a partition.

This humiliation of Belgium was in course of accomplishment whilst the Dukes d'Orléans and de Nemours were still at Brussels. Four days after

their departure, on the 25th October, the Chamber
of Representatives decided that the discussion of
the treaty should take place in secret committee.
But the chief speeches were published, and bore
witness to all the warmth, and, at the same time,
the grandeur of the debates.   M. Nothomb, who
was nearly every day with the king, explained, on
the 26th, with rare profundity, Belgium's conditions of existence. He acknowledged that Belgian
diplomacy had been beaten, but by causes beyond
anybody's control.   This speech contained the
germs of the beautiful book on Belgian nationality which will remain an imperishable monu-
ment of the Revolution of 1830.[18]

Leopold during these grave debates flattered
himself with no illusions : in his eyes the existence
of an independent Belgium was once more at
stake.   He had resolved therefore to appeal to
the country if the twenty-four articles were
rejected, and to abdicate if the new chamber
persisted in the negative vote.

But Belgium was spared this supreme trial.
On the first of November the twenty-four articles

---

[18] *Essay, Historical and Political, on the Belgian Revolution* (third edition, 1834).

were adopted by the Chamber of Representatives with a majority of fifty-nine to thirty-eight; on the third, the Senate likewise adopted them by thirty-five to eight.   In the forcible language of a historian, the treaty was accepted as you accept the law of the strongest.   The government attempted to obtain modifications of what concerned the boundaries, debts, and navigation. But the Conference replied that it was no longer even within the capacity of the Five Powers to accede to a single one.   On the 15th, M. Van de Weyer signed the treaty: the ratifications were to be exchanged within a period of two months.

This definitive sealing of Belgian independence encountered unforeseen obstacles.   The northern courts desired to obtain previously the adhesion, already problematical, of King William.   France and England, on their side, wished to come to an agreement about the defensive system of Belgium.

The powers who, after 1815, erected the fortresses of our country, had so managed that the Revolution of 1830 reacted in by no means an unforeseen manner on these bulwarks of Europe. They were the subject of a *reserved* protocol, a secret act, signed April 17, 1831, by the pleni-

potentiaries of Austria, Great Britain, Prussia, and
Russia. The four powers, to the exclusion of
France, decided that so soon as there existed in
Belgium a government recognized by them, a
negotiation should be opened between the four
courts and that government, with a view of
determining the fortresses which should be
demolished. The four powers had excluded
France from the protocol, because she had not
contributed to the expense of constructing the
fortresses. Further, they waited until the 14th
of July before communicating the fact to the
French plenipotentiaries. Louis Philip pretended
to mistake the meaning of the four courts.
At the opening of the French Chambers, July
23rd, he announced that "the fortifications
" raised to threaten France, not to protect
" Belgium, would be demolished." On the
28th, Count Sébastiani even declared to M. Le
Hon that the French government, before recognizing the new King of the Belgians, wished
to settle the matter of the fortifications. But
this recognition, as has been seen, was precipitated
by the abrupt invasion of the Dutch.

The haughty language of Louis Philip on

the 23rd of July had made the Belgians sore, and
the government had lost no time in protesting
against a declaration which seemed to place it
under the suzerainty of France. Whilst the
army of Marshal Gérard was still occupying
Belgium, the Cabinet of the Palais-Royal
attempted, through the Marquis de Latour-Mau-
bourg, to conclude a private agreement on the
subject of the fortresses directly with the government of King Leopold. This attempt was
abortive. However, the Belgian government
made a declaration, September 8, importing that
King Leopold agreed and engaged to take
measures, in concert with the four powers at
whose expense the fortresses were to a great extent
constructed, for the speedy demolition of
the forts of Charleroi, Mons, Tournay, Ath, and
Menin.

The king deputed General Goblet, formei
war minister under the Regency, inspector-general
of engineering and fortifications, to repair to
London in the capacity of special plenipotentiary
accredited to the four powers. Not only was
Leopold unwilling to offend France, he also
aimed at preventing the irritating discussions

which might have arisen in the English parliament between the Whig ministry and the Duke of Wellington, the originator of the fortresses in 1815. He believed that General Goblet, in consequence of his former connection with Wellington, might serve as a conciliator between him and the cabinet. This general officer, who had been a lieutenant of engineers under the First Empire, had at the capture of St. Sebastian in 1813 been a prisoner of the commander-in-chief of the English army; in 1815, political changes had placed him under his orders at Waterloo. Being employed after the peace in the fortifications of the southern frontier of the Netherlands, he had continued to keep up relations with the Duke, who even deigned to honour him with some kind attention. From the time of the war in the Peninsula he had also been very intimate with Colonel John Jones, who exercised great ascendancy over the mind of the Duke.

King Leopold's emissary arrived in London in the first half of September, 1831. He had first of all to do his utmost to efface the unfavourable impression produced in England by the declaration made on the eighth to the French

Cabinet; in the next place to bring out clearly the spirit in which the act was conceived; and finally to show that the Belgian Government by this conciliatory declaration had not departed from the principle laid down in the protocol of April 17. In respect of the particular fortresses to be destroyed, the Government, in conformity with the declaration made to France, had ordered him to bring all the negotiations to bear upon Charleroi, Mons, Tournay, Ath, and Menin.

The task accepted by General Goblet bristled with difficulties. To accomplish it there was need of all the sagacity, tact, cool energy, and perseverance with which this officer was in an eminent degree endowed; for he was not only a distinguished general but also a statesman. He has himself recounted in a remarkable work the manifold incidents of his laborious negotiation.[19]

At the moment of his departure King Leopold authorised him to correspond directly with himself on any points he considered calculated to interest him. From this unpublished correspon-

---

[19] *The Five Great Powers of Europe in their Relations, Political and Military, with Belgium. A Mission to London in* 1831. (Brussels, 1863, 8vo.)

dence are borrowed some details which will be read with interest.

After a first long conversation with Colonel Jones at Woolwich on the defensive system of Belgium, as a European question, General Goblet was received on the 21st of September by the Duke of Wellington. The Duke, displaying a lively interest in the prince whom he had known in England, commenced by asking all the particulars of the new king's life—about his health, his habits, his amusements. Touching then upon the question of the fortresses erected in 1815, he pronounced against their demolition. He maintained that a sovereign could not govern an independent state with a capital to which a powerful neighbour might at any moment come and levy contributions; that King Leopold could not sleep in security at Laeken if they were to destroy the fortresses which covered Belgium on the side of France. He added that he had no conception of a Belgian kingdom, which should be neutral, without the existence of these fortresses; and that a state, if it were not strong by nature, must be strengthened by art. He put off the development of his system to another and early interview. It took place, but the word *fortress* was not mentioned again. However, the conversation was not without importance. The Duke declared that the state of peace which was the most ardent desire of all nations gave King Leopold the most favourable opportunity which could exist for founding a durable throne; in the course of a century, according to him, there would seldom be found a more advantageous conjunction of circumstances. If the king employed his firmness of character in resisting whatever could incline him more towards one of the great powers than towards another, he might play a great part in Europe; on the other hand, if he did not show complete impartiality, he would find himself in one of the most difficult of positions. The Duke expressed his wishes for the glory and happiness of the King of the Belgians, and for that reason authorized General Goblet to transmit to him his opinion as to what should be the basis of the king's conduct. The general hastened to reply that if what the Duke had just said was intended to throw blame upon the Belgian government, he could not refrain from calling his attention to

the position in which Belgium had been.   When
death is imminent, is one bound to think of anything but self-preservation?   And, seeing the
English fleet still in the Downs, were the Belgians
bound to abstain from having recourse to France?
The Duke, nevertheless, continued his reflections.
He said that the first condition of proper conduct
is to see things as they are; that realities alone
are worth anything in the world; and that, from
this point of view, it was, at the present moment,
a very sad miscalculation to make a strict alliance
with a revolutionary power; and that the mere
adoption of foreign officers from one and the
same nation was a breach of Belgian neutrality.
The general explained that when Belgium had
reorganized her military institutions she would
doubtless produce good officers, but that his
illustrious interlocutor appeared to have forgotten
that the 10th of October was at hand, and that it
was for that date that the Belgian government
had been obliged to try to get an army well commanded in all parts.   The duke, however, did not
appear convinced.[20]   This account of the opinions

---

[20] General Goblet to King Leopold, London, 23rd and
26th of September, 1831.

expressed by Wellington made a great impression upon the king. He more than anybody else felt the necessity of gaining that historical personage whom M. Guizot called "the most "considerable of the considerable men in "England;" and whom Queen Victoria was one day to call "the pride, the glory, the hero of "Britain." He enjoined upon General Goblet to disabuse the mind of the duke, and to keep up the best relations with him; he told him to correct people's notions that he meant to "stuff" the whole Belgian army with French.[21]   But it was difficult to win back the Iron Duke, as the English called him. On the 13th of October he wrote to General Goblet that he must persist in the apprehensions suggested to him by the admission of French generals into Leopold's service. He maintained that the king at his parades was surrounded by French officers, and that General

---

[21] As long before as September 15 he had written to his Minister at Paris: "Do not neglect Lord Granville. We "are accused of being wholly French; we are friends, but "all we desire is *our independence.* France has the same "interests as we have; and the more the other powers ill-"treat us, the more they themselves will force us to approach "her. . . ."

Belliard, French ambassador at Brussels, was really at the head of the Belgian army.[22] Some days afterwards, on the 29th, he spoke strongly in the House of Lords against this intrusion of French officers into the Belgian army. " In submitting these remarks to you," he said, " I have but one " view, and that is, to make King Leopold some- " thing better than a French prefect."

The negotiation relative to the fortresses could not but be affected by these feelings. The Duke of Wellington opposed the dismantlement of Ath and Tournay, alleging the good service these places did in 1815, by forcing the Emperor Napoleon to attack by Charleroi. In spite of the energetic opposition of France, and to the great displeasure of King Leopold, who saw in the sub- stitution an increase of embarrassments, Philippe- ville and Marienburg replaced Charleroi and Tournay, the importance of which was far greater in the eyes of the English general. Prince Talleyrand thought of a singular expedient for putting an end to the discussions : he proposed

---

[22] General Belliard, whom Leopold used to call "that " good Belliard," died at Brussels, of apoplexy, January 28, 1832.

to the Conference to *cede* Philippeville and Marienburg to France. "No," replied almost simultaneously Baron Bulow, Prussian minister, and Lord Palmerston, "we should prefer war. If "those two fortresses give you umbrage, we will "destroy them."

The part King Leopold had to play became every day more troublesome. From gratitude and from interest, since he desired an alliance with the House of Orleans, and was urgent for its conclusion, he did not want to give France, in his own words, "any motive to complain of him." On the other hand, he could not bear up against England and the three courts in concert with her. He endeavoured, therefore, to serve as mediator by himself, invoking the kind intervention of the Duke of Wellington. "Do not neglect "the Duke of Wellington," he wrote to General Goblet; "say all that is kind to him from me; in "spite of our disputes about Greece, I must say "that I have always liked him very much."

At this time King Leopold was not only chagrined at the difficult business of the fortresses, but he was also under the melancholy effects of the death of his mother. The dowager-duchess of Saxe-Coburg had felt the sweet satisfaction of seeing her son on the throne of Belgium: she had even paid him a visit at the Castle of Laeken. But, on the 16th of November, a short time after her return to Germany, she expired at Coburg.

The negotiation with which General Goblet was intrusted, after being suspended during the negotiations relative to the twenty-four articles treaty, was resumed after the adoption of this treaty by the Belgian Chambers. A singular incident cropped up to complicate it. During General Goblet's temporary return to Belgium, M. Van de Weyer found himself in a manner obliged by the plenipotentiaries of the four courts to sign as a corollary of the principal treaty a special convention touching the fortresses; he put his signature but *sub spe rati (in hopes of ratification)*, so as not to engage his government. Without ratifying, and still without disavowing M. Van de Weyer's signature, the Cabinet of Brussels gave a sort of carte-blanche (free permission) to General Goblet to conclude and sign a definitive convention. King Leopold wrote to him: "Conclude as nearly as you can according " to my intentions, but conclude."

The definitive convention with the plenipotentiaries of the four powers was signed on the
14th December by General Goblet. It decreed
the demolition of the fortified places of Menin,
Ath, Mons, Philippeville, and Marienburg. It
contained also a secret article which promised the
King of the Belgians, in case the security of the
preserved fortresses should be threatened, the aid
of the courts of Austria, Great Britain, Prussia,
and Russia, always with the provision of Belgium's
neutrality. "I know not whether your majesty,"
wrote General Goblet on the same day, "will be
" of my opinion, but it appears to me that the
" negotiation you deigned to intrust to me is
" now accomplished in a way to cause the least
" possible jealousy, at the same time that Belgium
" is placed in the position destined for her by the
" four courts." Leopold replied that he approved
of the secret article drawn up in such a manner,
he remarked, as to be perfectly inoffensive, since
it said simply : "If your fortresses are in danger,
" call for assistance."

It seems opportune to give in this place some
characteristic correspondence about the Belgian
fortresses.

"*King Leopold to General Goblet.*

"Laeken, September the 25th, 1831.

" MY DEAR GENERAL,

"I read your letter with interest, and I am
" pleased to see that you are received in England
" as I desired.

"I do not, for my own part, see any objection
" in respect of the preservation of Charleroi, if
" you think it expedient; I am only afraid lest
" it cause France displeasure without giving us
" thereby a barrier against her.

"According to a letter from Lord Palmerston,
" the conference is very well satisfied with its
" relations with you; you will do well, therefore,
" to attempt to keep it of this mind.

"Here we are busy with fortifications, but I
" fear there is more talking than working.

"I have appointed you my aide-de-camp, to
" give you by that a fresh proof of my approbation
" of your conduct in the difficult times we have
" passed through. I reckon upon you equally
" for the future, and shall ever be,

"Your much attached,

"LEOPOLD."

"*King Leopold to General Goblet.*

(Extract.)

"Laeken, September the 29th, 1831.

" MY DEAR GENERAL,

"Thank you for your communications.
"Take a little pains to explain in London that
"our reverses were due to surprise. . . .

"It is very much to our interest that you
"should be able to see the Duke of Wellington
"from time to time. Say all manner of proper
"things to him on my behalf. Set people right
"also with respect to the notion that we want to
"stuff all our army with French. It is not that.
"We had need of inspectors who were obliged to
"be foreigners, as party-spirit could not be
"mixed up with the matter. (*See* Brouckere
"and the officers of the free corps.) They
"were obliged to be of high rank. In the army
"we shall take but few foreigners, and we shall
"take them from all nations. Get hold, how-
"ever, of a Colonel Smith, born at Brugger,
"whom the king countenances a great deal, and
"whom it would not be a bad thing to conciliate,

" as he cries out against our Gallicisms. M. de
" Stockmar will be able to tell you news of
" him. . . .

" LEOPOLD."

" I am off for Antwerp, and I am determined
" to keep and defend that city."

" The Duke of Wellington to General Goblet.

(In French.)

" London, October the 13th, 1831.

" GENERAL,

"I had the honour of receiving your letter
" of the 2nd, but I have been so much occupied
" since I received it, and the answer that I wish
" to make is of so little importance, that I per-
" mitted myself to put it off until to-day.

"I should not have taken the liberty of
" talking to you about the affairs of the King of
" the Belgians if you had not spoken to me
" about them. I then mentioned to you the
" reports which were circulating here and on the
" Continent about the entry of French officers
" into the service of King Leopold. These
" reports acquired some appearance of truth-
" fulness from the decrees of the Belgian legisla-

" ture, and by the orders of H. M. the King of
" the French, published abroad, which gave per-
" mission to French officers to enter the service
" of His Majesty (Leopold) on certain conditions.

" Since I had the honour of seeing you, I
" have again seen accounts of travellers who
" speak of having seen His Majesty surrounded
" by French officers at his parades.

" As His Majesty has thought it proper to
" take into his service three French generals as
" French inspectors-general, it is probable that
" the appointment of the French generals in
" question is their doing, not his. For my own
" part, I confess I see no happiness for His
" Majesty and for the country except in absolute
" independence of any power whatsoever. I repeat
" to you, no sovereign ever had so good an
" opportunity of taking up a positive attitude. A
" whole century could not give him the like. It
" is for His Majesty himself to seize upon it and
" profit by it. No power can point out to him
" the road or the measures he ought to take ; but
" His Majesty may rest assured that all the
" powers are watching him, with an anxiety pro-
" portioned to the importance of their policy as

" well as the fate of His Majesty, to see what
" position His Majesty is going to take up.

" From this point of view I confess to you
" that I have seen with pain that the ambassador
" of France at Brussels is Commander-in-Chief,
" or, whatever his title may be, in effect at the
" head of the army.

" I remember having heard of general officers
" in the service of King Joseph in Spain. But
" even in that case they had left the service of
" the Emperor Napoleon. There was no one
" who was ambassador of France in Spain and
" not even in the service of France.

" I have the honour, etc.

" WELLINGTON."

" *King Leopold to General Goblet.*

" Brussels, December the 2nd, 1831.

" I read with sincere satisfaction your
" despatch of November the 27th; it is written
" with great talent. The news you give me
" is generally good.

" I have just spoken to ministers to get you
" new instructions, which will give you *entire*

" *latitude* to finish matters and avail yourself of
" your full powers.

" I appreciate and approve of all you say.
" You know my views, and you will do all you
" can to accomplish them.   But if that is im-
" possible, you *will make the best ending* you can.
" It is desirable to conclude, and only you who
" are on the spot can judge of the facilities and
" difficulties of the thing.   I share your opinion
" about the secret article; even in London it is
" difficult to keep people from knowing all; here
" it is almost impossible.   The question should
" be, then, about putting ourselves in the position
" destined for us by the conference, but to
" manage the drawing-up in such a manner as
" not to create jealousies.

" I think the French government, which has
" given proof of the greatest moderation, and
" is placed in a difficult position, deserves to be
" treated with the very greatest consideration.

" Thank you for the sentiments you express
" on the sad loss I have lately suffered, and which
" has plunged me in very deep affliction.[23]

---

[23] The king alludes to the death of his mother.

" Do not neglect the Duke of Wellington, and
" say all that is friendly on my part to him.   In
" spite of our disputes about Greece, I must say
" I always liked him much.   Write to me often,
" and be assured of the feelings with which I
" regard you.

" LEOPOLD."

" King Leopold to General Goblet.

" Brussels, Dec. 13, 1831.

" MY DEAR GENERAL,

" I had you written to by M. Nothomb, to
" press you to finish the negotiation with which
" you are charged.   Your instructions give you
" the widest latitude, and it is desirable in the
" interests of Belgium to conclude, and soon after
" ratify, the treaty.   On receiving this letter, if
" contrary to all expectation you have not yet
" signed, I invite you to do so without loss of
" time.   I have informed King Louis Philip of
" the number of forts, as well as of the difficulties
" we have encountered in the conference.   France
" does not at all like Marienburg and Philippe-
" ville being in the treaty, and says, Why not
" leave to Belgium the initiative in demolishing

" them, without mentioning them in the treaty?
" I repeat, conclude as well as you can according
" to my views, but conclude. A motion in the
" House of Lords against the demolition of the
" fortresses might still add considerably to the
" embarrassments of the English government.
" They are wrong, however, about their Marien-
" burg and Philippeville, which should have
" been left out.

    " I pray for your success, and that I may
" soon hear good news from you.

" LEOPOLD."

" *King Leopold to General Goblet.*

" Brussels, December the 17th, 1831.

" MY DEAR GENERAL,

    " I approve of the secret article, which is
" drawn up in a manner perfectly inoffensive,
" since it merely says, If your fortresses are in
" danger, call for assistance. So that we have
" only to be left alone, and we shall have no need
" of that assistance.

    " If only Marienburg and Philippeville could
" have been left out! That is about to cause me
" much tribulation on account of France. . . . . .

" I am a little afraid of the Chambers in respect
" of the article about keeping in good repair.
" Try to explain to Prince Talleyrand that the
" Belgian government did everything in the
" world to obtain what France desired, and that
" the strongest proof is the non-ratification of the
" basis which Van de Weyer had been pressed to
" sign, which was a step not without danger.

" I place the ratification in your hands and
" Van de Weyer's. I am of opinion that we must
" *do nothing which can give France any reason*
" *to complain of us*. The important matter is
" that you have signed; ratification can change
" nothing, but to give it without demand, and
" without being able to assign any good *reason*,
" would *hurt* the French government. Lord
" Palmerston must be able to say to you, If you
" do not give your ratification, such or such
" danger will result. Then we can say it was a
" case of urgency.

" LEOPOLD.

" Try to see the Duke of Wellington, and
" give him my kind regards."

" King Louis Philip to King Leopold.

" Paris, Saturday morning,
" December the 17th, 1831

" MY VERY DEAR BROTHER AND EXCELLENT
" FRIEND,

" I receive with equal surprise and regret the
" news that your Majesty's plenipotentiary has
" permitted himself to sign a treaty in formal
" contradiction to engagements contracted with
" me.

" I confidently expect, therefore, that this
" treaty will not receive ratification from you, for
" I am bound to rely on your promises. I ought
" not to hide from you, my dear brother, that
" this affair is more serious than I can express to
" you, and the official steps which General
" Belliard and M. de Talleyrand are enjoined to
" take will sufficiently show it. I was far from
" expecting that the first act done in the name of
" your government, after the treaty of November
" the 15th, would have been of such a nature;
" but, indeed, I cannot doubt but that your
" efforts are about to be united with mine to
" preserve France, Belgium, and Europe from
" the evils which might result therefrom.

" I was engaged in writing to you at length
" when I received this sad news which stops my
" letter.   I therefore confine myself to returning
" you that which you had confided to me, and
" which you will find herewith.   You will under-
" stand that I am waiting with impatience for
" your answer.

" You know all my kind regard for you.

" Your Majesty's

" Good brother and faithful friend,

" LOUIS PHILIP."

" *King Leopold to General Goblet.*

" Brussels, December the 18th, 1831.

" MY DEAR GENERAL,

" Courier succeeds courier from Paris, and
" Marienburg and Philippeville cause extreme
" uproar in the ministry.   I am very sorry, for
" really I never thought it would attach so great
" an importance to this affair.   To mitigate the
" evil, and seeing that this arrangement relative to
" the fortresses has nevertheless in view the doing
" of something agreeable for France, I have pro-
" posed to the English government to have an
" additional article drawn up, wherein it should be

" stated, that at the proposal of the Belgian
" plenipotentiary, the four Courts consent to
" suspend the demolition of Marienburg and
" Philippeville.   Let Le Hon know all that
" passes, by English courier. The ratification
" which is in your hands must not *go out of them*
" *without my special commands*. This affair of
" the fortresses is very annoying for me : it is a
" matter of indifference to us, and is our torment.
" The minister writes to you to authorize you
" to take the step I speak of, relative to the
" additional article I desire.   Do anything in the
" world to obtain it, and believe me, with un-
" changed sentiments,

" LEOPOLD.

" Show this letter to Van de Weyer and
" Stockmar."

" Lord Palmerston to General Goblet.

(In French.)

" Foreign Office, December 20, 1831.

" MY DEAR GENERAL,
    " I am sending off this evening a courier to
" Melton, who will carry to Count Matuszewic
" copies of the convention on the fortresses, for

" the Count to sign. This courier will return the
" day after to-morrow, and I hope that on
" Saturday you will be able to exchange your
" ratification for ours.

" I assure you this is indispensably necessary,
" and I invite you to meet me here for that pur-
" pose on Saturday at five.

" I had to-day a long conversation on the
" subject with Prince Talleyrand, to whom I ex-
" plained the impossibility of making any change
" in the convention such as it is in its signed
" form.

" Yours, my dear General,

" PALMERSTON."

" *The Same to the Same.*

(In French.)

"Goodwood, December the 22nd, 1831.

" MY DEAR GENERAL,

" I have just received your letter of to-day,
" together with the paper which I restore to you.
" I entreat you to dispense with my giving you
" an opinion on the ground or form of a pro-
" ceeding which I forewarn you can have no
" result. I have too much respect for the king

" your master and the king I have the honour to
" serve to make it possible I could ever consent
" to yield to the insolent tone the French govern-
" ment has judged it proper to assume on the
" subject of these fortresses. Prince Talleyrand
." and General Sébastiani must learn that they are
" no longer the instruments of the imperious
" wishes of a Napoleon; and it is necessary also
" that Louis Philip should know that the laurels
" of Valmy and Jemmapes cannot serve as a
" bugbear to all Europe.

   "It would be ill consulting the interests of
" King Leopold to alter a single letter of the
" convention, and I expect you with your ratifi-
" cation at the place of meeting on Saturday,
" without troubling ourselves with the flourishes
" of Talleyrand and Sébastiani, which I cannot
" help stigmatizing as unseemly and unworthy.

"Yours,

"PALMERSTON."

"*King Leopold to General Goblet.*

"Brussels, December the 22nd, 1831.

   "They are furious at Paris, and take up
" severely what you so correctly estimated, that

" they pretend to see in the treaty a *return* to
" the system of 1815.

" I am extremely desirous of obtaining the
" modification about those unhappy fortresses of
" Marienburg and Philippeville.   I think this
" will be an act of justice towards France, who
" feels hurt thereby.   All the warlike rhodomon-
" tades I do not much believe in ; but it is very
" certain that those two plaguy fortresses are not
" worth the bad blood the matter causes.

" It is necessary therefore to do anything in
" the world to obtain your additional article for
" their preservation ; I lay great store by it.
" And if I could have foreseen the violence and
" injustice of the French attacks, I would have
" given my positive opposition to their insertion
" in the treaty.

" The French government is very desirous
" that you should confer with Prince Talleyrand.
" Come to an understanding with him according
" to circumstances ; tell him nothing he should
" not know ; but make him feel that our desire is
" to put these two forts out of the question, and
" ask his advice.   You must, however, impress
" upon him that in our neutrality resides our

" total change of position, since the system of
" 1815 cannot apply to our position except in
" the unheard-of case of French aggression.

"We must confine ourselves simply to this:
" we are ready to demolish the forts which
" France desires us to, but we have no means of
" binding the other powers to that. All that
" goes beyond that we cannot meddle with.

" Believe in the sentiments I feel towards you,

" Leopold."

" *King Leopold to General Goblet.*

"Brussels, December the 25th, 1831.

" My dear General,

" You and your fortresses get me much bad
" blood, and yet they interest me but little, and
" the country no more.

" Your observations are very just; but on the
" other hand, to have cut off France from all
" means of obtaining some additions to the treaty
" of December the 14th, would have caused
" extreme irritation.

" We are poor shuttlecocks amidst it all.

" It is therefore urgent and important to make
" the greatest efforts to obtain whatever France

" may desire, *without, however, putting in*
" *jeopardy the treaty of November the* 15*th.*
" The letter, herewith, from the minister gives
" you the same instructions.   All these demands
" should be made in a friendly manner, and as far
" as possible verbally.   I can in this respect rely
" upon your prudence and that of Van de Weyer.

  " It is however, for our tranquillity, very
" desirable that the treaty should not give the
" least possible hold for an accusation of a return
" towards 1815.   You always perceived this
" danger, and I think the powers should have
" thought only of essentials, and not have shocked
" the national self-love of France.   Perfectly
" pacific as they are, it might have forced the
" government in a false direction through sheer
" weakness.   Keep as good an understanding as
" you can with Prince Talleyrand.

  " I would willingly have had you recalled
" here, but, thank God, there is very little talk as
" yet about the treaty of December the 14th, and
" your return would cause a great deal of sensa-
" tion, which, at the present moment, we have
" reason to avoid as much as possible.   So you
" will have to sacrifice yourself, and still remain

" in London.   So long as Russia's ratification has
" not arrived, nothing presses for an exchange of
" ratifications of your treaty.

" With unchanged sentiments,

" LEOPOLD."

" *King Leopold to General Goblet.*

" Brussels, January the 2nd, 1832.

" MY DEAR GENERAL,

" I hold the fortress-treaty still a little under
" lock and key ('dark'), and you will find that
" we begin to keep a secret better since there is
" nothing said in our journals about these infernal
" fortresses.

" You are quite right in thinking that I shall
" be very pleased when this affair is . all over.
" Good faith is my second nature : an accusation
" of the contrary, and from France too, has
" deeply wounded me.   It is maintained at Paris
" that *we* proposed the treaty in its present form ;
" that is a little too much.   Only let the end
" come soon, and I will put on my mourning
" (will be resigned). .

" LEOPOLD."

"*King Leopold to General Goblet.*

(Extract.)

"Brussels, January the 7th, 1832.

" The ratification of the treaty of December
" the 14th shall remain in London, in the hands
" of M. de Stockmar.   As I consider Marl-
" borough House more safe than private houses,
" the baron will not let it out any more without
" *special commands* from me.

" Here we might probably want you till the
" fifteenth in your military capacity.   The Dutch
" are very threatening, so much so that I shall
" put everything in order to be able to repulse
" them when necessary."

"*King Leopold to M. Le Hon.*

" Brussels, December the 16th, 1831.

" I read with much interest your three de-
" spatches, and I approve heartily of all you have
" said relative to family alliance.

" To have to wait for the ratifications is
" perfectly natural, but to wait for the *quasi-assent*
" of the King of Holland would be really
" monstrous.

" Certes, the events which might yet over-
" throw me in Belgium would cause a little
" tottering to the throne of Louis Philip.
" When once the ratifications have arrived,
" Belgium is a power recognized by all Europe
" except Holland. Yet this King of Holland has
" *no other rights but those which these powers*
" *in question have been pleased to grant him*, not
" at all for 'his beautiful eyes' (his personal
" merits), but because they thought *thus* to
" establish a new *system of equilibrium* in
" Europe.

" Seeing I was elected, according to all the
" forms prescribed by the constitution, by the
" representatives of the nation, received with
" acclamations by this same nation, and recog-
" nized by the powers which had in 1814 and
" 1815 made the conquest of Belgium, I think
" that my position is *diplomatically and popularly*
" *one of the most* legitimate in Europe.

" To say that we must wait until the King
" of Holland has given his assent, is to offer
" himself a premium for not concluding an ar-
" rangement which, however, in the present state
" of things in France, is of some importance to

' the very existence of the kingship and a govern-
" ment in this country.—And it would be far
" more natural for me to commence by asking
" the elder branch of the Bourbons if they have
" truly abandoned their views on France, and the
" rights which were never disputed them for cen-
" turies ; since, if it were not the case, I might as
" their neighbour find myself at a later period in
" a *false position* as regarded them. I have just
" received good news from London, where there
" is no intention at all of altering the twenty-four
" articles. General Goblet was to have signed
" the fortresses-treaty on the 13th. This act is
" for the royal family of France a new guarantee,
" since it must be considered as a second recogni-
" tion almost more *special* than the first, as by it
" I am recognized as inheritor of the rights of
" King William.

　　" Consequently I will lose not an instant in
" ratifying it, and taking away all fresh pretence
" from the Northern powers of creating difficul-
" ties.

　　" I am glad that General Tiburce Sébastiani is
" enabled to form an opinion on the spot, not
" only of the perfect tranquillity of the country,

" but also of the excellent disposition of the
" people.

" The courier is off, and I must finish. . . . .
" Believe in the wishes I cherish for your success
" in everything.

" LEOPOLD.

" Commercial matters begin to interest us
" strongly. If you could obtain admission of
" cast iron for a year at a reasonable duty it
" would do us infinite good; not with a view of
" obtaining profit, but of enlivening, as a measure
" of policy, those populations to which we pay
" great attention; and it should be in this light
" chiefly that the matter should be presented to
" the French government."

" *King Leopold to M. Le Hon.*

" Brussels, December 20, 1831.

" It is particularly *distressing* that we should
" be plagued about an affair [24] which is one of
" perfect indifference to us. If we have mixed
" France up with it as little as possible, it is that it
" would in no way have helped France, but would
" certainly have complicated matters still further.

---

[24] The affair of the fortresses.

" You on your side must take good care not
" to speak of this treaty except to the king and
" the ministers.

" There is something queer in all this. It is
" doubtful if in France, in spite of *its* recognition,
" we were considered as existing before this treaty
" of November 15 ; and in the present transaction,
" which is a consequence of that treaty and of
" the very natural desire not to give any pretext
" to the three other powers not to recognize us,
" we are treated as ruffians, robbers, etc.

" I have proposed to adjoin an additional
" article to the treaty, whereby those two ever-
" lasting towns [25] should be put out of the ques-
" tion. I shall take, and have already taken, the
" most energetic steps to arrive at this end ; I
" shall not know the result for some days.

" All this is a question between the five
" powers, and in no way a matter which *interests*
" *us*. Raze Tournay and Ypres ; we shall see it
" with pleasure. In the declaration of M. de
" Muelenaere it is said : ' *in conformity* with
" ' the protocol of April 17 ; *in concert* with the
" ' five powers.' These two points include the true

---

[25] Philippeville and Marienburg.

" question. However, as the original intention
" was that that should be a compliment to
" France, I think the powers should have regard
" to it now, and change it so as not to annoy the
" French government.

" Write often, and believe in the feelings I
" have towards you.

" LEOPOLD."

" *King Leopold to M. Le Hon.*[26]

" Brussels, December 24, 1831.

" I owe you some answer for a great num-
" ber of letters. The Belgian government desired
" to conclude, to get out of its provisional position
" which kills the country ; that is the cause of all
" these invectives.

" It seems to me like looking for noon at
" two o'clock P.M., to say that Belgium will find
" itself established in a sense hostile to France, in
" fact in the sense of 1815. It is in its neutrality
" that lie the immense change in position of
" this country and the advantage of France.

---

[26] This letter has already been published in the work
dedicated to Count Le Hon, Minister of State, etc. ; but it is
too important and too characteristic not to be reproduced
here.

" Belgium covers its frontier from the North Sea
" to the Moselle.

" Belgium, established as it is, must be natu-
" rally bound by interest to France, so long as
" the latter shall not ill-treat her or think of
" invading her.

" It is only in the latter case that the co-
" signing powers ought to interfere in our favour;
" and that it is of the very highest importance
" for Belgium that this invasion should not be
" able to take place without dragging France
" into a war with the four great powers. If it
" were otherwise, if Belgium were to exist only
" during the good pleasure of one or other of
" the five powers, she would cease to deserve the
" name of State.   It is only, then, the aggression
" of France which would give the four powers the
" right to interfere.   It was not so in the treaties
" of 1815, and it is an advantage which France
" derives from the new order of things.

" I cannot sufficiently express to you my
" astonishment at the extreme violence and injus-
" tice, and I should add bad taste, of the expres-
" sions of the French government, and I am
" *very much hurt* thereby.

" I grant with pleasure to the French govern-
" ment all the time for trying to get some changes
" added to the treaty ; I say added, since accord-
" ing to the dispositions of Russia, the fortress-
" treaty will, perhaps, be one of the means of
" engaging her to ratify the treaty of Novem-
" ber 15.

" General Goblet had finally unlimited
" instructions *to conclude*, according to the
" possibilities he met with. He has done so, and
" I should have no excuse for not ratifying the
" treaty.

" France will do well to let one truth sink
" into her ; that if she do not soon revive at
" home public confidence, and industry and
" commerce, which without it cannot flourish,
" she will be ruined. So long as our affairs
" here are not arranged, or if amusement is found
" in deranging them for subtle reasons connected
" with a possibility of Holy Alliance which
" nothing in the present position of Belgium
" renders probable in the remotest degree, this
" confidence will not spring up again, and the
" condition of France will deteriorate in a fright-
" ful manner.

" France, rich, making war on Germany and
" Italy, as the Bourbons did on Spain, with
" crowns of five francs, might obtain some grand
" revolutionary results, which would always end
" by causing to itself a violent crisis which would
" unseat royalty and upset its institutions.   But
" the French, poor, coming as pillagers, will find
" armies very differently organized from hereto-
" fore, and fellows who will come down heavily
" on the friends who whilst preaching liberty
" will devour their substance.   Napoleon has left
" France a sorry inheritance, by compelling all
" Europe to put itself under arms at the slightest
" signal of alarm.

" For myself individually, I lay more store by
" my honour and reputation for loyalty than
" anything else in the world.   I have known how
" to preserve it in very difficult positions, and
" certainly it was not on occasion of a question
" of so little *importance* for me and the country
" as this affair of the fortresses that I should
" change my principles.

" The government likewise, as you know,
" had not for an instant the least thought of
" acting with bad faith, in anything whatever.

" It is its duty, however, to neglect nothing
" which may consolidate our independence, even
" if that must, however causelessly, irritate the
" self-love of another country.   Let France, if
" she has anything to say against the treaty,
" address herself to the four powers: we are
" indifferent about the names of the forts.

" Here is a long letter.   If you find occasion,
" you can show it wholly or in part to the French
" government, and express at the same time my
" discontent at the far from agreeable tone it has
" thought proper to adopt towards the Belgian
" government.   If all memory be not lost at
" Paris, there may be some recollection of
" services rendered, and of an absence of all
" hesitation in going to the front when it could
" be of any use to France; for example, in the
" very delicate affair of the departure of the
" troops for France.

" Be assured of the feelings I have towards
" you.

" LEOPOLD."

" *M. de Muelenaere, Minister of Foreign Affairs,
to M. Le Hon.*

" Brussels, December the 31st, 1831.

" There has rolled by a month and a half
" since the conclusion of the treaty of Novem-
" ber 15th ; a fortnight only separates us from
" the fateful end. At no period of our revolution
" have we been nearer the issue and in a state
" of greater uncertainty. This must certainly be
" acknowledged : after fifteen months of negotia-
" tion, strife, and toil, all is in suspense, all is
" thrown back into doubt ; the question is still of
" peace or war, as unsettled as it was on the first
" day which followed the revolution of September.
" If the act of November 15th be not ratified,
" all ulterior proposal and negotiation become
" impossible : there will have been played at our
" and France's expense a comedy of fifteen
" months' duration. Refusal of ratification will
" be the most signal homage to the opinion of
" the men who in France and in Belgium have
" criticized the course followed by the two
" governments. You know what efforts were
" required to obtain the acceptation of the

" twenty-four articles. I ask, then, who is the
" man in Belgium who would dare to propose
" a modification ? Who is the man who would
" consent to a modification ? There will be no
" more faith in diplomacy, if an act declared
" final and irrevocable can be retracted : the first
" modification might be followed by a demand
" for a fresh modification, and so on. It becomes
" henceforth impossible, even logically, to assign
" to any act a character of immutability. . . ."

" *King Leopold to M. Le Hon.*

" Brussels, April the 4th, 1832.

" I am afflicted to see by a letter from the
" king that an infamous advantage has been
" taken of the cholera to cause troubles in Paris.
" What a scoundrel must any one be to turn to
" account such a scourge as that.

" I have no positive news from London about
" anything. The Dutch army is concentrated on
" our frontier, under the notion, as they pretend,
" that we had an intention of attacking them.

" I renew my request with reference to some
" generals. If there is fear of scandal, they may
" at least be in readiness somewhere where they

" would be in disposability, and information
" might be given me so as to be able to have
" them at once when their presence becomes
" necessary. . . .

" I am grieved that the uncertainty which
" still prevails, and even the cholera, should be
" such obstacles to this union, which I desire
" very earnestly. I see that Russia has incor-
" porated Poland : it is a great event, from which
" a great deal may be made in favour of the
" conclusion of the Belgian business. This act
" of Russia is contrary to all stipulations ; Prussia
" and Austria must be hurt by it. If the powers
" consent to it, they ought to exact from Russia
" a frank adhesion to the twenty-four articles.

" Take care of my letter for the king.
" As ever,

" LEOPOLD."

The King of the Belgians had informed
Louis Philip of the number of places to be
dismantled, as well as of the difficulties he had
encountered at the Conference; but his explanations were far from satisfying the French
government. General Sébastiani gave himself

up to the most singular transports, threatening
not to ratify the principal treaty of November 15th, if the Belgian government ratified the
fortresses-convention.   Louis Philip himself, in
an autograph letter addressed to the King of the
Belgians, expressed himself with great bitterness.
He wrote to him on the 17th of December,
that he had learned with equal surprise and
regret the news that General Goblet had felt
himself at liberty to sign a treaty in formal contradiction of the engagements entered into with
himself. " I expect, then, with confidence," he
added, " that this treaty will not receive your
" ratification, for I am bound to rely on your
" promises."

M. de Talleyrand had attributed to *Belgian
intrigue* the extension of the treaty to Marienburg and Philippeville, as well as the secrecy of its
conclusion ; and General Sébastiani accused the
Cabinet of Brussels of dissimulation, weakness,
and duplicity.

It must have been deeply wounding to King
Leopold, to him who used to say, Good faith
is my second nature.   Accordingly he repudiated
energetically the unjust conclusions of the Cabinet

of the Tuileries.   He bade his minister at Paris
complain of the "far from agreeable tone" of the
French government towards the Belgian government, of the extreme violence, injustice, and bad
taste of its language.   He protested that the
Cabinet of Brussels had never for an instant had
the least idea of acting in bad faith in any case
whatever; that it was part of his duty, however,
to neglect nothing which consolidated Belgian
independence, even if he must thereby, however unreasonably, irritate the self-love of another
country.   The complaints of France, moreover,
were unjust, its pretensions certainly antiquated.
" It seems to me," added the King, "like looking
" for mid-day at two o'clock, to say that Belgium
" will be established in a sense hostile to France,
" in the sense in fact of 1815.   It is in the
" neutrality that are to be found the vast change
" in the position of this country and the gain of
" France.   Belgium covers her frontier from the
" North Sea to the Moselle.   Belgium, con-
" stituted as it is, must be naturally bound by
" the ties of interest to France so long as the
" latter abstains from ill-treatment and dreams
" not of invasion."   He then announced his

intention of ratifying the convention, because he was bound in honour to do so. Casimir Périer, on his side, showed a strong determination to refuse concurrence in the guarantee of the Belgian State if the convention of December the 14th were ratified. Such were also the views of Louis Philip and the Duke d'Orléans.

General Goblet, who had been in a position to appreciate the delicate conduct of King Leopold, did not hesitate to say that that of the French government had been revoltingly unjust. However, the King of the Belgians, wishing, in his own words, to mitigate the evil, forbade his plenipotentiary to let out of his hands the ratification of the fortresses-convention without a special injunction; and he bade him, further, present an additional article, importing that on his proposal the plenipotentiaries of the four courts consented to suspend the dismantlement of Philippeville and Marienburg. But the efforts of General Goblet failed. Before taking official steps, he thought it right to sound Lord Palmerston semi-officially, and to communicate to him the scheme of the note he proposed to address to the plenipotentiaries of the four courts.

Lord Palmerston, who, two days previously, had
written to General Goblet to press for an exchange of ratifications, did not conceal his lively
displeasure at the receipt of this communication.
He gave the general clearly to understand that
such a step could not have any result; and he
vented, without any circumlocution, in bitter
terms, his growing irritation against the French
government: "Prince Talleyrand and General
"Sébastiani," he said, "must learn that they are
"no longer instruments of the imperious will of
"a Napoleon, and Louis Philip also must be
"taught to know that the laurels of Valmy and
"Jemmapes will not serve as a bugbear to all
"Europe."

This violence was far from pleasing King
Leopold. "We are but poor shuttlecocks,"
he wrote, "amidst all that." He did not confine
himself to delaying the ratification: he expressed
a desire that new efforts might be made to
satisfy France, without however endangering the
principal treaty of November the 15th, which
guaranteed the independence of Belgium.
Being informed that a more healthy apprecia-
tion of facts was being shown in the high

places of the French government, the Cabinet
of Brussels, in concert with King Leopold, and
assured of the assent of Louis Philip, suggested
at last to the Conference the idea of an explanatory note of a nature to satisfy the Cabinet
of the Tuileries. This expedient was adopted.
Consequently, the plenipotentiaries of the four
Courts, by their declaration of January the 23rd,
1832, placed beyond a doubt the fact that all the
clauses of the convention of December the 14th
were in perfect harmony with the character of
an independent and neutral power which had
been allowed to Belgium by Austria, England,
France, Prussia, and Russia. King Leopold had
awaited not without ill-humour the end of this
difference. If the fortress-convention had but
little interest for him, he attached vital importance to the prompt ratification of the treaty
of the twenty-four articles. But lately, December
15th, he had remarked that it would be "a
" really monstrous thing " to wait, before recognizing him as a legitimate king, for the
quasi-consent of the King of Holland.
" Elected," he said, " with all the forms pre-
" scribed by the constitution, received with ac-

" clamation by the nation, recognized by the
" powers who, in 1814 and 1815, had made the
" conquest of Belgium, I think my position is—
" diplomatically and popularly—one of the most
" legitimate in Europe." France and England,
after having compounded over the affair of the
fortresses, put off no longer the ratification of
the treaty of November the 15th. This important formality was completed in London,
January the 31st, 1832.

As King Leopold had foreseen, the final
adhesion of the other courts to the cause of
Belgian independence seemed to be really
subordinated to the preliminary assent of King
William.[27]

---

[27] The following information is borrowed from one of the
unpublished letters of Baron Stockmar (London, December
19th, 1831) : " Immediately after having cognizance of the
" treaty concluded between Belgium and the Powers, the
" Cabinet of Berlin declared that it would ratify, and would
" send its ratification within a few days, to be exchanged.
" Scarcely had this news gone forth, when letters from King
" William came to beg the King of Prussia most urgently
" not to give his ratification. Thereupon he declared,
" through his ambassador at the Hague, that at all events
" he would ratify, but that he would defer the despatch, so
" as to leave King William time to arrange with the Confer-

" It is," he wrote on the 20th of February,
" unworthy conduct on the part of the three
" courts, a dishonourable failure of their word."
He said again to his representative in France:
" You may assure the presiding minister of the
" council that I am far from provoking war, but I
" am sure that the only way of avoiding one with
" Holland is to show one's perfect ability to make
" it."

Leopold had worked unrelaxedly at the re-

" ence. Two days after the departure of this declaration
" for the Hague, a communication from the Cabinet of
" Vienna appears to have been made to that of Berlin,
" according to which Prince Metternich had not been quite
" satisfied with the sudden manner in which the treaty had
" been made, but would have desired that the Conference
" should have fixed a period for King William's acceptance
" of the twenty-four articles, declaring to him that at the ex-
" piration of that period a treaty would be made with Belgium
" without further scruple. At the same time the Cabinet
" of Vienna had to ask the Cabinet of Berlin whether the
" latter really intended to ratify or not. The latter, it is
" said, gave the same answer it had given to the Hague,
" inviting Vienna to do likewise. Accordingly Vienna pro-
" mised to ratify simultaneously with Berlin. . . . I have
" reason to believe that Russia has not yet replied. . . . In
" case Russia should refuse her ratification, Austria and
" Prussia do not appear less determined to give theirs. . . . "

organization of the national army. Aided by
Charles de Brouckere, minister of war, who in his
turn was seconded by General Evain, one of the
best-trained general officers of the First Empire,
and by Desprez, the chief of the staff, for whom
the king had a particular regard, calling him
" My very dear Desprez," he had already
obtained satisfactory results. Before the end of
1831 Belgium had an effective force of 87,000
men. When spring came the king resolved
to take into his service some of the Polish
generals who were in France, keeping clear,
however, " of all the heads that might be too
" hot," and to incorporate with the Belgian army
the Polish soldiers who had sought refuge at
Dantzig and Elbing.

That this arrangement was unpleasant to the
French, is clear from the following letter :—

" *King Leopold to M. Le Hon.*

" Brussels, April the 9th, 1832.

" I am not astonished at the repugnance of
" the French government with reference to the
" Poles : I even expected it.

" However, I have a way of getting out of

" the affair. Eight thousand men out of the
" twelve thousand of this year's contingent are
" called out; they are all young, *too young*, in
" fact, and will be infinitely better at home. The
" budget finds funds for them as well as for the
" four foreign battalions. Instead, then, of
" forming a foreign regiment, I shall form Polish
" battalions, which will allow of their being
" mingled with the army as substitutes.

" The same with the cavalry. I am going
" *incontinently* to form six new squadrons; we
" want men and officers; I shall be enchanted to
" be able to form them of Poles; since as we
" are going to have the horses we shall only have
" to get them accoutred and mounted.

" This cannot cause more talk than the
" thousands of Germans and Swiss in the Dutch
" army, and the Prussian and Hanoverian troopers
" to be found in their regiments of cavalry.

" I want also gunners and some officers of
" artillery. There are three arms, essential ones,
" of which I am in want. The most urgent are
" the cavalry and artillery.

" Represent the matter from this point of
" view to the French government, who, un-

" happily, are at present a prey to that terrible
" malady of cholera and to fear. All I ask on their
" part will be to let these people file to the left,
" instead of letting them go to the left southward.
" Let them abstain from being mixed up with
" it, but let them not *prevent* it any the more.

" It would be very important for me to have
" the cavalry as soon as possible; we want two
" thousand at least.

" I am sorry General Chranowski remains in
" Germany.   I desire to have colonel of cavalry,
" Krusewski.   If we could only get at least a
" good Polish general!

" I am of the French government's opinion
" that it will be more wise not to form a separate
" corps of Poles, and I flatter myself that this will
" tranquillize it, and cause it not to hinder us,
" especially in respect of the cavalry, of which we
" have the most urgent need, since the Dutch
" have *at least* two thousand more cavalry than
" we have. . The French government cannot
" deny this inferiority on our part.

" Your despatch is wise, and you have seen
" things as they are.   I think the French
" government would be sorry to see us form a

" Polish legion, and perhaps Russia would make it
" a pretext for further chicanery with us. By
" taking the Poles, then, as substitutes for my
" young reserves, I am perfectly master of them,
" and do not run the risk of seeing the corps
" take a direction which would be inconvenient.
" We have no *party of movement* here, but that
" is a fact which we cannot make the French
" government comprehend. . . .

" France will not make war, or, if she do, it is
" probable that she and Belgium will march on
" the same line.

" You see then I adopt the king's views to
" please him, and I think that in this way he
" will not see *any* inconvenience. . . .

" Beg the French government to send me a
" list of the generals it could place at my
" disposal.

" The ratifications go on very slowly.
" Energy on the part of the French and English
" might have advanced them, but there is
" nothing listened to but fear.

" Keep yourself clear of cholera, and let me
" soon hear news—good news—from you. Say
" all sorts of things from me to MM. Périer

" and Sébastiani. I charge them to reflect that
" their lives are very precious to us.

" LEOPOLD.

" I have written to the king that there are
" but two things to be done ; either let the treaty
" be executed by the powers, or, if that does not
" suit them, let us be permitted by these same
" powers to execute it for better or worse.

" I have been a thousand times interrupted,
" and my letter betrays it. . . ."

On the 28th of February was promulgated
the law which, pursuant to the prescriptions of
the Constitution, was to settle the Civil List for
the whole duration of the reign of Leopold I.
The sovereign's settlement was fixed at
(2,751,322 francs) 110,053*l.*, and, besides, he
had at his disposal the palaces at Brussels,
Laeken, and Antwerp. Though the figure
proposed to the legislature, in virtue of the
right of initiation, by some of its members,
was relatively reduced, the king did not wish
that any pressure whatever, direct or indirect,
should be exercised upon the deputies of the
country. He organized his household, aided by

the counsels of Baron Stockmar, who had previously been at the head of the arrangements at Claremont. "He wisely resolved to adapt " this organization to the nature of circum- " stances and the spirit of the age. Instead of " appointing a host of chamberlains and other " ordinary officers of courts, he confined himself " to appointing a grand marshal, a master of the " horse, a comptroller of the privy purse, and " private secretary. He added to them four " aides-de-camp and two extra aides-de-camp."[28]

At this juncture, when Belgium was still on the eve of a fresh struggle with Holland, and when the three powers still refused to irrevocably cement its independence, Leopold saw that the duties he had to accomplish as a sovereign were as yet rather military than civil. He kept up with General Desprez a correspondence, in which he paid the most anxious attention to the security of the country, and to the moral and physical condition of the troops; no incident, no detail, escaped his notice.[29]   " A long absence,"

---

[28] *White, Revolution of* 1830, vol. iii. chap. 4.

[29] *See* the *Conservative:* an international law review (Utrecht, 1868), p. 135, *seq.*

he wrote from Paris, "might offer strange
"temptations to the Dutch, and you know I am
"the Atlas on whose shoulders rests our little
"kingdom." On another occasion he said, still
more clearly : "As regards Belgium in its present
"condition, the State means myself."

Belgium was, in truth, a nascent state, over
which the Head had to watch with a solicitude
which could not be for a moment relaxed.
Always able, prudent, and far-seeing as he was, he
had to guard at the same time against galling
France and awakening the jealousy or suscepti-
bilities of England. If Leopold tried to gain the
Duke of Wellington, he was no less engaging in
his relations with the Tuileries. They were
wrong, he said, to imagine at Paris that there
existed about him influences hostile to France.
" My policy towards her will always be the same ;
" she will always find in me an equally faithful and
" devoted friend, so long as she shall not invade
" Belgium. He prophesied besides, that this idea
" of invasion, to which the party of movement
" was still so much attached, would be false policy
" and cost France dear."

To consolidate Belgian independence, Leopold

asked only that a period should be fixed for the ratifications still wanting to the treaty of November the 15th, and that this treaty should be carried out to the full. Belgium, without outlets, without regular relations with other peoples, could only, he maintained, vegetate in the provisional state she was in. He blamed the French government freely for not showing more energy towards Russia. What risk was there, according to his own words, in showing courage in the right place? In spite of assurances given him, the king despaired of seeing the ratifications of the three northern powers. "As long as we " have them not in our hands," he wrote on the 20th of April, " I don't believe in them." Now, two days previously, the plenipotentiaries of Austria and Prussia had proceeded to an exchange of ratifications of the treaty of November the 15th, but under a reservation of the rights of the Germanic Confederation, with respect to the articles concerning the cession and exchange of a part of the Grand Duchy of Luxemburg. When he heard of the restrictions Leopold did not show that he was much affected by them. "We have only to think," he said, "of

" the ratifications of a treaty which has been
" imposed upon us, which we have accepted with
" chagrin, but which we will not exchange for
" still worse conditions."

On the 18th of April, however, Russia had
not joined Austria and Prussia. It was understood that the Emperor Nicholas wished to
humour as long as possible the royal family of
the Netherlands, and above all the Prince of
Orange, his brother-in-law. But he ought not
to have forgotten that the House of Coburg
was also allied to the Romanows, and that Prince
Leopold had served bravely under the Emperor
Alexander. Respect was due also to the
signature given on November the 15th. The
King of the Belgians, under the influence of
these reflections, could not then speak of the
Russian government without bitterness. He
wrote, fourteen days before the Austrian and
Prussian ratifications : " I see that Russia has
" incorporated Poland : it is a great event, from
" which we can draw a great deal in favour of the
" conclusion of the Belgian business. This act of
" Russia is contrary to all stipulations. Austria
" and Prussia must be hurt by it. If the

" powers consent to it, they should exact from
" Russia a frank adhesion to the twenty-four
" articles." At last the Russian government
came in its turn to sanction the independence of Belgium ; the ratification which
was still wanting was given on the 4th of May.[30]

Half the work of the powers was then accomplished, in spite of the reservations expressed by
the Courts of Austria and Prussia and the conditions formulated by the Cabinet of St. Petersburg. This conditional ratification on the part
of Russia had at first been very galling to the
King of the Belgians. "By accepting it," he
wrote on the 9th, "we give up our position,
" abandon our treaty, and drop into ambiguity."
However, he showed himself to be quite determined not to allow the introduction in the treaty
of November the 15th of modifications or
changes without compensation. Besides, he soon
acknowledged that there had been unreasonable
apprehension respecting the Russian ratifications,
although, as he said, they might have been more
satisfactory. " Leopold was in a hurry to com-

[30] The convention relative to the fortresses was ratified
next day.

" plete his task.   It was not by any means all to
" have got Belgian independence acknowledged;
" it was necessary to get this independence
" respected by obliging the enemy to evacuate
" the national territory; it was necessary to exact
" without delay the execution of the treaty
" sanctioned by Europe. 'Heaven,' said the
" king, 'has been graciously pleased to grant
" ' me two qualities, courage and patience; and I
" ' reckon on turning them to account.'"

Whilst tracing some time previously the
picture of the monarchy of July, its vicissitudes
and its successes, an eminent writer, reserved as a
statesman for so brilliant and strange a destiny,
expressed himself in these terms :[31]   "We could
" not suffer the republic or the imperial dynasty
" that we desired not at home to establish itself
" beside us, and gather, excite, and throw up again
" our malcontents. We could not give the Duke
" de Nemours; for that was really no union for
" us, though for the powers it was equal to union ;
" it was, consequently, war for a simple family
" interest. Leopold alone suited us, not because

---

[31] *The Monarchy of* 1830, by A. Thiers, deputy from the
Rhone-Mouths (Paris, 1831, 8vo.), p. 108.

" he was English, for one is always of the country
" over which one is called to reign, but because
" with the English manner he was sure to be a
" good true Belgian. He has proved it. So much
" the worse for those who cannot see the wisdom of
" such a combination.   To reassure Europe, and
" not make an enemy for ourselves, was all that
" could be done."

APPENDIX.

———◦◦✦✦◦◦———

Certificate of Birth and Baptism.

(Extract from the Baptismal Register of the Parish of the Ducal Court at Coburg.)

Leopold George Christian Frederick, third prince and eighth child of his Ducal Highness Francis Frederick Anthony, Hereditary Prince of Saxe-Coburg-Saalfeld, etc., etc., and Augusta Caroline Sophia his wife, Hereditary Princess of Saxe-Coburg-Saalfeld, Countess Reuss by birth, was born between one and two o'clock A.M. of December 16th, 1790, at Coburg, and baptized on the following day, December 17th, between four and five P.M.

The Sponsors were :—

1. His Roman Imperial Majesty Leopold II.
2. His Electoral Highness Clemens Wenzeslaus, Elector of Trier; Royal Polish Prince of Saxony.
3. His Ducal Highness Albert Casimir, Duke of Saxe-Teshen.

4. His Ducal Highness George of Saxe-Meiningen.
5. His Ducal Highness Christian Francis, Prince of S.C.S.
6. His Ducal Highness Frederick Josias, Prince of S.C.S.
7. His Serene Highness Maximilian Joseph, Prince of Pfalze-Zweibrück.
8. His Serene Highness Charles Louis, Prince of Hohenlohe-Langenburg.
9. His Highness Henry XIII., Hereditary Prince of Graiz.

Decree proclaiming H.R.H. the Prince of Saxe-Coburg King of the Belgians.

In the Name of the Belgian People.

The National Congress

Decrees :

1st Article.

H.R.H. Leopold George Christian Frederick, Prince of Saxe-Coburg, is proclaimed King of the Belgians, on condition of accepting the Constitution as it has been decreed by the National Congress.

2nd Article.

He is not to take possession of the throne until after he has solemnly taken, in the midst of Congress, the following oath :—" I swear to observe the Constitution and laws of the Belgian people, to maintain the national independence and territorial integrity."

The executive power will see to the execution of the present decree.

Brussels, Palace of the Nation, June 4, 1831.

President of the National Congress,
E. C. DE GERLACHE.

Secretaries, Members of the National Congress,

> LIEDTS.
> NOTHOMB.
> VICOMTE VILAIN XIV.
> HENRI DE BROUCKERE.

Official Report of the Inauguration of Leopold I., King of the Belgians.

At one o'clock the National Congress of Belgium met under the presidency of M. de Gerlache.

His Majesty the King of the Belgians, *Leopold the First*, and the Regent of Belgium, Baron Erasmus Surlet de Chokier, attended the Assembly.

The Regent resigned the powers confided to him by the National Congress.

The President gave the Regent official acknowledgment of his declaration.

The President caused to be read out the Constitution decreed by the National Congress, February 7, 1831.

His Majesty the King took the following oath :—" I swear to observe the Constitution and laws of the Belgian people, to maintain the national independence and territorial integrity."

The President gave the King official acknowledgment of the taking of the oath.

In proof whereof was drawn up this report, signed by H.M. the King, the Regent, the President, and the Secretaries of the Congress.

Brussels, the twenty-first of July, one thousand eight hundred and thirty-one.

LEOPOLD.

E. SURLET DE CHOKIER.

President of the Congress,
E. C. DE GERLACHE.

Vice-Presidents of the Congress,
RAIKEM.
DESTOUVILLES.

The Secretaries, Members of the National Congress.

LIEDTS.
VICOMTE VILAIN XIV.
NOTHOMB.
H. DE BROUCKERE.

Treaty of November 15th, 1831.

The courts of Austria, France, Great Britain, Prussia and Russia, taking into consideration the events which have taken place in the United Kingdom of the Netherlands since the month of September, 1830, the obligation they lie under of preventing those events from disturbing the general peace, and the necessity, resulting from these events, of applying some modifications to the transactions of 1815, whereby was created and established the United Kingdom of the Netherlands, and H. M. the present King of the Belgians being a party to these intentions of the Courts above mentioned, have named for their plenipotentiaries, to wit :

H.M. the King of the Belgians, Sieur Sylvan Van de Weyer, his envoy extraordinary and minister plenipotentiary to His Britannic Majesty ;

H.M. the Emperor of Austria, King of Hungary and Bohemia ;

Prince Paul d'Esterhazy, Knight of the Golden Fleece, etc., now a privy councillor of His Imperial and Royal Apostolic Majesty, and his ambassador extraordinary to His Britannic Majesty ;

And Sieur John Philip Baron de Wessenberg, Grand Cross of the Royal Order of St. Stephen, etc., chamberlain, now a privy councillor of his Imperial and Royal Apostolic Majesty ;

H.M. the King of the French, Sieur Charles Maurice de Talleyrand-Périgord, Prince-duke de Talleyrand, peer of France, ambassador extraordinary and minister plenipotentiary of his said Majesty to his Britannic Majesty, Grand Cross of the Legion of Honour, etc., etc., etc. ;

H.M. the King of the United Kingdom of Great Britain and Ireland, the Right Honourable Henry John Viscount Palmerston, Baron Temple, peer of Ireland, of his Britannic Majesty's Privy Council, member of parliament and his principal Secretary of State having the Department of Foreign Affairs ;

H.M. the King of Prussia, Sieur Henry William Baron de Bulow, his Chamberlain, Privy Councillor of Legation, envoy extraordinary and minister plenipotentiary to his Britannic Majesty, and Knight of several orders;

And H.M. the Emperor of All the Russias ;

Sieur Christopher, Prince de Lieven, General of Infantry in his armies, his aide-de-camp-general, ambassador extraordinary and plenipotentiary to his Britannic Majesty, Knight of the Orders of Russia, etc. ;

And Sieur Adam, Count Matuszewic, privy councillor of his said Majesty, Knight of the Order of St. Anne, of the First Class, etc. ;

Who, having exchanged their full powers, found in good and due form, have concluded and signed the articles which follow : [1]

Article 1.

The Belgian territory consists of the provinces of South Brabant, Liège, Namur, Hainault, West Flanders, East Flanders, Antwerp, and Limburg, such as they were when part of the United Kingdom of the Netherlands established in 1815, with the exception of the districts of the Province of Limburg designated in Article 4. The Belgian territory shall, moreover, comprise that part of the Grand Duchy of Luxemburg specified in Article 2.

Article 2.

H.M. the King of the Netherlands, Grand Duke of Luxemburg, consents that in the Grand Duchy of Luxemburg the boundaries of Belgian territory be such as they are about to be described below.

Starting from the frontier of France, between *Rodange*, which shall remain in the Grand Duchy of Luxemburg,

---

[1] The first twenty-four articles are in textual conformity with the twenty-four articles of the Treaty of Separation of October 15, 1831.

and *Athus*, which shall belong to Belgium, there shall be drawn, according to the chart here annexed, a line which, leaving to Belgium the road from *Arlon* to *Longwy*, the town of *Arlon* with its district, and the road from *Arlon* to *Bastogne*, shall pass between *Messancy*, which will be in Belgian territory, and *Clemency*, which will remain in the Grand Duchy of Luxemburg, to end at *Steinfort*, which place will likewise remain in the Grand Duchy; from *Steinfort* this line shall be prolonged in the direction of *Eischen*, from *Hecbus*, *Guirsch*, *Oberpalen*, *Grende*, *Nothomb*, *Paretth*, and *Perlé*, up to *Martelange; Hecbus*, *Guirsch*, *Grende*, *Nothomb*, and *Paretth* to belong to Belgium, and *Eischen*, *Oberpalen*, *Perlé*, and *Martelange* to the Grand Duchy. From *Martelange* the said line shall descend the course of the *Sûre*, of which the *thalweg* (waterway) shall serve for boundary between the two states as far as opposite to *Tintange*, whence it shall be prolonged as directly as possible towards the present frontier of the arrondissement of *Diekirch*, and shall pass between *Surret*, *Harlange*, and *Tarchamps*, which it will leave to the Grand Duchy of Luxemburg, and *Honville*, *Livarchamp*, and *Loutermange*, which will form part of the Belgian territory; then reaching, in the neighbourhood of *Doncols* and of *Sonlez*, which will remain in the Grand Duchy, the present frontier of the arrondissement of *Diekirch*, the line in question shall follow the said frontier as far as that of the Prussian territory. All the territories, towns, forts, and places situated to the west of this line shall belong to Belgium, and all territories, towns, forts, and places situated to the east of this same line shall continue to belong to the Grand Duchy of Luxemburg.

It is understood that in tracing this line, and in conforming as closely as possible to the description which has been given above, as well as to the indications in the chart, added for greater clearness to the present article, the demarcation commissioners, of whom mention is made in Article 5, will have regard to localities as well as to considerations of convenience which may result therefrom reciprocally.

Article 3.

H.M. the King of the Netherlands, Grand Duke of Luxemburg, shall receive for the cessions made in the preceding articles a territorial indemnity in the province of Limburg.

Article 4.

In execution of the part of Article 1 relative to the province of Limburg, and in consequence of cessions which H. M. the King of the Netherlands makes by Article 2, his said Majesty shall possess, whether in his capacity of Grand Duke of Luxemburg, or for the purpose of being reunited to Holland, the territories whereof the boundaries are indicated below.

1st. On the right bank of the Meuse :

To the old Dutch enclaves on the said bank in the province of Limburg shall be added the districts of this same province on this same bank which did not belong to the States-General in 1790, in such fashion that the part of the present province of Limburg situated on the right bank of the Meuse, and comprised between this river on the west, the frontier of the Prussian territory on the east, the present frontier of the province of Liège on the south, and Dutch Guelderland on the north, shall belong henceforth wholly and entirely to H. M. the King of the Netherlands, whether in his capacity of Grand Duke of Luxemburg, or to be reunited to Holland.

2nd. On the left bank of the Meuse:

Starting from the most southern point of the Dutch province of North Brabant, there shall be drawn, according to the chart hereto annexed, a line which shall end at the Meuse above [2] *Wessem*, between this place and *Stevenweet*, at the point where meet, on the left bank, the frontiers of the present arrondissement of *Ruremonde* and *Maestricht*, in such fashion that *Bergerot, Stamproy, Neer-Itteren, Ittervoord*, and *Thorn*, with their districts, as well as all the other places situated to the north of this line, shall form part of the Dutch territory.

The old Dutch enclaves in the province of Limburg on the left bank of the Meuse shall belong to Belgium, with the exception of the town of *Maestricht*, which, with a territory of 1200 toises (about 8000 feet) in radius, starting from the outer glacis of the fort on the said bank of this river, shall continue to be possessed in full sovereignty and proprietorship by H. M. the King of the Netherlands.

Article 5.

H. M. the King of the Netherlands, Grand Duke of Luxemburg, shall come to an understanding with the Germanic Confederation and the agnates of the House of Nassau about the application of the stipulations included in Articles 3 and 4, as well as about all other arrangements which the said Articles might render necessary, whether with the agnates, above mentioned, of the House of Nassau, or with the Germanic Confederation.

Article 6.

In consideration of the above territorial arrangements,

---

[2] The French is "au dessus;" the English, as given in the Annual Register, is "below." The translator simply translates. Transl.

each of the two parties gives up reciprocally and for ever, all pretension to the territories, towns, forts, and places situated within the other's boundaries, such as they have been settled to be in Articles 1, 2, and 4.

The said boundaries shall be traced in conformity with these same Articles by demarcation-commissioners, Belgic and Dutch, who shall meet as soon as possible in the town of Maestricht.

Article 7.

Belgium, within the limits specified in Articles 1, 2, and 4, shall form an independent and perpetually neutral State. She shall be bound to observe this same neutrality towards all other States.

Article 8.

The *drainage* of the waters of the two Flanders shall be regulated between Holland and Belgium according to the stipulations laid down on this head in Article 6 of the definitive treaty concluded between H. M. the Emperor of Germany and the States-General, November 8, 1785 ; and, in conformity with the said Article, commissioners named by each party shall come to an understanding on the application of the provisions it sanctions.

Article 9.

The provisions of Articles 108–117, inclusive, of the general act of the Congress of Vienna, relative to the free navigation of navigable streams and rivers, shall be applied to the streams and navigable rivers which separate or traverse simultaneously the Belgian and Dutch territory.

As touching especially the navigation of the Scheldt, it shall be agreed that piloting and buoying, as well as the preservation of the channels of the Scheldt below Antwerp, shall be under a common supervision ; that this common supervision shall be exercised by commissioners, named for this purpose on both sides ; that moderate pilotage-dues shall be fixed by common agreement, and that these dues shall be the same for Dutch commerce and for Belgian commerce.—It is likewise agreed that the navigation of the waters intermediate between the Scheldt and the Rhine, for going from Antwerp to the Rhine and *vice versâ*, shall remain reciprocally free ; and that it shall be subject only to moderate tolls, which shall be provisionally the same for the commerce of both countries.

Commissioners shall meet, on both sides, at Antwerp, within the space of a month, both to fix the definitive and permanent amount of these tolls, and to agree upon a general regulation for the execution of the provisions of the present article, and to comprise therein the exercise of the right of fishing and the fishery trade along the whole extent of the Scheldt, on a footing of perfect reciprocity in favour of the subjects of both countries. Meanwhile, and until the said regulation be fixed, the navigation of the navigable streams and rivers above mentioned shall remain free to the commerce of both countries, which shall adopt provisionally on this head the tariff of the convention signed on the 31st of March, 1831, at Mayence, for the free navigation of the Rhine, as well as the other provisions of that convention so far as they can apply to the navigable streams and rivers which separate or traverse simultaneously the Dutch territory and the Belgian territory.

Article 10.

The use of the canals which traverse simultaneously both countries shall continue to be free and common to their inhabitants. It is understood that the enjoyment thereof shall be reciprocal and on the same conditions, and that, on both sides, there will be on the canals only moderate navigation-dues.

Article 11.

Commercial communications by way of the town of Maestricht and that of Sittard shall remain entirely free, and shall not be impeded on any pretext whatsoever.

The use of the roads which, by traversing these two towns, lead to the frontiers of Germany, shall be subject only to a payment of moderate turnpike tolls for the keeping up of these roads, in such sort that transit traffic may meet with no obstacle, and that, in consideration of the tolls above mentioned, these roads may be kept in good condition and fit to facilitate this traffic.

Article 12.

In case there should have been, in Belgium, a new road made, or a new canal dug, ending at the Meuse opposite the Dutch canton of Sittard, then Belgium would be entitled to demand of Holland, who may not refuse in such a case, that the said road or said canal should be lengthened after the same plan, entirely at the charges and expense of Belgium, through the canton of Sittard up to the frontiers of Germany. This road or canal, which should serve only for commercial communication, would be constructed, at the choice of Holland, either by engineers and workmen whom Belgium would obtain authority to employ for this purpose in the canton of Sittard, or by engineers and workmen whom Holland would provide, and who would execute at the charges of Belgium the works agreed upon, the whole with-

out any cost at all to Holland, and without prejudice to her
exclusive rights of sovereignty over the territory traversed by
the road or canal in question.

The two parties would fix by common accord the
amount and mode of collection of the dues and tolls which
should be levied on this same road or canal.

Article 13. § 1.

From and after the 1st of January, 1832, Belgium, for
its share of the public debt of the United Kingdom of the
Netherlands, shall remain charged with a sum of 8,400,000
florins (£717,500) of the Netherlands in annual interests,
whereof the capitals shall be transferred from the debit of
the Great Book at Amsterdam, or the debit of the general
treasury of the United Kingdom of the Netherlands, to the
debit of the Great Book of Belgium.

§ 2.

The capitals transferred to, and the interests inscribed in
the debit of the Great Book of Belgium, in pursuance of the
preceding paragraph, to the amount of the sum total of
8,400,000 florins of the Netherlands in annual interests
(£717,500), shall be considered as making part of the
Belgian National Debt, and Belgium engages to make either
now or for the future no distinction between this portion of
the public debt, arising from her union with Holland, and
any other Belgian National Debt already created or here-
after to be created.

§ 3.

The payment of the sum of annual interests above
mentioned, of 8,400,000 florins (£717,500) of the Nether-

lands, shall take place regularly, from half-year to half-year, either at Brussels or at Antwerp, in ready money, without any deduction of any kind whatsoever, either now or for the future.

§ 4.

In consideration of the creation of this sum of 8,400,000 florins (£717,500), Belgium shall be discharged from all obligation to Holland on account of the division of the public debts of the United Kingdom of the Netherlands.

§ 5.

Commissioners appointed on both sides shall meet within a fortnight in the town of Utrecht, to proceed to a liquidation of the accounts of the Sinking Fund Syndicate and of the Bank of Brussels charged with the service of the general treasury of the United Kingdom of the Netherlands. From this liquidation there shall arise no new charge for Belgium, the sum of 8,400,000 florins (£717,500) of annual interests comprising the whole of her liabilities. But if there be a balance from the said liquidation, Belgium and Holland shall share it in the proportion of the imposts paid by each of the two countries during their union, according to the budgets voted by the States-General of the united Kingdom of the Netherlands.

§ 6.

In the liquidation of the Sinking Fund Syndicate shall be comprised the credits secured on the public lands, called *Domein-los-renten*. They are mentioned in the present Article only by way of note.

The Dutch and Belgian commissioners mentioned in § 5 of the present Article, and who are to meet in the town of

Utrecht, shall proceed, besides the liquidation with which they are charged, to the transfer of the capitals and annual interests which upon the division of the public debts of the United Kingdom of the Netherlands should fall to the charges of Belgium, up to the amount of 8,400,000 florins (£717,500) of annual interests. They shall proceed also to the extradition of all archives, charts, plans, and documents whatsoever, belonging to Belgium or concerning her administration.

Article. 14.

Holland having exclusively made, since November 1st, 1830, all the advances necessary for the discharge of the totality of the public debts of the kingdom of the Netherlands, and having to do so still for the half-year expiring on January 1st, 1832, it is agreed that the said advances, calculated from November 1, 1830, to January 1, 1832, for fourteen months, in proper ratio with the sum of 8,400,000 florins (£717,500) of the Netherlands in annual interests, with which Belgium remains charged, shall be repaid in three parts to the Dutch treasury by the Belgian treasury. The first third of this repayment shall be settled by the Belgian treasury with the Dutch treasury on January 1, 1832, the second on April 1, and the third on July 1, in the same year. On these two last thirds there shall accrue further to Holland, interest calculated at the rate of 5 per cent. per annum, until the whole is discharged at the aforesaid dates of expiry.

Article 15.

The port of Antwerp, agreeably to the stipulations of Article 15 of the treaty of Paris, May 30, 1814, shall continue to be solely a commercial port.

Article 16.

Works of public or private utility, such as canals, roads, or others of a similar kind, constructed entirely or partly at the expense of the United Kingdom of the Netherlands, shall belong, with the advantages and charges attached to them, to the country in which they are situated. It remains understood that the capitals borrowed for the construction of these works, and which are specifically appropriated thereto, shall be comprised in the said charges so far as they are not yet repaid, repayments already effected not giving any claim for liquidation.

Article 17.

Sequestrations which may have taken place in Belgium during the troubles, on political grounds, of any properties and hereditary estates whatsoever, shall be taken off without delay, and the enjoyment of the said properties and estates shall be forthwith restored to the lawful owners.

Article 18.

In the two countries whereof the separation takes place in consequence of the present articles, inhabitants and owners of property, if they desire to change their domicile from one country to the other, shall have two years' leave to dispose of their property, movable or immovable, of whatsoever kind it may be, to sell it, and to take away the produce of the sales, either in coin or in other equivalents, without hindrance or payment of other duties than those which are now in force in the two countries upon changes and transfers. It is understood that renunciation is made now and for the future of the collection of all *droits d'aubaine et de détraction* on the persons and properties of Dutch in Belgium and Belgians in Holland.

Article 19.

The quality of mixed subject, as to property, shall be recognized and maintained.

Article 20.

The provisions of Articles 11 to 21 inclusive of the treaty concluded between Austria and Russia, May 3, 1815, which forms an integral part of the General Act of the Congress of Vienna, provisions relative to mixed properties, to the choice of domicile they are bound to make, to the rights they shall exercise as the subjects of one or the other state, and as regards neighbourhood in properties cut by the frontiers, shall be applied to such owners of property as well as properties as in Holland, in the Grand Duchy of Luxemburg, or in Belgium, shall be found to come within the cases provided for by the aforesaid provisions of the Acts of the Congress of Vienna. The *droits d'aubaine et de détraction* being henceforth abolished as between Holland, the Grand Duchy of Luxemburg, and Belgium, it is understood that, amongst the provisions herein-above mentioned, those which related to the *droits d'aubaine et de détraction* shall be considered null and void in the three countries.

Article 21.

No one in the countries which undergo a change of rule shall be called to account or molested in any way because of any kind of participation direct or indirect in political events.

Article 22.

Pensions and allowances of expectants, of unemployed or retired persons, shall be paid for the future on either side to all claimants, civil as well as military, who have a right thereto conformably with the laws in force before

November 1, 1830. It is agreed that the pensions and allow-ances aforesaid of claimants born in the territories which now constitute Belgium, shall remain at the charge of the Belgian Treasury, and the pensions and allowances of the claimants born in the territories which now constitute Holland, at that of the Dutch Treasury.

Article 23.

All claims of Belgian subjects on private establishments, such as widows' funds and funds known under the deno-mination of *fonds des leges*, and of the chest of retired allowances, civil and military, shall be examined by the mixed commission of liquidation, of whom it is treated in Article 13, and decided after the rules which regulate those funds or charts.

The securities furnished and the payments made by Belgian accountants, the judical deposits and consignments, shall likewise be restored to the claimants on presentation of their proofs. If under the head of the liquidations called *French*, any Belgian subjects had still rights of inscription to make good, these claims shall likewise be examined and liquidated by the said Commission.

Article 24.

Immediately after the exchange of ratifications of the treaty to come between the two powers, the necessary orders shall be sent to the commandants of the respective troops for the evacuation of the territories, towns, forts, and places which change masters. The civil authorities there shall receive also at the same time the necessary orders for the surrender of those territories, towns, forts, and places, to the commissioners who shall be appointed for that purpose on either side. This evacuation and surrender shall take effect in such wise as to be able to be terminated within a fortnight, or if possible sooner.

Article 25.

The Courts of Austria, France, Great Britain, Prussia, and Russia, guarantee to H.M. the King of the Belgians the execution of all the articles preceding.

Article 26.

Consequent upon the stipulations of the present treaty, there shall be peace and amity between H.M. the King of the Belgians on the one part, and T.M. the Emperor of Austria, the King of the French, the King of the United Kingdom of Great Britain and Ireland, the King of Prussia, and the Emperor of All the Russias, on the other part, their heirs and successors, their states and subjects respectively, for ever.

Article 27.

The present treaty shall be ratified, and the ratifications thereof exchanged in London, within the space of two months, or sooner if can be.

In witness whereof the plenipotentiaries respectively have signed it and put to it their seals of arms.

Done in London, the fifteenth of November, in the year of grace one thousand eight hundred and thirty-one.

> (L. S.) ESTERHAZY.
> (L. S.) WESSENBERG.
> (L. S.) TALLEYRAND.
> (L. S.) PALMERSTON.
> (L. S.) BULOW.
> (L. S.) LIEVEN.
> (L. S.) MATUSZEWIC.

L. S. SYLVAN VAN DE WEYER.

Fortresses-Convention concluded and signed in London,
December 14, 1831.

T. M. the Emperor of Austria, etc., the King of the
United Kingdom of Great Britain and Ireland, the King of
Prussia, and the Emperor of All the Russias, on the one
part, and H. M. the King of the Belgians on the other,
having taken into consideration the present state of Belgium,
and the changes worked in the relative position of that
country by its political independence, as well as by the
perpetual neutrality which has been guaranteed to it, and
wishing to concert the modifications which this new situation
renders indispensable in the system of military defence
which had been adopted therein in consequence of the
treaties and engagements of 1815, have resolved to consign,
with this view, to a private convention, a series of determi-
nations concerted in common.

To this end, their said Majesties have appointed as
their plenipotentiaries, to wit :—

H. M. the King of the Belgians, Sieur Albert Goblet, etc. ;

H. M. the Emperor of Austria, Prince Esterhazy, etc.,
and Baron Wessenberg, etc. ;

H. M. the King of Great Britain and Ireland, Viscount
Palmerston, etc. ;

H. M. the King of Prussia, Baron Bulow, etc. ;

H. M. the Emperor of All the Russias, Prince Lieven
etc., and Count Matuszewic, etc.

Who, after having exchanged their full powers, found to
be in good and due form, have drawn up and signed the
following articles :—

Article 1.

In consequence of the changes which the independence
and neutrality of Belgium have brought upon the military

situation of that country, as well as on the means it will have at disposal for its defence, the high contracting parties agree to cause to be demolished, amongst the fortified places erected, repaired, or extended in Belgium since the year 1815, altogether or in part, at the expense of the Courts of Austria, Great Britain, Prussia, and Russia, those of which the maintenance would henceforth constitute only a useless charge.

On this principle, all the works of fortification of the strong places of Menin, Ath, Mons, Philippeville, and Marienburg, shall be demolished within terms herein-below fixed.

Article 2.

The artillery, munitions, and all objects forming part of the equipment given to the fortified places, of which the demolition has been decided on in the preceding article, shall be withdrawn from the said places within a month, counting from the ratification of the present convention, or sooner, if can be, and transported to the fortified places which are to be maintained.

Article 3.

In each of the places destined to be demolished, pro-ceedings shall at once be taken for the demolition of two fronts, as well as of the works which happen to be before these fronts, and of the means of inundation which might serve to cover them, in such wise that each of these places may be regarded as open through this demolition, which shall be effected within two months after the ratification of the present convention.

As for the total demolition of the works of fortification of the places herein above designated, it shall be terminated December 31, 1833.

Article 4.

The fortresses of Belgium which are not mentioned in Article 1 of the present convention as being destined to be demolished shall be preserved. H. M. the King of the Belgians engages to keep them constantly in good repair.

Article 5.

In case, in consequence of the balance which shall be struck, the Four Courts (or one of them) shall be found to have at its disposal a residue of the sums originally applied to the defensive system of Belgium, this residue shall be remitted to H. M. the King of the Belgians, to serve the object to which the said sums were destined.

Article 6.

The Courts of Austria, Great Britain, Prussia, and Russia, reserve to themselves the securing, at the terms fixed in Articles 2 and 3, of the full and entire execution of the said articles.

Article 7.

The present convention shall be ratified, and the ratifications thereof shall be exchanged in London within the space of two months, or sooner, if can be.

In witness whereof the respective plenipotentiaries have signed, etc.

Done in London, December 14, in the year of grace 1831.

> (L. S.) ESTERHAZY.
> (L. S.) WESSENBERG.
> (L. S.) PALMERSTON.
> (L. S.) LIEVEN.
> (L. S.) MATUSZEWIC.

(L. S.) GOBLET.

LONDON:
PRINTED BY WILLIAM CLOWES AND SONS, STAMFORD STREET
AND CHARING CROSS.

A List of Books

PUBLISHING BY

SAMPSON LOW, SON, AND MARSTON,

Crown Buildings, 188, Fleet Street.

[*September, 1868.*

NEW ILLUSTRATED WORKS.
Gray's "Elegy" in Colours, Uniform with the Illustrated
"Story Without an End."

N ELEGY IN A COUNTRY CHURCHYARD. By
Thomas Gray. With Sixteen Water-Coloured Drawings, by
Eminent Artists, printed in Colours in facsimile of the Ori-
ginals. Royal 8vo. cloth, 12s. 6d.; or in morocco, 25s.
[*In preparation*

THE STORY WITHOUT AN END. From the German of
Carové. By Sarah Austin. Illustrated with Sixteen Original Water-
Colour Drawings by E. V. B., printed in Fac-simile and numerous Illustrations on wood. Small 4to. cloth extra, 12s.; or inlaid on side with
floral ornament on ivory, 15s.; or in morocco, 21s.

** Also a Large Paper Edition, with the Plates mounted (only 250
copies printed), morocco, ivory inlaid, 31s. 6d.

" *Nowhere will he find the Book of Nature more freshly and beautifully
opened for him than in ' The Story without an End,' of its kind one of the
best that was ever written.*"—Quarterly Review.

" *We have here a most beautiful edition of Mrs. Austin's well-known
translation of ' The Story without an End,' illustrated by E. V. B. with
even more than her accustomed poetical grace and fancy. It is difficult to
select when all the illustrations are so delicately beautiful, but we cannot
help pointing out several that strike us especially. . . . But it is quite
impossible to describe these illustrations. We must refer our readers to
the book itself if they wish to see a perfect development of the grace, fancy,
and true poetical genius for which the pictures of E. V. B. have long been
remarkable.*"—Spectator.

Also, illustrated by the same Artist,

Child's Play. Printed in fac-simile from Water-Colour Drawings, 7s. 6d.
Tennyson's May Queen. Illustrated on Wood. Large Paper Edition,
7s. 6d.

CHRISTIAN LYRICS. Chiefly selected from Modern Authors.
138 Poems, illustrated with upwards of 150 Engravings, under the superintendence of J. D. Cooper. Small 4to. cloth extra, 10s. 6d.; morocco, 21s.

The Poetry of Nature. Selected and Illustrated with Thirty-
six Engravings by Harrison Weir. Crown 8vo. handsomely bound
in cloth, gilt edges, 5s.; morocco, 10s. 6d.
⁎ Forming the new volume of Low's Choice Editions of Choice Books.

Choice Editions of Choice Books. New Editions. Illustrated by
C. W. Cope, R. A., T. Creswick, R. A., Edward Duncan, Birket Foster,
J. C. Horsley, A. R. A., George Hicks, R. Redgrave, R.A., C. Stonehouse,
F. Tayler, George Thomas, H. J. Townshend, E. H. Wehnert, Har-
rison Weir, &c. Crown 8vo. cloth, 5s. each; mor. 10s. 6d.

Bloomfield's Farmer's Boy.	Keat's Eve of St. Agnes.
Campbell's Pleasures of Hope.	Milton's l'Allegro.
Cundall's Elizabethan Poetry.	Poetry of Nature.
Coleridge's Ancient Mariner.	Rogers' Pleasures of Memory.
Goldsmith's Deserted Village.	Shakespeare's Songs and Sonnets.
Goldsmith's Vicar of Wakefield.	Tennyson's May Queen.
Gray's Elegy in a Churchyard.	Wordsworth's Pastoral Poems.

"*Such works are a glorious beatification for a poet. Such 'works as
these educate townsmen, who, surrounded by dead and artificial things, as
country people are by life and nature, scarcely learn to look at nature till
taught by these concentrated specimens of her beauty.*"—Athenæum.

Bishop Heber's Hymns. An Illustrated Edition, with upwards
of one hundred Designs. Engraved, in the first style of Art under the
superintendence of J. D. Cooper. Small 4to. handsomely bound, price
Half a Guinea; morocco, 21s.

The Divine and Moral Songs of Dr. Watts: a New and very
choice Edition. Illustrated with One Hundred Woodcuts in the first
style of the Art, from Original Designs by Eminent Artists; engraved
by J. D. Cooper. Small 4to. cloth extra, price 7s. 6d.; morocco, 15s.

Artists and Arabs; or Sketching in Sunshine. By Henry
Blackburn, author of "The Pyrenees," &c. Numerous Illustrations.
Demy 8vo. cloth. 10s. 6d.

The Pyrenees; a Description of Summer Life at French
Watering Places. By Henry Blackburn, author of "Travelling in Spain
in the Present Day." With upwards of 100 Illustrations by Gustave
Doré. Royal 8vo. cloth, 18s.; morocco, 25s.

Travelling in Spain in the Present Day by a party of Ladies and
Gentlemen. By the same Author. With numerous Illustrations and
Map of Route. Square 8vo. 16s.

Two Centuries of Song; or, Melodies, Madrigals, Sonnets,
and other Occasional Verse of the English Poets of the last 200
years. With Critical and Biographical Notes by Walter Thornbury.
Illustrated by Original Pictures of Eminent Artists. Drawn and Engraved especially for this work. Printed on toned paper, with coloured
borders, designed by Henry Shaw, F.S.A. Very handsomely bound.
Cloth extra, 21s.; morocco, 42s.

Milton's Paradise Lost. With the original Steel Engravings of
John Martin. Printed on large paper, royal 4to. handsomely bound,
3*l.* 13*s.* 6*d.*; morocco extra, 5*l.* 15*s.* 6*d.*

Light after Darkness: Religious Poems by Harriet Beecher
Stowe. With Illustrations. Small post 8vo. cloth, 3*s.* 6*d.*

Poems of the Inner Life. Selected chiefly from modern Authors,
by permission. Small post 8vo. 6*s.*; gilt edges, 6*s.* 6*d.*

Favourite English Poems. *Complete Edition.* Comprising a
Collection of the most celebrated Poems in the English Language, with
but one or two exceptions unabridged, from Chaucer to Tennyson. With
300 Illustrations by the first Artists. Two vols. royal 8vo. half bound,
top gilt, Roxburgh style, 1*l.* 18*s.*; antique calf, 3*l.* 3*s.*

. Either Volume sold separately as distinct works. 1. " Early
English Poems, Chaucer to Dyer." 2. " Favourite English Poems,
Thomson to Tennyson." Each handsomely bound in cloth, 1*l.* 1*s.*

*" One of the choicest gift-books of the year, " Favourite English
Poems" is not a toy book, to be laid for a week on the Christmas table and
then thrown aside with the sparkling trifles of the Christmas tree, but an
honest book, to be admired in the season of pleasant remembrances for its
artistic beauty; and, when the holydays are over, to be placed for frequent
and affectionate consultation on a favourite shelf."—*Athenæum.

Schiller's Lay of the Bell. Sir E. Bulwer Lytton's translation;
beautifully illustrated by forty-two wood Engravings, drawn by Thomas
Scott, and engraved by J. D. Cooper, after the Etchings by Retasch.
Oblong 4to. cloth extra, 14*s.*; morocco, 25*s.*

An Entirely New Edition of Edgar A. Poe's Poems. Illustrated
by Eminent Artists. Small 4to. cloth extra, price 10*s.* 6*d.*

A History of Lace, from the Earliest Period; with upwards of
One Hundred Illustrations and Coloured Designs. By Mrs. Bury Palliser.
One volume, 8vo. New Edition. [*In preparation.*

The Royal Cookery Book. By Jules Gouffé, Chef de Cuisine of
the Paris Jockey Club. Translated and Adapted for English use. By
Alphonse Gouffé, Head Pastrycook to Her Majesty the Queen. Illustrated with large Plates beautifully printed in Colours, and One Hundred and Sixty-One Woodcuts. One volume, super-royal 8vo. cloth
extra, 2*l.* 2*s.*

The Bayard Series.

CHOICE COMPANIONABLE BOOKS
FOR HOME AND ABROAD,

COMPRISING

HISTORY, BIOGRAPHY, TRAVEL, ESSAYS,
NOVELETTES, ETC.

Which, under an Editor of known taste and ability, will be very choicely printed at the Chiswick Press; with Vignette Title-page, Notes, and Index; the aim being to insure permanent value, as well as present attractiveness, and to render each volume an acquisition to the libraries of a new generation of readers. Size, a handsome 16mo. bound flexible in cloth extra, gilt edges, averaging about 220 pages.

Each Volume, complete in itself, price Half-a-crown.

THE STORY OF THE CHEVALIER BAYARD. From the French of the Loyal Servant, M. de Berville, and others. By E. Walford. With Introduction and Notes by the Editor.

> " Praise of him must walk the earth
> For ever, and to noble deeds give birth.
> This is the happy warrior; this is he
> That every man in arms would wish to be."—*Wordsworth.*

SAINT LOUIS, KING OF FRANCE. The curious and characteristic Life of this Monarch by De Joinville. Translated by James Hutton.

> " St. Louis and his companions, as described by Joinville, not only in their glistening armour, but in their every-day attire, are brought nearer to us, become intelligible to us, and teach us lessons of humanity which we can learn from men only, and not from saints and heroes. Here lies the real value of real history. It widens our minds and our hearts, and gives us that true knowledge of the world and of human nature in all its phases which but few can gain in the short span of their own life, and in the narrow sphere of their friends and enemies. We can hardly imagine a better book for boys to read or for men to ponder over."—Times.

The Bayard Series,—

THE ESSAYS OF ABRAHAM COWLEY. Comprising all his Prose Works; the Celebrated Character of Cromwell, Cutter of Coleman Street, &c. &c. With Life, Notes, and Illustrations by Dr. Hurd and others. Newly edited.

"Praised in his day as a great Poet; the head of the school of poets called metaphysical, he is now chiefly known by those prose essays, all too short, and all too few, which, whether for thought or for expression, have rarely been excelled by any writer in any language."—Mary Russell Mitford's Recollections.

"Cowley's prose stamps him as a man of genius, and an improver of the English language."—Thos. Campbell.

ABDALLAH AND THE FOUR-LEAVED SHAMROCK. By Edouard Laboullaye, of the French Academy. Translated by Mary L. Booth.

One of the noblest and purest French stories ever written.

TABLE-TALK AND OPINIONS OF NAPOLEON THE FIRST.

A compilation from the best sources of this great man's shrewd and often prophetic thoughts, forming the best inner life of the most extraordinary men of modern times.

THE KING AND THE COMMONS: Cavalier and Puritan Poems. Selected and Arranged by Henry Morley, Professor of Literature, London University. Forming the New Volume of "The Bayard Series."

_{*} *It was in working on this volume that Mr. Morley discovered the New Poem attributed to Milton, about which there is so much controversy. A facsimile of the Poem and Signature J. or P. M., with parallel passages, and the whole of the evidence pro and con, will be given in the prefatory matter, so that the scholar can form his own conclusion.*

VATHEK. An Oriental Romance. William Beckford.

"Beckford's 'Vathek' is here presented as one of the beautifully got-up works included in Messrs. Low and Co.'s 'Bayard Series,' every one of which is a gem, and the 'Caliph Vathek' is, perhaps, the gem of the collection. We may as well add that every one of the works included in this series is well worth possessing, and the whole will make an admirable foundation for the library of a studious youth of polished and refined tastes."—Illustrated Times.

" If the publishers go on as they have begun, they will have furnished us with one of the most valuable and attractive series of books that have ever been issued from the press."—Sunday Times.

" There has, perhaps, never been produced anything more admirable, either as regards matter or manner."—Oxford Times.

" 'The Bayard Series' is a perfect marvel of cheapness and of exquisite taste in the binding and getting up. We hope and believe that these delicate morsels of choice literature will be widely and gratefully welcomed."

Nonconformist.

The Gentle Life Series.

Printed in Elzevir, on Toned Paper, and handsomely bound,
forming suitable Volumes for Presents.

Price 6s. each; or in calf extra, price 10s. 6d.

I.

THE GENTLE LIFE. Essays in Aid of the Formation of
Character of Gentlemen and Gentlewomen. Ninth Edition.

> " *His notion of a gentleman is of the noblest and truest order.* . . . .
> *The volume is a capital specimen of what may be done by honest reason,
> high feeling, and cultivated intellect.* . . . *A little compendium of
> cheerful philosophy.*"—Daily News.

> " *Deserves to be printed in letters of gold, and circulated in every
> house.*"—Chambers's Journal.

> " *The writer's object is to teach people to be truthful, sincere, generous :
> to be humble-minded, but bold in thought and action.*" —Spectator.

> " *Full of truth and persuasiveness, the book is a valuable composition,
> and one to which the reader will often turn for companionship.*"—Morning
> Post.

> " *It is with the more satisfaction that we meet with a new essayist who
> delights without the smallest pedantry to quote the choicest wisdom of our
> forefathers, and who abides by those old-fashioned Christian ideas of duty
> which Steele and Addison, wits and men of the world, were not ashamed
> to set before the young Englishmen of 1715.*"—London Review.

II.

ABOUT IN THE WORLD. Essays by the Author of " The
Gentle Life."

> " *It is not easy to open it at any page without finding some happy idea.*"
> Morning Post.

> " *Another characteristic merit of these essays is, that they make it their
> business, gently but firmly, to apply the qualifications and the corrections,
> which all philanthropic theories, all general rules or maxims, or principles,
> stand in need of before you can make them work.*"—Literary Churchman.

III.

FAMILIAR WORDS. An Index Verborum, or Quotation Handbook. Affording an immediate Reference to Phrases and Sentences that have become embedded in the English language. Second and enlarged Edition.

" *Should be on every library table, by the side of ' Roget's Thesaurus.' "* —Daily News.

" *Almost every familiar quotation is to be found in this work, which forms a book of reference absolutely indispensable to the literary man, and of interest and service to the public generally. Mr. Friswell has our best thanks for his painstaking, laborious, and conscientious work.*"—City Press.

IV.

LIKE UNTO CHRIST. A new translation of the " De Imitatione Christi," usually ascribed to Thomas à Kempis. With a Vignette from an Original Drawing by Sir Thomas Lawrence.

Think of the little work of Thomas à Kempis, translated into a hundred languages, and sold by millions of copies, and which, in inmost moments of deep thought, men make the guide of their hearts, and the friend of their closets."—Archbishop of York, at the Literary Fund, 1865.

V.

ESSAYS BY MONTAIGNE. Edited, Compared, Revised, and Annotated by the Author of "The Gentle Life." With Vignette Portrait.

" *The reader really gets in a compact form all of the charming, chatty Montaigne that he needs to know.*"—Observer.

" *We should be glad if any words of ours could help to bespeak a large circulation for this handsome attractive book ; and who can refuse his homage to the good-humoured industry of the editor.*"—Illustrated Times.

VI.

THE COUNTESS OF PEMBROKE'S ARCADIA. Written by Sir Philip Sidney. Edited, with Notes, by the Author of "The Gentle Life." Dedicated, by permission, to the Earl of Derby. 7s. 6d.

" *All the best things in the Arcadia are retained intact in Mr. Friswell's edition, and even brought into greater prominence than in the original, by the curtailment of some of its inferior portions, and the omission of most of its eclogues and other metrical digressions.*"—Examiner.

" *The book is now presented to the modern reader in a shape the most likely to be acceptable in these days of much literature and fastidious taste.*"—Daily News.

" *It was in itself a thing so interesting as a development of English literature, that we are thankful to Mr. Friswell for reproducing, in a very elegant volume, the chief work of the gallant and chivalrous, the gay yet learned knight, who patronized the muse of Spenser, and fell upon the bloody field of Zutphen, leaving behind him a light of heroism and humane compassion which would shed an eternal glory on his name, though all he ever wrote had perished with himself.*"—London Review.

VII.

THE GENTLE LIFE. Second Series. Third Edition.

"*There is the same mingled power and simplicity which makes the author so emphatically a first-rate essayist, giving a fascination in each essay which will make this volume at least as popular as its elder brother.*" Star.

" *These essays are amongst the best in our language.*"—Public Opinion.

VIII.

VARIA : Readings from Rare Books. Reprinted, by permission, from the *Saturday Review, Spectator*, &c.

CONTENTS:—The Angelic Doctor, Nostradamus, Thomas à Kempis, Dr. John Faustus, Quevedo, Mad. Guyon, Paracelsus, Howell the Traveller, Michael Scott, Lodowick Muggleton, Sir Thomas Browne, George Psalmanazar, The Highwaymen, The Spirit World.

" *The books discussed in this volume are no less valuable than they are rare, but life is not long enough to allow a reader to wade through such thick folios, and therefore the compiler is entitled to the gratitude of the public for having sifted their contents, and thereby rendered their treasures available to the general reader.*"—Observer.

IX.

A CONCORDANCE OR VERBAL INDEX to the whole of Milton's Poetical Works. Comprising upwards of 20,000 References. By Charles D. Cleveland, LL.D. With Vignette Portrait of Milton.

*** This work affords an immediate reference to any passage in any edition of Milton's Poems, to which it may be justly termed an indispensable Appendix.

" *An invaluable Index, which the publishers have done a public service in reprinting.*"—Notes and Queries.

X.

THE SILENT HOUR : Essays, Original and Selected. By the Author of "The Gentle Life."

CONTENTS.

How to read the Scriptures	From the Homilies.
Unreasonable Infidelity . . .	Isaac Barrow.
The Great Loss of the Worldling . . .	Richard Baxter.
Certainty of Death	Dean Sherlock.
On the Greatness of God	Massillon.
Our Daily Bread	Bishop Latimer.
The Art of Contentment	Archbishop Sandys.
The Foolish Exchange	Jeremy Taylor.
Of a Peaceable Temper	Isaac Barrow.
On the Marriage Ring	Jeremy Taylor.
Nearer to God	Archbishop Sandys.
The Sanctity of Home	John Ruskin.
The Thankful Heart	Isaak Walton.
Silence, Meditation, and Rest.	

And other Essays by the Editor. Second Edition.

LITERATURE, WORKS OF REFERENCE, ETC.

THE Origin and History of the English Language, and of the early literature it embodies. By the Hon. George P. Marsh, U. S. Minister at Turin, Author of " Lectures on the English Language." 8vo. cloth extra, 16s.

Lectures on the English Language; forming the Introductory Series to the foregoing Work. By the same Author. 8vo. Cloth, 16s. This is the only author's edition.

Man and Nature; or, Physical Geography as Modified by Human Action. By George P. Marsh, Author of " Lectures on the English Language," &c. 8vo. cloth, 14s.

"*Mr. Marsh, well known as the author of two of the most scholarly works yet published on the English language, sets himself in excellent spirit, and with immense learning, to indicate the character, and, approximately, the extent of the changes produced by human action in the physical condition of the globe we inhabit. In four divisions of his work, Mr. Marsh traces the history of human industry as shown in the extensive modification and extirpation of animal and vegetable life in the woods, the waters, and the sands; and, in a concluding chapter, he discusses the probable and possible geographical changes yet to be wrought. The whole of Mr. Marsh's book is an eloquent showing of the duty of care in the establishment of harmony between man's life and the forces of nature, so as to bring to their highest points the fertility of the soil, the vigour of the animal life, and the salubrity of the climate, on which we have to depend for the physical well-being of mankind.*"—Examiner.

Her Majesty's Mails: a History of the Post Office, and an Industrial Account of its Present Condition. By Wm. Lewins, of the General Post Office. 2nd Edition, revised and enlarged, with a Photographic Portrait of Sir Rowland Hill. Small post 8vo. 6s.

" *Will take its stand as a really useful book of reference on the history of the Post. We heartily recommend it as a thoroughly careful performance.*"—Saturday Review.

A History of Banks for Savings; including a full account of the origin and progress of Mr. Gladstone's recent prudential measures. By William Lewins, Author of " Her Majesty's Mails." 8vo. cloth. 12s.

The English Catalogue of Books: giving the date of publication of every book published from 1835 to 1863, in addition to the title, size, price, and publisher, in one alphabet. An entirely new work, combining the Copyrights of the " London Catalogue" and the " British Catalogue." One thick volume of 900 pages, half morocco, 45s.

Index to the Subjects of Books published in the United Kingdom during the last Twenty Years—1837-1857. Containing as many as 74,000 references, under subjects, so as to ensure immediate reference to the books on the subject required, each giving title, price, publisher, and date. Two valuable Appendices are also given—A, containing full lists of all Libraries, Collections, Series, and Miscellanies—and B, a List of Literary Societies, Printing Societies, and their Issues. One vol. royal 8vo. Morocco, 1*l.* 6*s.*

A Dictionary of Photography, on the Basis of Sutton's Dictionary. Rewritten by Professor Dawson, of King's College, Editor of the "Journal of Photography;" and Thomas Sutton, B.A., Editor of "Photograph Notes." 8vo. with numerous Illustrations. 3*s.* 6*d.*

Dr. Worcester's New and Greatly Enlarged Dictionary of the English Language. Adapted for Library or College Reference, comprising 40,000 Words more than Johnson's Dictionary, and 250 pages more than the Quarto Edition of Webster's Dictionary. In one Volume, royal 4to. cloth, 1,834 pp. price 31*s.* 6*d.* Half russia, 2*l.* 2*s.* The Cheapest Book ever published.

"The volumes before us show a vast amount of diligence; but with Webster it is diligence in combination with fancifulness,—with Worcester in combination with good sense and judgment. Worcester's is the soberer and safer book, and may be pronounced the best existing English Lexicon."—*Athenæum.*

The Publishers' Circular, and General Record of British and Foreign Literature; giving a transcript of the title-page of every work published in Great Britain, and every work of interest published abroad, with lists of all the publishing houses.

Published regularly on the 1st and 15th of every Month, and forwarded post free to all parts of the world on payment of 8*s.* per annum.

A Handbook to the Charities of London. By Sampson Low, Jun. Comprising an Account of upwards of 800 Institutions chiefly in London and its Vicinity. A Guide to the Benevolent and to the Unfortunate. Cloth limp, 1*s.* 6*d.*

Prince Albert's Golden Precepts. *Second Edition,* with Photograph. A Memorial of the Prince Consort; comprising Maxims and Extracts from Addresses of His late Royal Highness. Many now for the first time collected and carefully arranged. With an Index. Royal 16mo. beautifully printed on toned paper, cloth, gilt edges, 2*s.* 6*d.*

Our Little Ones in Heaven: Thoughts in Prose and Verse, selected from the Writings of favourite Authors; with Frontispiece after Sir Joshua Reynolds. Fcap. 8vo. cloth extra, 3*s.* 6*d.*

Rural Essays. With Practical Hints on Farming and Agricultural Architecture. By Ik. Marvel, Author of "Reveries of a Bachelor." 1 vol. post 8vo. with numerous Illustrations. 8*s.*

The Book of the Hand; or, the Science of Modern Palmistry. Chiefly according to the Systems of D'Arpentigny and Desbarolles. By A. R. Craig, M.A. Crown 8vo. 7*s.* 6*d.*

BIOGRAPHY, TRAVEL, AND ADVENTURE.

THE Life of John James Audubon, the Naturalist, including his Romantic Adventures in the back woods of America, Correspondence with celebrated Europeans, &c. Edited, from materials supplied by his widow, by Robert Buchanan. 8vo. [*Shortly.*

Christian Heroes in the Army and Navy. By Charles Rogers, LL.D. Author of " Lyra Britannica." Crown 8vo. 3s. 6d.

Leopold the First, King of the Belgians; from unpublished documents, by Theodore Juste. Translated by Robert Black, M.A. [*In preparation.*

Fredrika Bremer's Life, Letters, and Posthumous Works. Edited by her sister, Charlotte Bremer; translated from the Swedish by Fred. Milow. Post 8vo. cloth. 10s. 6d.

The Rise and Fall of the Emperor Maximilian: an Authentic History of the Mexican Empire, 1861-7. Together with the Imperial Correspondence. With Portrait, 8vo. price 10s. 6d.

Madame Recamier, Memoirs and Correspondence of. Translated from the French and edited by J. M. Luyster. With Portrait. Crown 8vo. 7s. 6d.

Plutarch's Lives. An entirely new Library Edition, carefully revised and corrected, with some Original Translations by the Editor. Edited by A. H. Clough, Esq. sometime Fellow of Oriel College, Oxford, and late Professor of English Language and Literature at University College. 5 vols. 8vo. cloth. 2l. 10s.

Social Life of the Chinese: a Daguerreotype of Daily Life in China. Condensed from the Work of the Rev. J. Doolittle, by the Rev. Paxton Hood. With above 100 Illustrations. Post 8vo. price 8s. 6d.

The Open Polar Sea: a Narrative of a Voyage of Discovery towards the North Pole. By Dr. Isaac I. Hayes. An entirely new and cheaper edition. With Illustrations. Small post 8vo. 6s.

The Physical Geography of the Sea and its Meteorology; or, the Economy of the Sea and its Adaptations, its Salts, its Waters, its Climates, its Inhabitants, and whatever there may be of general interest in its Commercial Uses or Industrial Pursuits. By Commander M. F. Maury, LL.D Tenth Edition. With Charts. Post 8vo. cloth extra, 5s.

Captain Hall's Life with the Esquimaux. New and cheaper Edition, with Coloured Engravings and upwards of 100 Woodcuts. With a Map. Price 7s. 6d. cloth extra. Forming the cheapest and most popular Edition of a work on Arctic Life and Exploration ever published.

" *This is a very remarkable book, and unless we very much misunderstand both him and his book, the author is one of those men of whom great nations do well to be proud.*"—Spectator.

The Black Country and its Green Border Land; or, Expeditions and Explorations round Birmingham, Wolverhampton, &c. By Elihu Burritt. 8vo. cloth, price 12s.

A Walk from London to John O'Groats, and from London to the Land's End and Back. With Notes by the Way. By Elihu Burritt. Two vols. price 6s. each, with Illustrations.

"*No one can take up this book without reading it through. We had thought that Elihu Burritt's ' Walk to John O'Groat's House' was the most perfect specimen of its kind that had ever seen the light, so genial, lively, and practical were the details he had brought together; but he has beaten his former literary production out of the field by this additional evidence of acuteness, impartiality, and good round sense.*"—Bell's Weekly Messenger.

The Voyage Alone; a Sail in the " Yawl, Rob Roy." By John M'Gregor, Author of " A Thousand Miles in the Rob Roy Canoe." With Illustrations. Price 5s.

A Thousand Miles in the Rob Roy Canoe, on Rivers and Lakes of Europe. By John M'Gregor, M.A. Fifth edition. With a Map, and numerous Illustrations. Fcap. 8vo. cloth. Price 5s.

The Rob Roy on the Baltic. A Canoe Voyage in Norway, Sweden, &c. By John Macgregor, M.A. With a Map and numerous Illustrations. Fcap. 8vo. Price 5s.

NEW BOOKS FOR YOUNG PEOPLE.

 TORIES of the Gorilla Country, narrated for Young People, by Paul Du Chaillu, author of " Discoveries in Equatorial Africa," &c. Small post 8vo. with 36 original Illustrations, 6s.

"*It would be hard to find a more interesting book for boys than this.*"—Times.

"*Young people will obtain from it a very considerable amount of information touching the manners and customs, ways and means of Africans, and of course great amusement in the accounts of the Gorilla. The book is really a meritorious work, and is elegantly got up.*"—Athenæum.

Life amongst the North and South American Indians. By George Catlin. And Last Rambles amongst the Indians beyond the Rocky Mountains and the Andes. With numerous Illustrations by the Author. 2 vols. small post 8vo. 5s. each, cloth extra.

"*An admirable book, full of useful information, wrapt up in stories peculiarly adapted to rouse the imagination and stimulate the curiosity of boys and girls. To compare a book with ' Robinson Crusoe,' and to say that it sustains such comparison, is to give it high praise indeed.*"—Athenæum.

The Marvels of Optics. By F. Marion. Translated and edited by C. W. Quin. With 80 Illustrations. Cloth extra. 5*s.*
"*A most instructive and entertaining volume, comprising not only a carefully-written and popular account of the phenomena of vision and the laws of light, as illustrated by the latest discoveries and experiments of our wise men, but a history of 'Natural Magic' from its earliest to its latest wonders.*"—*Observer.*

Also uniform.
Thunder and Lightning. From the French of De Fonvielle, by D. T L. Phipson. With 36 full-page Woodcuts. 5*s.*

Alwyn Morton; his School and his Schoolfellows. A Story of St. Nicholas' Grammar School. Illustrated. Fcap. 8vo. 5*s.*

The Silver Skates; a Story of Holland Life. Edited by W. H. G. Kingston. Illustrated, small post 8vo. cloth extra, 3*s.* 6*d.*

The Voyage of the Constance; a tale of the Polar Seas. By Mary Gillies. New Edition, with 8 Illustrations by Charles Keene. Fcap. 3*s.* 6*d.*

The Boy's Own Book of Boats. A Description of every Craft that sails upon the waters; and how to Make, Rig, and Sail Model Boats, by W. H. G. Kingston, with numerous Illustrations by E. Weedon. Second edition, enlarged. Fcap. 8vo. 3*s.* 6*d.*
" *This well-written, well-wrought book.*"—Athenæum.

Also by the same Author,
Ernest Bracebridge; or, Boy's Own Book of Sports. 3*s.* 6*d.*
The Fire Ships. A Story of the Days of Lord Cochrane. 5*s.*
The Cruise of the Frolic. 5*s.*
Jack Buntline: the Life of a Sailor Boy. 2*s.*

The True History of Dame Perkins and her Grey Mare, and their run with the Hounds. Told for the Countryside and the Fireside. By Linden Meadows. With Eight Coloured Illustrations by Phiz. Small 4to. cloth, 5*s.*

Great Fun Stories. Told by Thomas Hood and Thomas Archer to 48 coloured pictures of Edward Wehnert. Beautifully printed in colours, 10*s.* 6*d.* Plain, 6*s.* well bound in cloth, gilt edges.

Or in Eight separate books, 1s. each, coloured. 6d. plain.
The Cherry-coloured Cat. The Live Rocking-Horse. Master Mischief. Cousin Nellie. Harry High-Stepper. Grandmamma's Spectacles. How the House was Built. Dog Toby.

Great Fun and More Fun for our Little Friends. By Harriet Myrtle. With Edward Wehnert's Pictures. 2 vols. each 5*s.*

A Book of Laughter for Young and Old.
A Bushel of Merry-Thoughts, by Wilhelm Busch. Including the Naughty Boys of Corinth, the Children that took the Sugar Cake, Ice Peter, &c. Annotated and Ornamented by Harry Rogers, plain 2*s.* 6*d.*; coloured 3*s.* 6*d.*

Under the Waves; or the Hermit Crab in Society. By Annie
E. Ridley. Impl. 16mo. cloth extra, with coloured illustration Cloth,
4s.; gilt edges, 4s. 6d.

Also beautifully Illustrated :—

Little Bird Red and Little Bird Blue. Coloured, 5s.
Snow-Flakes, and what they told the Children. Coloured, 5s.
Child's Book of the Sagacity of Animals. 5s.; or coloured, 7s. 6d.
Child's Picture Fable Book. 5s.; or coloured, 7s. 6d.
Child's Treasury of Story Books. 5s.; or coloured, 7s. 6d.
The Nursery Playmate. 200 Pictures. 5s.; or coloured, 9s.

Golden Hour; a Story for Young People. By Sir Lascelles
Wraxall, Bart. With Eight full page Illustrations, 5s.

Also, same price, full of Illustrations :—

Black Panther; a Boy's Adventures among the Red Skins.
Stanton Grange; or, Boy Life at a Private Tutor's. By the Rev. C. J.
Atkinson.

Paul Duncan's Little by Little; a Tale for Boys. Edited by
Frank Freeman. With an Illustration by Charles Keene. Fcap. 8vo.
cloth 2s.; gilt edges, 2s. 6d. Also, same price,
Boy Missionary; a Tale for Young People. By Mrs. J. M. Parker.
Difficulties Overcome. By Miss Brightwell.
The Babes in the Basket : a Tale in the West Indian Insurrection.
Jack Buntline ; the Life of a Sailor Boy. By W. H. G. Kingston.

The Swiss Family Robinson; or, the Adventures of a Father and
Mother and Four Sons on a Desert Island. With Explanatory Notes and
Illustrations. First and Second Series. New Edition, complete in one
volume, 3s. 6d.

Geography for my Children. By Mrs. Harriet Beecher Stowe.
Author of "Uncle Tom's Cabin," &c. Arranged and Edited by an Eng-
lish Lady, under the Direction of the Authoress. With upwards of Fifty
Illustrations. Cloth extra, 4s. 6d.

Stories of the Woods ; or, the Adventures of Leather-Stocking :
A Book for Boys, compiled from Cooper's Series of "Leather-Stocking
Tales." Fcap. cloth, Illustrated, 5s.

Child's Play. Illustrated with Sixteen Coloured Drawings by
E. V. B., printed in fac-simile by W. Dickes' process, and ornamented
with Initial Letters. New edition, with India paper tints, royal 8vo.
cloth extra, bevelled cloth, 7s. 6d. The Original Edition of this work
was published at One Guinea.

BELLES LETTRES, FICTION, &c.

DAVID GRAY; and other Essays, chiefly on Poetry. By Robert Buchanan, author of "London Poems," "North Coast," &c. In one vol. fcap. 8vo. price 6s.

"*The book is one to possess as well as read, not only for the biographical essay on David Gray,—an essay of much more than deep interest, of rare power, and a strange unimpassioned pathos,—but also for certain passages of fine original criticism, occurring in essays—thickly sprinkled, we admit, with foreign substances—on poetry, and the religion and aims which modern poets should put before them.*"—Spectator.

The Book of the Sonnet; being Selections, with an Essay on Sonnets and Sonneteers. By the late Leigh Hunt. Edited, from the original MS. with Additions, by S. Adams Lee. 2 vols. price 18s.

"*Reading a book of this sort should make us feel proud of our language and of our literature, and proud also of that cultivated common nature which can raise so many noble thoughts and images out of this hard, sullen world into a thousand enduring forms of beauty. The 'Book of the Sonnet,' should be a classic, and the professor as well as the student of English will find it a work of deep interest and completeness.*"—London Review.

English and Scotch Ballads, &c. An extensive Collection. Designed as a Complement to the Works of the British Poets, and embracing nearly all the Ancient and Traditionary Ballads both of England and Scotland, in all the important varieties of form in which they are extant, with Notices of the kindred Ballads of other Nations. Edited by F. J. Child, new Edition, revised by the Editor. 8 vols. fcap. cloth, 3s. 6d. each.

The Autocrat of the Breakfast Table. By Oliver Wendell Holmes, LL.D. Popular Edition, 1s. Illustrated Edition, choicely printed, cloth extra, 6s.

The Professor at the Breakfast Table. By Oliver Wendell Holmes, Author of "The Autocrat of the Breakfast-Table." Cheap Edition, fcap. 3s. 6d.

"*A welcome book. It may be taken up again and again, and its pages paused over for the enjoyment of the pleasant touches and suggestive passages which they contain.*"—Athenæum.

Bee-Keeping. By "The Times" Bee-master. Small post 8vo. numerous Illustrations, cloth, 5s.

"*Our friend the Bee-master has the knack of exposition, and knows how to tell a story well; over and above which, he tells a story so that thousands can take a practical, and not merely a speculative interest in it.*"—Times.

Queer Little People. By the Author of "Uncle Tom's Cabin." Fcap. 1s. Also by the same Author.
The Little Foxes that Spoil the Grapes, 1s.
House and Home Papers, 1s.
The Pearl of Orr's Island, Illustrated by Gilbert, 5s.
The Minister's Wooing. Illustrated by Phiz, 5s.

Entertaining and Excellent Stories for Young Ladies, 3s. 6d. each,
cloth, gilt edges.
Helen Felton's Question : a Book for Girls. By Agnes Wylde.
Faith Gartney's Girlhood. By Mrs. D. T. Whitney. Seventh thousand.
The Gayworthys. By the same Author. Third Edition.
A Summer in Leslie Goldthwaite's Life. By the same Author.
The Masque at Ludlow. By the Author of " Mary Powell."
Miss Biddy Frobisher : a Salt Water Story. By the same Author.
Selvaggio ; a Story of Italy. By the same Author. New Edition.
The Journal of a Waiting Gentlewoman. By a new Author. New Edition.
The Shady Side and the Sunny Side. Two Tales of New England. By
    Country Pastors' Wives.

Marian ; or, the Light of Some One's Home. By Maud Jeanne
Franc. Small post 8vo., 5s.
Also, by the same Author.
Emily's Choice : an Australian Tale. 5s.
Vermont Vale : or, Home Pictures in Australia. 5s.
    Each Volume, cloth flexible, 2s. ; or sewed, 1s. 6d.

Tauchnitz's English Editions of German Authors. The following are now ready :—
    1. On the Heights. By B. Auerbach. 3 vols.
    2. In the Year '13. By Fritz Reuter. 1 vol.
    3. Faust. By Goethe. 1 vol.
    4. Undine, and other Tales. By Fouqué. 1 vol.
    5 L'Arrabiata. By Paul Heyse. 1 vol.
    6. The Princess, and other Tales. By Heinrich Zschokke. 1 vol.
Other volumes are in preparation.

Low's Copyright Cheap Series of American Authors.
Each complete in itself, printed from new type, with initial letters and
ornaments, to be published at the low price of 1s. 6d., stiff cover or cloth.
The first Volume in the New Series will appropriately be the Novel with
which the Anglo-American Copyright battle has been fought and won, so
long known in our Law Courts and so long suspended in publication. By
the recent Judgment its English copyright is established, and the property
therein secured to the present Publishers, entitled—

Haunted Hearts · A Tale of New Jersey. By the Author of
    " The Lamplighter."   [On the 1st October.
                    And the second,
The Guardian Angel. By the Author of " The Autocrat of
    the Breakfast Table."   [On the 1st December.
    To be followed by a New Volume on the first of every alternate month.

LONDON : SAMPSON LOW, SON, AND MARSTON,
    CROWN BUILDINGS, 188, FLEET STREET.
English, American, and Colonial Booksellers and Publishers.

Chiswick Press :—Whittingham and Wilkins, Tooks Court, Chancery Lane.

Ingram Content Group UK Ltd.
Milton Keynes UK
UKHW021823110623
423271UK00003B/11

9 781017 972979